THE DARK SIDE OF DESIRE

The moon had risen in the dusk, a big yellow ball that bathed Zach's tanned face and shock of wheat-toned hair. Such a beautiful man, truly he was. Her ardor became physical, a rising heat low in her belly. . . .

Liz took a step toward him, wondering if his skin and hair would feel as smooth as they looked in the moonlight, not quite sure what she was doing or why.

"If you're a voodoo queen, after all, tell me now."

She stopped short, feeling once again exposed, as much a victim to those superstitious rumors as she'd been before.

"That's silly. I'm not doing anything." Why was she defending herself?

"Just a joke," he said. "If I really thought you were into voodoo, I wouldn't've come on this trip."

She buried her hands in her hair. It gleamed like polished ebony in the moonlight, and her cheeks were rich with color that the moon turned tawny pink.

"You're so beautiful, *cher*," he said almost in a whisper. "No way you could be a witch."

THE
FIRE OPAL

Connie Flynn

AN ONYX BOOK

ONYX
Published by the Penguin Group
Penguin Putnam Inc., 375 Hudson Street,
New York, New York 10014, U.S.A.
Penguin Books Ltd, 27 Wrights Lane,
London W8 5TZ, England
Penguin Books Australia Ltd,
Ringwood, Victoria, Australia
Penguin Books Canada Ltd, 10 Alcorn Avenue,
Toronto, Ontario, Canada M4V 3B2
Penguin Books (N.Z.) Ltd, 182–190 Wairau Road,
Auckland 10, New Zealand

Penguin Books Ltd, Registered Offices:
Harmondsworth, Middlesex, England

First published by Onyx, an imprint of Dutton NAL,
a member of Penguin Putnam Inc.

First Printing, December, 1998
10 9 8 7 6 5 4 3 2 1

 REGISTERED TRADEMARK—MARCA REGISTRADA

Printed in the United States of America

PUBLISHER'S NOTE
This is a work of fiction. Names, characters, places, and incidents either
are the product of the author's imagination or are used fictitiously, and
any resemblance to actual persons, living or dead, events, or locales is
entirely coincidental.

To Karen, who, alas, will always be
younger than me, no matter
how much I lie.

Chapter One

"Come back from the dead . . ."

"Best-kept secret I've ever . . ."

"Her folks never said . . ."

They huddled together, casting furtive glances and whispering among themselves from behind their hands. A misting rain shrouded the gathering, and wind blew through the moss-hung cypress and oak with an eerie whine that made a somber backdrop for the rites the priest performed.

Liz Deveraux gathered the hood of her lightweight raincoat around her face, as much to block out their voices as to protect herself from the cold and the rain. The townspeople were trying to be kind, she told herself. They were trying not to show their qualms about the woman they were putting to rest, about the daughter who'd somehow climbed out of a grave to attend the funeral, but their hushed murmurs and thinly veiled wariness made her feel exposed.

She'd run from this so long ago, from the sly looks and whispers. From that odd mixture of love, respect, and fear that Port Chatre residents had always shown Ellie Deveraux, and by proxy, her only daughter.

But Liz had loved the way a child loves. And she'd always believed her mother would live forever, providing time to resolve their differences. Wrong, oh so wrong, as the rain-slick marble cover leaning against the vault attested.

The priest finished the rites. Attendants from the mortuary took up the sides of the cover, sliding it into place with a baleful clunk. The finality of the sound sent a shudder through Liz, but her eyes still remained as dry as they'd been throughout the funeral.

"Come, Izzy. The time is now to go to the wake."

Liz turned to her father. Even at this sorrowful time, she felt an urge to correct his fractured syntax, and with it came a pang of guilt. Her parents were who they were, and if she'd learned to accept that, she wouldn't now be feeling the weight of the unresolved issues her mother had taken with her to her crypt.

"Weep, *mon fille*, you must weep. Keep tears inside, they poison your soul."

"In my own time," she replied softly. She wanted

so much to cry. Her throat and chest ached, but somehow the tears just wouldn't flow.

He acknowledged her answer with a nod of his bowed head, and returned to staring at the freshly sealed vault. Unlike most of the other men, he wore no suit. Raindrops had collected on the felt bill of his hunting cap and on the nappy surface of his checked flannel jacket, making him look exactly like the swamper he was.

Liz moved to the impressive crypt that she had ordered, glad she could give at least this much. The marble was fresh and smooth, and the indentations of the inscription were already filling with rain. She could feel the rough edges left by the chisel as she traced the letters of her mother's name, hoping the act would somehow fill the empty space inside her. But it didn't.

When she touched the epitaph, she stilled her finger and looked at her grandmother's adjacent vault. It bore the very same words.

Guardian of the Fire Opal
At Last She Rest

"This makes it sound like a blessing that Mama died," she said sadly, running the flat of her hand across the markings.

"A blessing, no. But now she finally be free of

Ankouer and the burden of caring for the opal. That, *mon fille,* is a blessing for true."

"But . . . it's so disturbing. Please have it changed, Papa."

He fixed her with a bloodshot stare.

"*Non.* Every guardian have this on her vault. And every defender, if there be one, carve it there as an act of love."

"It's total superstition."

"Superstition. Yeah. I think that, too. Once."

He ran his hand across his strong, stubbled jaw, and Liz wondered how long it had been since he'd shaved. He wasn't prone to be slovenly or to talk about things such as Ankouer and the purpose of the opal. It was her mother who had followed the mystic ways that awestruck the townspeople and had caused Liz such embarrassment.

"Then I seen him with my own eyes." He tapped the marble as he spoke. With each word, the taps grew harder and faster, until they sounded like angry cries. "Giantlike and black, swirling with evil. And he suck my Ellie's life breath. I can do nothing, I, to stop him, though I try so very hard."

"See what I mean, Papa?" She leaned over to stop his tapping hand, then reached up to caress his face. He was grief crazed, that was it. His sorrow had warped his judgment. "A stroke killed Mama, just like *Grandmère,* but you're blaming yourself. That's

10

what superstition does. Please don't do this to yourself."

"No one else to blame." He covered her hand with his other one and smiled sadly. It was the smile she remembered from childhood, the one that said she was loved. "We talk no more of this. Richard has been so kind to offer his home for your *maman's* wake. We not keep them waiting, no?"

"No, of course not," she replied, giving a wan grin to hide her dread.

Holding his hand, she turned to head out of the cemetery, but a sudden drag signaled that her father had stopped. She lifted her eyes to him in question.

"Tomorrow I give you the opal."

She shook her head. "I want you to have it."

"I cannot. The opal is now yours to guard. There be no one else to carry on."

"To guard . . ." she repeated dully, involuntarily glancing back at the twin vaults with their twin inscriptions.

"*Oui.* Only you can keep the stone from *le fantôme noir*. You be the last guardian. There be no one else."

Her legacy, she thought bitterly. Instead of bone china or jewelry like everyone else, she was inheriting an icon of superstition. She started to protest again, then realized no argument would keep her father from giving her that stone.

"I am sorry, Izzy," he said, tightening his grip on her hand, and gazing at her with lost, haunted eyes. "For true I am."

"Glad, you responded to my fax in person, son. I'm no expert coroner"—Doc Allain stated this humbly, but his chest puffed up with pride—"just a small-town doctor doing my best, and I didn't want to put my suspicions in writing. Pretty sure you'll understand why when you see what I got."

"Looking forward to it," replied Zach Fortier, thinking that the guy was kind of an amazement. Had to be nearly ninety, and the last time he'd seen the man, he'd been tottering on a cane. Now here he was looking a healthy sixty, if that.

"Used to get a lot of notifications," Zach went on to tell the doctor, "but the last year they kind of petered out. Yours is the first I've seen in months."

"None of 'em panned out I suppose."

"Nope. Maybe this time. A man can always hope."

"Sure can. Probably should." Allain tilted his head. "But what makes you doubt the official findings?"

Zach hesitated. He wasn't crazy about examining his reasons too close. They were hazy, sort of, and came more from the gut than the brain. But Allain deserved some answer, he supposed.

"Jed knew the swamp as well as any man, and

he swam like a gator. It doesn't make sense he'd drown out there. Plus that, the escaped con he was chasing had drug ring connections. Throwing a body in the swamp's a good way to cover up the real cause of death." He'd explained enough, Zach thought, and he was impatient to see the evidence the doc had faxed about. "So what have you got?"

"Nothing conclusive, you understand."

"You never know until you see the evidence."

"Right, but let me give it to you in a nutshell. I compared the results of Ellie Deveraux's examination with the stuff you put on the wire about your brother, and—" The man's short cough almost seemed to be for effect. "Well, there's reason to believe Frank killed his wife."

"What?" Zach sputtered. "What did you find?"

"Just this." He handed Zach a medical file. "Couldn't do an autopsy without Frank throwing a fit. But I have plenty."

The thick folder was old, the edges bent, and it contained the records of every member of the Deveraux family. Unusual these days to see a family file, but Port Chatre was still a small, old-fashioned town. Some of the papers looked the worse for wear, but a new top sheet contained the results of the doctor's examination.

Zach read the doctor's report carefully. Ellie Deveraux had died in her sleep. Frank found her the next morning.

Just the idea of waking up to discover your wife lying dead beside you gave Zach the creeps. Just as creepy was the act of going through the family folder of the first girl he'd ever loved.

Were the results of Izzy's examinations in here? Did they mention her vitality? Her love of life? Those remarkably flecked amber eyes that always reminded him of the stone called cat's eye? Did those pages tell all these things about a young woman whose life was wiped out so early?

An unwelcome thickness in his throat made him turn his attention back to the report. Except for the lividity about the lips, the same unexplained blue cast Jed's desecrated body had also borne, nothing looked unusual about Ellie's death. A stroke, Doc Allain had written, causing paralysis of the lungs, resulting in anoxia and eventual asphyxiation. A blood test revealed no oxygen in the bloodstream. There was tissue decay of the fingers and toes.

Hell, Zach wasn't a coroner. But he didn't have to be to see this was another wild goose chase. This sweet old guy was one of those backwoods physicians with an honorary coroner's title who fancied himself a forensic expert.

He leafed through the folder, telling himself he wasn't really looking for something about Izzy, and when he came across a sheet on her, he quickly passed it by. Near the back he found a report on Catherine Deveraux, Ellie's mother. She, too, had died of a stroke. Same lividity about the lips, and decay of the digits.

"Those the same kind of marks found on your brother?" Allain asked.

"The bluish lips, yes," Zach said. "There wasn't enough left . . ."

"Petechiae under the eyelids?"

"Yeah." At least on what was left of the lids.

"You identify the body yourself?"

Zach reached for a cigarette. One thing about small Louisiana towns, no one objected to smokers, not even in a doctor's office. "Yeah," he said after lighting up. "I did."

"Must've been rough seeing him chewed up that way."

"Wasn't the easiest." He looked back down at Catherine's sheet. "Looks like strokes run in the family."

"Or maybe murders. Frank brought Catherine in, too."

"You examine Catherine yourself?"

"Yes, but those days I didn't know what I know now."

Bull's-eye. Yep, give a man a little knowledge. One thing was clear, Allain sure did want to prove he'd found a killer.

But accusing Frank Deveraux? Zach remembered the man's dark laughing eyes, the way his big, rough hands could so gently touch a kid's shoulder.

Investigators didn't put much stock in coincidence, and he'd given years to the business, but connecting these deaths was a stretch he couldn't quite make.

True, Ellie's lips had shown a blue cast; so had Catherine's—and Jed's. Not uncommon in asphyxiation, but this particular marker was unusual because color on the lips usually faded rapidly as uncirculated blood pooled in the body. Another medical anomaly that would suddenly start popping up again and again? Maybe, maybe not. Regardless, despite the similarities to the findings on Jed's body, there was nothing in these reports that a stroke couldn't explain away.

"Frank's gone half bonkers," Allain went on, "saying Ellie died of *la maladie maléfique*. Shows a guilty conscience, you ask me." The man chuckled derisively. "Evil illness, indeed. These swamp Cajuns and their hocus-pocus. Have to admit, though, it's one I haven't heard in a while. Hell of it is, some take him seriously enough they'd never think murder."

"Sure, Doc," Zach replied absently as he spied Izzy's name at the top of a sheet. This time he paused to look. She'd been in to see Doc about a sore throat. Strep, the doctor had diagnosed, prescribing an antibiotic. Odd, considering her mother's reputation as a natural healer, but maybe the problem had gone on too long.

"Don't get many murders around here. Last one

happened in eighty-nine. Old Pete Bourg went off half-cocked in Tricou's cafe, shot Louis Martin clean through the chest. Boy, what a mess. Pete carried Louis in, bleating like a goat that Ankouer made him do it, blood spurting all over the place, like to never clean it . . .''

Zach hardly heard. His mind drifted to his teenage years. He and Izzy paddling through the swamps, sometimes alone, but more often than not with Jed tagging along. Lots of mischief, lots of laughs. Now he was the only one left.

How could that be? Sagging belly or not, he wasn't even forty. Too young to have lost two people so close to him who were even younger.

"Town's not the same since your folks left," Allain remarked. "Cannery's gone, tourists all over the place. I miss the old days."

Zach abandoned his trip down memory lane, and looked up.

"Ma couldn't run the cannery herself with Pa gone," he replied. "Too bad the buyers couldn't make a go of it. Times change, I suppose."

"Sure do." The doctor chuckled again, for no apparent reason. Then out of the blue he asked, "Think we should demand an autopsy? Get a court order, need be?"

Zach stared at the doctor blankly, reflecting on the possibility that the man's brain hadn't fared as well as his body. "That would just add to Frank's grief, and he's already had enough. Besides, your toxicology came up negative."

"But the presence of petechiae . . ."

"Look, Doc, I'm no coroner, but wouldn't a bit of hemorrhaging be normal from a stroke?"

"Not necessarily in the eyes and nose. And the same type were found in your brother's body, and in the prisoner's."

Zach swallowed an impatient sound and dropped his gaze back to the notes on Izzy. "I don't want to rain on your parade, partner, but there's only a slim connection. Not enough to warrant an autopsy. Thanks for contacting me, but—"

"The wake's being held right now over at Cormier's house. How 'bout just talking to Frank? See if I'm not right about his bizarre behavior. You could speak with the girl, too."

Zach's head snapped up so hard the bones in his neck cracked. "Who?"

"Frank and Ellie's girl, Lizette I think. Yeah, Lizette. In her mid-thirties now, but you must remember her. You used to sniff around her enough."

"Izzy?" Zach choked out. "No. Izzy's dead."

"Seems not. Drove in last night pretty as you please to attend her mama's funeral. Care to come see for yourself?"

The wake was abuzz with quiet speculation about Liz's reappearance in Port Chatre and about her mother's fate in the afterlife. Discussion ended quickly at her approach. The gossipers then turned en masse with cautious and sympathetic smiles to rev up their Southern charm and drawl polite questions in soft, lazy voices that never revealed their true thoughts.

Liz pried herself loose from the latest gossip pod and had drifted only a few feet away before the morbid topic was resumed.

"The girl's cursed, just like her mama."

"Not cursed, a witch. Runs in the blood."

"I hear she rose outta her vault."

A short, tubby man snickered uneasily. "Sure she did. Like one of them *Tales from the Crypt* episodes."

"No, no," a woman interjected, lifting her hands and wiggling her fingers. "Ankooooor helped her."

The snickers got louder and longer, but still sounded spooked.

What rubbish, Liz thought. They couldn't honestly believe she was a zombie or that Ankouer truly existed. Judging by the anxious edge in their laughter, it was easy to believe they did. And it didn't help any that her father was sitting in the kitchen, telling his old cronies that Ankouer had sent *la maladie maléfique* to kill his wife.

Wandering aimlessly through the spacious Cormier home, feeling very much like the young girl she'd left behind so many years ago, she sipped on a rum and Coke someone had pressed in her hand.

Liquor was always present at Cajun wakes, along with enormous platters of shrimp and crawdads and plump grilled sausage, bottomless bowls of etouffee, and dirty rice with beans.

Quite a feast, and one provided by the generosity of Richard and family. When she'd lived here, the Cormiers had been struggling to make their grocery a success, living upstairs, giving credit that wasn't always repaid. Seemed as if these twenty years had been kind to them.

According to the others—who were more than happy to fill Liz in—when the Fortier cannery folded, Richard Junior snapped up the wharf that once fed it. He renamed it a marina—a title as grandiose as this tiny town's name—and with the air finally freed of the stench of rotting fish, tourism picked up. Cash customers arrived, needing supplies, needing rental boats, which Richard supplied for a small king's ransom. The Cormiers then used those profits to build an inn. And so it went.

Regular entrepreneurs. Judging by this mansion, a faithful replication of a Creole plantation house, she wouldn't be surprised to see their industries show up as her next hot penny stock. But their current kindness couldn't erase her memories of their constant bullying during her childhood.

Witch's child. Raggedy swamp girl. Those were the gentler taunts. Other times they claimed she curdled milk or made babies sick with her evil eye.

One day she hurled a curse at Richard in retaliation and he broke his arm that afternoon, adding fuel to their accusations.

Liz stopped before one of the large stone hearths to warm herself by the fire. It was unusually cold for an afternoon in the middle of May, and she was grateful for the heat. As she rubbed her hands, she found herself staring up at a crucifix hanging over the mantel, something that graced almost every Cajun home. To most this represented all that was holy, but to Liz it symbolized everything she'd fled.

"Praying for your mama's soul?"

It took a moment for Liz to realize the question had been directed at her. When she turned, a chill crept up her spine.

"Hello, Maddie," she said coolly.

"Lord Jesus watch out for your mama, Izzy. You must trust."

Liz regarded Maddie for a long moment, deciding not to bother with asking if she'd call her Liz. She noted with mild surprise that Maddie, who was ten years her senior, somehow did not look a day over thirty. Although painfully thin, a fact her sleeveless, scoop-necked gown emphasized, Maddie was nonetheless striking. Her dark skin and large almond-shaped eyes gave her an exotic beauty, and her bearing revealed a self-possession that even her ungrammatical speech couldn't belie.

"I pray for her." Maddie brushed back an imagi-

nary stray hair. "I pray God take her soul to heaven
and she be very happy."

"How can you pretend you care?" Liz asked
acidly.

"It weren't like that between Ellie and me. I love
her like a sister. Some things you don't understand,
with them big city ways you got now."

Liz placed her glass beneath the feet of the cruci-
fied Jesus. "If you'll excuse me."

Instead of replying, Maddie stared at her long
and hard. For a peculiar second, Liz felt as if those
slanted dark eyes were searching her soul. But she
met them boldly. As she did, an electric charge ran
from the top of her head and down her spine.
Words spilled involuntarily from her lips.

"You will die a violent death," she said in a
strangely altered voice. "Fortunately, it will be
quick."

"Ah, you is the daughter of your mama, after
all." A cynical smile crossed Maddie's face. "And
got her gift of second sight."

The words shattered Liz's trancelike state. Somewhat stunned, she turned away from Maddie and
rushed through the open French doors to the veranda outside.

She walked to the edge, propped her elbows on
the carved railing, and stared into the distance. The
dipping sun glowed behind a curtain of misting
rain. Tiny drops of water fell from the trees and

clung to the Spanish moss, where they glittered like rhinestones. The splash of a fish breaking the water of the bayou not far away added an alto note to the high chirrups of the crickets. Thunder rumbled softly in the distance.

What had happened in there?

Lord, she thought with despair, as intensely as she disliked Maddie, nothing justified what she'd said. And it scared the hell out of her that she'd said it. She suspected that somewhere in her morass of deliberately buried memories she might discover similar incidents. That scared her even more.

Everything about Port Chatre frightened her, in fact. The memories it held. The flood of suspicion and fear directed her way. The possibility that the false life she'd built for herself would be exposed. Even the potential risk that listening to these gently slurred accents would cause her to slip back into the speech patterns of her girlhood.

She didn't want to go back. Didn't want to remember. Which was why she'd vowed that nothing would ever make her return to Port Chatre. Nothing, that is, but her mother's funeral.

An event she'd somehow never taken into account.

Chapter Two

"Zach-ar-ree For-tee-ay." Frank's drawl boomed across the large room as he walked in Zach's direction.

Doc Allain nudged his elbow. "Go ahead, see what I'm saying. Meantime, I'm checking out the eats."

The doctor faded into the crowd, leaving Zach to wait while Frank came forward with his huge hand extended.

"Frank," he said warmly, taking the man's hand and shaking it firmly. "How're you holding up, partner? I'm sorry about Ellie."

Frank's face sagged as he whispered. "*Oui. La maladie maléfique.*"

"That's as good as anything to call it. Though the doctor calls it a stroke." Zach surreptitiously scanned the room. His knees were quaking and the air felt thick, but hiding his true feelings came naturally to him.

"Men of science know nothing," Frank countered, then went on in the same conspiratorial voice. "Ankouer come for Ellie—he take her breath and freeze her blood."

The remark caused Zach to turn on his zoom lens and focus it on Frank. Bloodshot, slightly crazed eyes. Disheveled appearance. So the doc had been right. Frank had taken a dive off the deep end. Finding himself a little at a loss for words, he mumbled something about never knowing.

He could hear fragments of conversations that let him know that others were aware of Frank's delusions. Some voices held fear, some pity. Some were downright scornful. Well, grief did odd things to people, and Zach didn't necessarily think the man's behavior revealed a guilty conscience.

He found himself unable to keep his attention honed the way he usually did. He'd come back to Port Chatre looking for Jed's killer. Instead he'd found . . .

"Is— I mean— Izzy, I heard she's here."

"*Oui*. She come and say good-bye to her *maman*."

"Frank, I—" He hesitated. How did you ask a man such a question on the day he'd interred his wife? "I'd been, that is, well, I'd been told Izzy was dead."

"A body washed up in the bayous, yes, and they

told us it were Izzy. Mistake of identity. She were up in the Saint Louie all along." He gravely made the sign of the cross. "For them other poor souls who was grieving for their daughter when the truth came out," he explained.

The quaking in Zach's knees spread like wildfire through his entire body. *Why didn't you tell me?* he wanted to shout. *Why?* Instead he asked for a drink.

Frank's eyes lost their wild edge as they drifted to Zach's visibly shaking hands. "That I can do, yes."

It only seemed like seconds later when Frank pressed a tumbler into Zach's hand. Zach swallowed quickly, demanding his heart to stop racing, demanding his lungs to inhale. After downing half the glass, he asked, "Where is she?"

"On the *galerie*, I think I seen."

"Thanks." Zach finished the rest of the glass and put it down on a nearby table. "I'll go look her up. Nice talking to you, partner, and hang in there."

"I do my best."

Turning slowly so as not to betray his eagerness, Zach headed for the open doors that led outside. He saw a slender figure looking up at Richard Cormier. Her shoulders were slightly bent as if they bore a great weight, but she listened in apparent fascination while Richard talked about his businesses. She wore a black knit kind of thing, with a long coat-jacket that skimmed the hemline of the skirt and clung rather enticingly to her slim hips.

Her smooth cap of hair almost matched the color of her outfit and revealed the curve of her neck.

Izzy? Where were her curls? That long mane of gloriously tousled hair?

Deciding he was about to find out, Zach straightened the knot of his tie, sucked in his stomach, and took a step into a moment that, until then, he hadn't known he'd been hoping for all his adult life.

"Afternoon, Richard," he said with forced nonchalance. "Nice spread you've put on for the folks."

"Fortier," Richard replied evenly, making very little effort to cover up his annoyance at being interrupted. "Come back to see what I've done with your town?"

Before Zach answered, the woman turned around.

His sharp hiss of breath occurred at the same moment her face broke into a delighted smile.

"Zach!"

She rushed toward him, still smiling. His heart exploded with joy.

"Izzy, I— Why didn't you . . . ?"

"A shock, isn't it?" Richard said archly. "We were all surprised out of our boots."

She stopped, her smile vanishing.

"Oh that." A nervous laugh bubbled in her throat. "Everyone seems to think I came back from the grave. I just— For the longest time I didn't know I'd been reported dead. Later . . . when I did, well, it seemed better this way."

"Better? How's that?" Didn't she realize what a kick in the gut she'd given him?

She made a sweeping motion with her hand. "Hard to explain. It just did, that's all."

Zach stared down at her, taking in the monumental changes. Gone were Izzy's soft consonants and drawn-out vowels. This was the studied accent of an expensive Northeastern prep school. And she had taken off weight. Where Izzy had been sensuously round, she was chicly slim. Actually, chic described her perfectly, and if it weren't for those flecked golden eyes meeting his, he'd hardly know this was the same person.

He let out his breath, allowing his stomach to sag. He'd almost forgotten he'd been holding it in. They'd both changed through these years, and not for the better in his opinion. But he had more to conceal than a softening belly. His damned emotions seesawed like crazy. His stomach twisted with disappointment, yet, stupidly, his heart still skipped with excitement. The faint spice of her perfume made it even harder for him to breathe. One thing he knew, though—he wasn't going to dump his feelings at her feet.

"It's not important, just a surprise. But I am glad to see you, Izzy." He thrust out his hand for a manly shake, feeling a sick kind of satisfaction when he saw hurt flicker on her face. She recovered quickly and by the time she took his hand, he wondered if he'd imagined that look.

"I use the name Liz now. Papa's the only one who calls me Izzy anymore." Smooth, flawless white teeth flashed at him. The best dentistry money could buy, he'd be willing to wager. Izzy's smile had once revealed overlapping incisors, with a small chip that he had quixotically adored.

"Is it still Deveraux?" he asked, for lack of anything better. He sure wasn't holding up his reputation for glib charm this afternoon.

"Yes." She tilted her head slightly. "How about you?"

"It's still Fortier."

She laughed again, a relaxed sound this time. "That's not what—"

"Actually, Zach here's proved his magic touch with the ladies," Richard interrupted. "Caught three of them. Too bad he doesn't know how to keep them."

Liz slanted Richard a scowling look.

"Hey, partner, thanks for not leading off with my faults," Zach retorted with studied laziness. Then he looked back at Liz. "Divorce . . ." For no reason in particular, he lamely added, "Two kids."

Richard made another snide remark that Liz didn't quite register. From the moment Zach came onto the veranda, her heart had been tripping like an old-fashioned ticker tape. He was taller than she remembered, broader in the shoulders, narrower in the hips. His body revealed a dedication to keeping fit that went well beyond a few hours a week at the gym, and the wind swept back his tawny sun-streaked hair, revealing the high forehead, the slash of brutal cheekbones, and the squareness of jaw that had remained etched in her mind.

"What happened to all those blue-black curls, *cher*?"

"People change in twenty years. At least some of us do." She tilted her head. "But it seems you haven't, except maybe you're a little taller."

Zach laughed. The sound was rich and delightful and it felt as though she'd heard it just yesterday. She'd always loved Zach's laugh and the rich Cajun rhythm to his speech, which also hadn't changed.

"I thought you'd be mayor of Port Chatre by now."

His laugh vanished immediately. "Nah, I got a football scholarship. Never came back after that."

"He wouldn't have beat out my pa, anyway," Richard interjected.

Liz barely acknowledged the remark. Neither did Zach. Since he'd walked into their conversation, Richard had faded into the background.

"Where're you staying?" Zach asked.

"Staying?" His eyes were as blue as ever. "Oh, in your family's house."

"In my old house?" The news obviously startled him. "Your pa buy the place?"

"It's his, yes. But he's probably going to sell it, now that Mama's gone."

"Seems strange, thinking of him living where I grew up. We shared so many memories there, you and me."

"Yes," she replied uneasily, refraining from telling him that her parents had never lived there. Although the place wasn't as large as Richard's, it was a true plantation house rather than a replica. The real thing, a spot where she'd spun so many dreams. For an instant she shared Zach's memories, almost hearing her girlish squeals as she burst through the open shutter doors onto the second-story balcony, Zach hot on her heels after some treasure she'd swiped.

In those days, she'd expected to raise his babies in that house, to plant pretty flowers in well-tended beds, and breathe magnolia fragrance in the spring. In those days before . . .

Liz frowned. Before what? Why had she fled Port Chatre so long ago? And fled she had, with nothing to her name except a flour sack full of ratty clothes and the thirty dollars she'd squirreled away for an extra-special dress to wear to Zach's senior prom.

"Something wrong, *cher*?" Zach asked.

"She's probably tired," Richard said, putting a

possessive hand on her arm, and clearly preparing to steer her inside.

"I'm fine, Richard, thanks." She subtly shook off his arm and kept her eyes on Zach. "Just fine. So how's Jed these days?"

For a second Zach looked as stunned as if someone had slapped him. "Jed died," he said flatly. "Almost three years ago."

"Jed? Oh, no, Zach. How?"

"Drowned in the bayou, they say."

"I liked him so much." Liz shook her head, weighed down by the shock of news that added to her grief for her mother. "I just can't believe it."

"Hey, Fortier," Richard said, "you might lighten up. Liz just put her ma to rest, remember?"

Zach had dealt with Richard's earlier jibe without much effort, but now he felt confused. Until Liz had asked about Jed, he'd completely forgotten his purpose for coming to Port Chatre. Since he'd identified his brother's body, not a moment of a day had passed when finding his killer wasn't Zach's main reason for living. Seeing Liz had completely erased it from his mind. "Sorry," he said distractedly. "My timing is piss poor."

Richard opened his mouth, probably to add another sarcastic comment, but a hollow ring sounded before he got a chance. Liz reached for the handbag draped over her shoulder and came out with a cellular phone.

"Oh, hi, Stephen," she said, after snapping it open and identifying herself. "Well, yes, this is a bad time. I'm at my mother's wake."

Then she was quiet.

Who was this guy that he'd call her at a time like this? Zach wondered sourly.

"Uni-Tech? Okay, fill me in."

Another thoughtful silence followed, then Liz looked up and met his eyes. Zach realized he'd been staring, and when she turned around and drifted farther down the *galerie*, softening her voice to make it harder to hear, he felt rebuked.

What kind of woman talked business during her mother's wake?

The same kind who ran off in the night and let her boyfriend think she'd died. The same kind who never called or wrote to let him know it wasn't true. The same kind who had caused him to momentarily forget his brother's unsolved murder.

He was a fool to have let his youthful dream come alive again. A complete fool. And if he had any illusions about renewing their lost love, he'd be a bigger fool if he didn't kiss them good-bye.

"When we sell this other stock, I've no idea where to put the funds," Stephen said. "You got any more of those hunches?"

Normally his remark would have amused Liz. But she had no right even being on the phone with

33

him, so her reply was stiff. "I don't have hunches. Just educated guesses like everyone else."

"Sure you do. That's why you've got an eighty-percent success rate."

"I've got other things on my mind at the moment, okay?"

"Right," Stephen replied, without a hint of contrition, which didn't surprise her. Tunnel vision, that was Stephen.

"So how's it going in Philly?" he asked in a dutiful tone.

"Groversfield," Liz corrected.

"Right. You holding up?"

"As well as can be expected."

"When are you coming back?"

"I'm not sure. My father's not taking this well. I want to stay around a few more days until he's over the hump."

She saw Zach crook his neck to look in her direction and deliberately turned away from him. Did he realize what she was doing? What she had done all along? Suddenly she wanted to spill it all, tell Stephen she wasn't really from Groversfield, Pennsylvania, and that her father wasn't a banker, but a Cajun tour guide who believed in ghosts and phantoms and had just gone over the edge because her mother had died.

Just then her father dashed through the doors, heading straight for Zach.

"Bâtard!" he roared. *"Bâtard!"* He followed this with a tirade in French that told Liz how deeply upset he was.

"I've got to go, Stephen." She slammed the cell phone shut and hastily shoved it in her purse, then hurried to keep her father from making a bigger scene than he already had.

"What is it, Papa?"

He fixed her with crazed eyes. "Zacharie! He wanna take you *maman* out of her crypt!"

"What? Why?"

"Where did you hear that, partner?" Zach asked, looking as if he knew, but didn't want to believe it.

"Blasphème! Ellie be a good woman, and here he want to keep her soul from heaven."

"Zach?" Liz said, moving to stand between the two men.

Her father didn't look too stable, while Zach simply looked flustered as he asked, "Who told you that?"

"Allain, that who! He telling everyone who listen!" Her father's fists were balled, and Liz worried that one of them would soon find its way to Zach's jaw.

"Well, it's a damned lie," Zach shot back, his eyes narrowing.

"He saying you wanna prove I kill Jed! Kill that boy, me, why would I wanna kill that boy?"

"Stop it, both of you!" Liz commanded, sotto voce.

She had no idea what this was about. Jed murdered? Her father suspect? And why was Richard just standing there, grinning as though this was the greatest show on earth?

"Papa." She touched her father's arm, startled when he jerked around. But the minute he saw it was her, his expression softened. The raised fists lowered.

"Ankouer kill Jed," he said with sudden sadness, "just like you *maman*, and I ain't risking her soul to prove it. Tell him, Izzy, tell Zacharie what be true." He whirled back toward Zach. "You ain't pulling her body outta her eternal resting place, no way, no how! Hear me, boy?"

"Whoa, partner," Zach said in a soothing tone, his anger apparently under control now. "Nothing's going to happen. Okay?"

"You'd better go, Zach," Liz said more sharply than she intended. When he made no move, she added, "Now."

"Sure, sure." He took a few steps toward the door, then stopped. "Trust me, Frank, I have nothing like what you're thinking in mind." Then he nodded at her, a bitter smile pasted on his face. "Have a good life, Liz Deveraux."

And though she knew it wasn't a heartfelt statement, Liz surprised herself by whispering, "You, too, Zach."

She watched him make his way inside and through the crowd, and kept her eyes on him, even though she heard Richard egging her father on. Very soon, Zach tracked down the doctor, and from her vantage point, she saw the conversation was heated, at least on Zach's side.

Which made her conclude that he'd told the truth. How much better if he hadn't. A life waited for her in Chicago, where no one knew about the warped world in which she'd grown up. She didn't belong in this town with its undercurrents of hostility and superstition. But when Zach had walked through those French doors, her joyous heart had betrayed how deeply she'd felt his absence over the years and made her regret the lie she'd built about her background. To let Zach back in would expose it, and she already felt exposed enough.

"Ellie fight him with all her strength."

Her father's statement forced Liz to tear her attention from Zach, and when she did, she experienced a flash of anger at the glint of amusement in Richard's eyes. In defense, she put a protective hand on her father's shoulder.

"Papa," she pleaded, "you don't know what you're saying. You're overwrought."

"Where you learn those big words, girl?"

He'd had too much to drink. Although his stance

was steady and his voice clear, she could see the signs she remembered well from girlhood.

"You're tired. Let's go home so you can get some rest."

"Not now, no. I wanna talk to Richard."

He raised his hand like a traffic cop's, the same warning he'd used when she'd sass back as a kid. For an instant she felt uncomfortably like that kid. I'm an adult now, she reminded herself, and her father needed her to act like one. "Please come home."

"*Non*, it not my home."

"It is. I wanted you and Mama to have it."

She saw Richard taking it all in, not even bothering to hide his interest. She looked over at him. "Could you give us a private moment?"

"Sure, Liz. My other guests need me anyway."

In the space left by his absence, a gaping silence loomed.

"You embarrass me, girl," her father finally said.

"I'm sorry." And she was. She'd displeased him. She was always displeasing him. The house had displeased him most of all, and she wondered why she was so obsessed he take it.

"That old Fortier house . . . it all the time make you angry with us 'cause we not live there." His dark eyes grew darker. "When you give it, it seem you are shamed by who we are, where we live. It cut you *maman* deep in the heart."

Liz almost gasped at that information. Her mother had never told her that; she'd only said her father didn't want to move out of the bayou.

"No, *mon petite*, it not my home. I will not live there."

He turned away, propped his elbows on the railing, and stared in the direction of the swamp.

Three years. Three years, during which she barely spoke to her parents because they refused to live in Zach's childhood home. Now her mother was dead and they'd never heal that rift. Her father was the only one she had left.

"I . . . oh, Papa, I wish I'd done it differently."

He met her eyes, and in them she saw not liquor or dementia, but deep love and compassion.

"I know that, Izzy. But go on now, go to that big old house. I come in the morning to give you the stone and watch you drive away. Cause, leave you must. Soon as you got that opal, *le fantôme noir*, he is gonna come for you. That why I say, run. Run fast, far away from Port Chatre."

The leaden weight already bearing down on Liz's heart got heavier. This was so crazy. There, she'd said it, if only to herself. Crazy.

She was tired, too. She'd made a red-eye flight from Chicago, then driven the remaining distance in a rental car. She'd stared at her mother's lifeless body in the casket for hours the night before, stood in front of her crypt, wandered through the house of a man who used to torment her, and listened to the cruel whispered remarks of his guests. But none of it compared to the pain her father's words ignited.

"All right," she said wearily. "But will you come by before you leave for the bayou?"

"*Oui.*"

She gave him a weak smile, kissed his prickly cheek, then went to say good-bye to Richard. When her father got to the house, she'd try to persuade him to come to Chicago with her. She'd put him in a quiet little hospital for rest and treatment.

But how would she explain him? She couldn't. Not without admitting the truth, which showed how completely she'd built her tangled web.

Expose herself or abandon him? Those were her choices. Both sent her stomach into jitters.

Chapter Three

Zach cut off the motor on the flat-bottomed aluminum boat and let momentum carry him the final distance to the pier. A big, battered aluminum craft was tied to a cypress mooring. It cried out for a new coat of paint, and its lettering, which said DEVERAUX SWAMP TOURS, was so badly chipped that the V and the W were missing. Two pirogues, the canoe of choice in the bayous, were lashed to the boat, one on each side.

The tall old cypress still stood, its twisting, moss-hung branches reaching to the sky and sheltering the steep roof of the cabin. And there, on a limb forking out over the water, a frayed and dirty rope swung in the morning breeze. The tire was gone now, probably taken by water rot. He wished his memories had gone with it. Ghosts of Izzy, laughing as she swung over the water to jump when the tire hit its apex, floated around him.

She always came up laughing, too. That's what Zach remembered most about her. She laughed all the time.

A crystal-clear image arose in his mind of the day he and Jed had come across the Deveraux cabin while paddling into the backwaters. Missus Ellie had come out on the dock, smiling, inviting them in for some cool lemonade. Behind her stood a young girl, all curly haired and grinning, and he'd been captivated by her sparkling spirit even then. She'd been barely seven, he soon learned, closer to Jed's age, who was eight. But even at ten, Zach recognized a link between himself and Izzy, one he'd come to believe could never die.

He made a scoffing sound. So much for that conviction. In a love that could never die, one partner didn't desert the other.

His boat hit the dock with a soft thud, breaking his anguished train of thought. Water was high this year, covering all but the last few steps to the dock. Spiderwebs glistened with dew beneath the final riser and, choosing to avoid them, he stood on a seat and jumped from the boat. He'd had that goddamn dream last night, and his skin still crawled. Spiders—who in the hell dreamed of spiders? He knew some dreamed of snakes—a Freudian thing, he'd heard tell—but thousands of creepy, eight-legged arachni-thingees? Maybe he should get his head examined.

He discarded that thought. Everyone had nightmares, although maybe not the same one, two to three times a week. And he could probably attribute last night's dream to the excessive amount of Smirnoff's he'd downed in the lounge at the Cormier Inn. To cope with his grief, he'd somehow found a way to tuck Liz's memory into a small mental box, opened only when he had too many under his belt, and then quickly closed when sobriety returned.

He had a hell of a time sleeping last night, thinking of her. His insides still quivered from the shock of finding her alive. At the time, he'd thought the day she'd run away was the worst day of his life, but that pain hadn't compared to the torture of hearing she'd been found dead.

Why? he again asked himself. Why hadn't Frank or Ellie had the decency to let him know it wasn't true, that even though Izzy had abandoned him, at least she was alive? Why? And even more painful to dwell upon was the question of why Izzy hadn't told him herself. She'd been the heart of his heart, his soul mate. As corny as it sounded it was true. He'd known it even then, and always thought that she had, too. So, why, why, why?

An osprey shrieked in the silence left by the killed boat engine as if to remind him he was driving himself nuts with these questions. If he kept it up, he *would* need a shrink. Then a roar as loud as a low-flying airplane jerked him fully from his reverie. The wildlife lapsed into silence. The day grew deathly still except for the slap of water against the rocking boats.

Rutting alligators. He hadn't boated through a bayou in ten, twelve years. Just his luck to come in May, right in the middle of mating season.

Close by, frogs soon croaked. Something stirred in the grasses, probably a nutria. He used to shoot those suckers, had once covered a wall in his room with their pelts. He'd promised Izzy he'd make her a coat from them for a wedding present, but he never—

He shook his head so hard he could almost hear his brain rattle. There was no Izzy. She'd vanished twenty years ago. Now an unfathomable woman named Liz claimed her place, which was almost as disorienting as learning she'd been alive all these years.

Zach remained on the end of the dock for a moment, taking in the changes to the house. Lots of gabby people at that wake, and several had mentioned Frank's new prosperity. Here were signs they spoke of. The enclosed second floor had been a screened-in room during the years he'd visited. An expensive job, especially when you lived twenty miles into the swamp. He'd spied power poles during his boat ride, and judging from the absent hum of the trusty generator, the Deverauxs must have hooked up. He wondered if Frank had paid the levy to have the wiring brought in.

Even more startling had been the news that they'd purchased his old family house, then had never moved in, although according to the scuttle-butt they kept it well maintained. And now Liz was staying there. He'd been sorely tempted to make a call on her last night, but just thinking of her roaming his childhood home brought back poignant memories he'd prefer to avoid.

No lights were on. Zach headed for the door any-way. Maybe Frank wasn't up yet or maybe he'd stayed with Liz. He peered in the windows, but the shade trees filtered the morning light too much to see clearly. Should he go in? Despite the remote location, breaking and entering was still against the law, and he hadn't notified the Vermillion authori-ties he was conducting an investigation inside their parish.

But why should he have? He *wasn't* conducting an investigation. He was here to apologize . . . and maybe, just maybe, check out the doctor's wild ac-cusations. He'd been furious at the man for spread-ing his theory at the wake, but after listening to Zach vent, Allain had introduced him to people who were more than happy to discuss Frank's change in fortune.

Where had the money come from? Even more, could it somehow be connected with Jed's death?

Considering Zach's drug dealer theory, it wasn't a completely illogical jump. But to think Frank would also kill his wife and mother-in-law for the same reason, and some twenty years apart? That *was* illogical.

He put his hand on the doorknob. It turned in his hand, but he was unable to make himself open it. If Frank was inside, he'd be furious, and they hadn't parted on the best of terms. And what if Liz was here? He refused to admit even to himself that she was the primary reason he'd boated all this way, but it was that thought that made him release the knob.

Not sure what to do next, he quite automatically reached in his back pocket and pulled out a silver flask, unscrewed the cap and took a few small sips of the vodka inside. As the liquor warmed his stomach he found it easier to keep his mind off Liz.

Standing around made him jittery, and as he returned the flask to his pocket, he decided to check the premises. Looking for what, he didn't know, probably just a reason to hang out until someone showed up.

He walked along the *galerie* toward the back of the cabin, ducking under the outside staircase, then rounding the corner of the building.

It was like stepping back in time. Frank's gin mill still occupied the center of the yard, but the revenuers must have put him out of business because no steam came from its rusty pipes. The big iron kettle was there. A reasonably clean apron was tied to its handle, and the ashes beneath looked fresh. Then there was the water pump, and the tool shed with its bent metal roof.

Nostalgia sucker punched him so suddenly he took a sharp, deep breath. He'd not been one of their people, these Deverauxs, these odd French-speaking Cajuns. Although of the same Acadian heritage, he'd been a town boy, son of the mayor, living in the biggest house. But the Deverauxs had opened their home and hearts to him.

The painful wave immobilized him momentarily, and it was a while before he took heed of the persistent scratching coming from the far edge of the property. He looked in the direction of the noise, and saw the striped tail of a raccoon.

Several striped tails, actually, and as he fixed his attention, a head lifted, staring at him with black-ringed eyes. He hurried down the stairs. Most of the animals scattered instantly, but a few waited until he was almost on them, appearing to issue a challenge with their dark eyes.

Even they retreated when he got within a foot or two. All except one, which held a scrap of fabric in its clever paw. Acutely interested in what had drawn these coons out in broad daylight, Zach bent for a stone and lobbed it, hoping the animal would drop the fabric before turning tail.

The creature jumped when the stone landed at its feet, then whirled and ran away, leaving the cloth behind. Zach walked over and bent to pick it up.

It was a coarse heavy cotton, and by the way it was folded and creased, Zach suspected it was the placket of a shirt. When he turned it in his hand, he caught some faded lettering. Needing better light, he lifted it, then let out a whoosh of breath as he clearly saw the identifying stencil of a Louisiana State Penitentiary uniform.

From long habit he always carried evidence bags in his pants pocket. He reached in for one in which to store the fabric, then returned the bag to his pocket, wanting to check out the site where the animals had been digging.

Although the soil was richly black from eons of rotting flora and fauna, something still blacker lay on top, and he dug out another bag, using it to protect the object from his fingers as he picked up a small black rectangle.

He expelled another rush of air as he saw the Fortier Security Corporation logo.

God, oh, God, he'd ordered the card case inscribed himself. The sting of salt nipped at his eyes, and he bit his lower lip against the pain as he read the words inscribed on a silver bar across the bottom edge: JEDEDIAH FORTIER, CHIEF PAIN IN THE BUTT.

Something was terribly wrong. Papa always kept his promise.

Liz's agitated pulse beat in time with the *putt-putt-putt* issuing from her small rented motor boat as she headed for her father's cabin. Richard Cormier had flashed an oily smile when he'd told her all the faster boats were out for the weekend, then assured her this one'd get her there. Yeah, Liz now thought irritably. At ten miles an hour tops, the trip should take only two or three hours, and the snail's pace only increased her dark mood.

Why hadn't her father shown up as he said he would? The most reassuring reason was he'd gone to Maddie's and was even now sleeping it off in that woman's arms. While the image of him betraying her mother's memory revolted Liz, the other possibilities popping into her mind were worse, much worse.

After settling her things in Zach's old room the night before, Liz had made up the bed, then prepared the master bedroom for her father, with barely acknowledged hope that sleeping here might make him feel he really owned the place. Later, she scrambled some eggs in the remodeled kitchen.

Her father still hadn't shown up by the time she'd

finished eating, so she called Stephen to plan their strategy for the next day, then rattled around the house, waiting and waiting. And waiting some more.

Several hours after dark, she bundled up and went hunting for him. She walked to the Cormier house. Everyone had gone, and the lights were dimmed for the night. She checked Tricou's café, even looked in the lounge at the Cormier Inn. He wasn't in any of those places, and the last anyone remembered he'd been talking to Maddie on the veranda. The recollection of their knowing looks made Liz angry, even now, which kept her fear at bay while she guided her small boat through the swamp.

Floods and droughts had a way of altering the bayou, but at the tip of a narrow peninsula she recognized a lone cypress, so hung with moss it looked like a dying weeping willow, and she turned there into boggier water, reasonably certain she was headed in the right direction.

At first the cypress knees appeared infrequently, but marshy islands of alligator grass narrowed the channel, and she saw ripples on the water that warned of submerged debris. She cut back on the gas, bringing the tiny craft to a crawl, then weaved easily through the obstacles, surprised to find she'd retained so much of her earlier skill. With renewed confidence, she upped the craft's speed. Soon the twisted knobby roots, so reminiscent of aged limbs, thickened. Still she navigated without difficulty. The dense cypress branches filtered the sun until the light dimmed to the level of a smoky bar. She peered through the gloom, looking for familiar landmarks and impatient to move ahead.

Creatures chittered in the grasses. Something screamed from afar. A bird, Liz told herself, tension creeping into her shoulders. Her hand tightened on the tiller.

Water splashed to her left.

She jerked around. Foolish, she told herself, when she saw it was only a diving fish, feeling more so when she turned back in barely enough time to avoid being decked by a low-hanging branch.

She was afraid, and she wasn't used to fear anymore, not like she once had been. These days she lived in a high-rise condominium that teemed with security guards, and she drove or took taxis everywhere. She felt invulnerable in the city, safe, protected, sheltered from harm.

Why did the bayou evoke such terror in her? She had once known these waters like the back of her hand and had loved roaming them. Especially when she was with Zach. He'd been her constant girlhood companion and eventually her lover. They'd planned to marry when they got old enough. Forever, they'd sworn. Forever.

Sparks of that long-ago love stirred in her heart. With a burst of panic, she doused them. But they made her wonder what had frightened her so badly that she'd fled in utter terror and snapped the almost unbreakable bond between them. This watery land was raw and full of dangers, true, but it hadn't always filled her with such trepidation. There must have been a reason, but if there was she couldn't remember it and was reluctant to try. Even the thought of dredging it up made her shudder.

Some things are best left to the past, she concluded, but she still found herself regretting that Zach had been among them.

Soon the cypress grove thinned, and not long after that she emerged on a wide waterway she clearly remembered. When the cabin finally appeared, her regret intensified, even as her death grip on the tiller relaxed. She saw the dock with the family name carved on one of the tall pilings. The familiar tour boat bobbed gently in the water, its dented canopy frame creaking in time with the motion. A good-sized aluminum craft stood at anchor nearby.

The house seemed taller, bigger. As she boated closer, she saw the remodeling her father had told her about, which brought back the day he'd tersely announced he'd added rooms and hooked up to city power, "Case she wanted to come home."

Home. She hadn't thought of the place as home in oh so long, but suddenly it felt that way.

Tears rushed up, and she blinked, hoping they would flow at last. Her eyes burned briefly, then were dry, leaving a thickness in her throat. Swallowing hard, she steered toward the dock until the bow hit wood, then formed a noose in the tie rope and threw it over a piling.

The front door was closed. A plastic holder had been mounted beside it and was filled with printed material about Deveraux Swamp Tours. She smiled. Electricity, advertising. Her father had finally gone twentieth-century. Maybe they even had running water.

"Papa," she called out. Getting no answer, she hopped onto the cypress steps, then climbed up to the dock, passing a loop of dirty rope as she headed for the door.

The rope uncoiled and slithered toward Liz's feet. Her eyes froze open, allowing her to stare in horror as two feet of reptile undulated over the toe of her shoe toward the edge of the pier with an agonizing lack of haste. It hung on the drop-off for a beat of her racing heart, then slid languidly out of sight.

A mewing sound squeaked inside her closed throat, and she stumbled backward, barely grabbing a piling in time to keep from falling off the dock. As she clung tightly, struggling to regain control, she heard a noise. Slowly she turned.

"Papa?"

Chapter Four

Zach hadn't meant to scare her. When he'd heard the boat approaching, he'd thought it was Frank coming back. The wimpy-sounding engine had made him a bit doubtful—he couldn't quite figure an old Cajun going out in a kid's boat—but he wanted it to be Frank. Wanted it bad. He was the only one who could give him answers to what Zach had found out back.

But as Liz stared at him wide-eyed, pale skinned, looking as if she'd seen a ghost, she seemed more like Izzy than the crisp, controlled powerhouse who'd taken a cell-phone call at her mother's wake.

He stepped around the corner of the house and crossed the *galerie*. "Are you all right?"

"I ran across a snake." She looked down at her shoes and laughed nervously. "It must be a snake with fashion sense, because it took its time examining my Doc Martens."

So much for seeming like Izzy, which left Zach in no mood for jokes. But he put on the old Fortier grin anyway as Liz continued examining her shoes. After a second or two, she raised her head. "What brings you out here?"

"Looking up your pa." He hesitated, fascinated with the gemlike shimmer in her eyes. "I wanted to explain—oh, hell, I wanted to apologize for last night. Allain was way out of line."

"People in the Port do and say funny things," she said. A pair of shallow lines appeared between her eyebrows. "Even . . . Someone told me that you think Jed was murdered. Is it true?"

"I've got reason to think so." He didn't want to talk about it right now, not with those unexplained items in his pocket, and he glanced over at the little fishing boat tied beside the steps. Wasn't much more than a flat-bottomed canoe. "You come out here in that, Izzy?"

"Liz," she corrected distractedly, looking at the boat. "Yes. Why not?"

"Gators are rutting this time of year. If one'd come after you in that piece of tin, it would have overturned you in a second. Christ, where does Richard keep his brains?"

"I'm here, aren't I?" Her voice held an irritable edge. "Where's Papa? Sleeping it off inside?"

"I don't think so. Only boat here is that tour boat. I'd think he'd use a smaller one to go to the Port."

"He does."

She then turned toward the door, clearly unwilling to share her worries. If not for the dimming highlights in her cat's eyes, Zach might have thought she'd been telling him her *Wall Street Journal* failed to arrive that morning. Then he saw her knock on the door.

Knock? She grew up in that house.

No one answered. She knocked again.

"This isn't Manhattan, *cher*. Why don't you try turning the knob?"

If she noticed his sarcasm, she didn't betray it. She just did as he suggested and the door swung open.

She took a step forward, then stopped. "Oh."

Zach's nerves were already primed for danger, and he instinctively nudged Liz out of the doorway and entered in front of her.

He'd expected mayhem. Instead he saw a typical Cajun living room. The furniture had changed since he'd last been there, but not much—just different patterns covering the plump cushions on the cypress sofa and chairs, and a recliner he didn't recall. The crucifix still hung over the simple oak mantel, and the wrought-iron rack that held the fireplace tools was the same one Frank himself had welded almost twenty-five years before.

Liz squeezed past him. "Goodness, Zach. You act like you were expecting an ax murderer." Inside, she turned to look back. "I'm sorry. I meant it as a joke. It's only . . ."

She swung her arms helplessly.

"It's only—the tortoise-shell table is gone. And where's the oak sideboard Mama kept the dishes in?" She gazed around wistfully. "Silly isn't it? How could I expect everything to be just the way I left it?"

"In case you haven't noticed, the kitchen's moved, too." He glanced at an archway leading to another room. He moved to enter the curved opening, then stopped. "Uh-oh."

He turned to look at her, hoping his expression didn't reveal his shock. But she looked as unflappable as ever, merely quickening her step and peering around his body.

Another quiet "Oh," left her mouth, but other than that, and the faint tightening of her jaw, she calmly surveyed the mess.

The sideboard was still around after all, but overturned, and its shattered doors lay open. Blue pottery dishes were spilled on the ground, some so badly crushed, they'd turned to rubble. And there were jars, dozens and dozens of clear glass jars, many of which were also broken. Crumbled leaves and twisted roots mingled with the pottery dust.

Liz walked slowly into the kitchen, crouching beside the pile of glass. Zach stepped in after her, his toe brushing an unbroken jar. It rolled, struck another jar, which also rolled to strike another, which struck another. The floor became filled with rolling jars, clicking and clanking in a crazy domino effect. One of the larger ones tumbled like a hamster's wheel, then came to rest at Liz's feet. She looked down at it dispassionately.

"Who on earth could have done this?" she asked. Softly, unemotionally, completely without feeling.

"I expected you to be more upset by finding your folk's place trashed," he said. "Most people would be."

She looked up, her eyes clear. "It is what it is. Nothing I can do now, except clean it up. I learned that lesson a long time ago."

If Zach had harbored any hope that Izzy still existed, this response wiped it away completely. Izzy would have burst through the front door the minute her father hadn't answered. She would have wailed out her despair in the face of this destruction. Izzy wouldn't have talked business on a cell phone at her mother's wake. She would have stayed at the cemetery, throwing herself on her mother's rain-wet vault, pounding and sobbing loud enough to wake the dead.

Maybe your pa did it, Zach thought. Maybe your pa killed your ma, your grandma. Maybe he even killed my funny, loyal, too-courageous-for-his-own-good kid brother and that poor sonuvabitch whose biggest crime was holding an ounce and a half of cocaine. Maybe there is an ax murderer, and maybe his name is Frank Deveraux.

Some part of him wanted to say all that, and if he'd had more booze inside his belly, he might have. But he didn't. Could be that he was too good an investigator to forget you couldn't judge a man by how he reacted to tragedy. Could be that some of his early optimism about people had survived the loss of Jed. So he kept his peace. But that didn't change the connection between Frank and his brother, and someday he might be forced to speak those words, regardless of his present restraint.

He remained silent as Liz picked up a large jar that had rolled to a stop at her feet. Furry tentacles came alive, clawing at the glass, but Liz stared at it unaffected, then put the jar back on the floor.

"Is that a tarantula?" Zach asked over the sudden tightening of his throat.

"Where?" She sounded dazed. "Oh, the jar. Yes. Mama liked to keep them around. Said they were good luck." She tilted her head in question. "Don't you remember?"

"Some things are better forgotten." He toed one of the jars closest to his foot, hoping nothing moved inside. It was labeled in French and contained a gray powder that broke apart in chunks as the jar rocked back and forth. He looked down at the others, all filled with various powders, crushed leaves, and other substances he wasn't sure he wanted to identify. Each jar had a label, with names written in careful handwriting, some in English, but mostly in French. Some were medicines, but some could easily be poisons meant for *gris-gris* bags to ward off evil.

He hadn't seen jars like this in years. Not since he'd attended college, met and married Rita, with her round, full-busted body, her sloe eyes and dark curly hair, her soft, slurred voice and sweet dependence. They'd settled in Baton Rouge and only went to the Port on holiday weekends.

But in the sweet days of his childhood, the ladies of Port Chatre furtively boated out to see Ellie, begging her to gaze in her crystal ball or lay out the Tarot and reveal the loves and fortunes coming their way. Nor were the men immune, but they came by night to learn how to defeat a rival or to get a concoction to cure baldness or impotence or other ailments Zach hadn't even known the meaning of at the time.

And always there was Izzy, impulsive, irrepressible, emotional. As unpredictable as the winds.

"Do you still read Tarot cards?"

Liz gave him a look that said she doubted his sanity, then stood up and grabbed one edge of the sideboard. "Can you help me lift this?"

"I'll do it for you."

"No, no. It's too much for one person." In contradiction, she already had one foot on the base and was doing her best to lever the huge cabinet up. Zach took a few hasty steps and took hold of the top.

When the piece was back in place, she picked up the jar with the tarantula and put it on a shelf. Next, she got the single unbroken dinner plate and turned it around in her hands.

"Mama was so proud of this set," she said. "I mean, look at it. It's just stoneware she got from a grocery in Abbeville, one place setting at a time, but she always kept them in the sideboard to use when papa boiled crawdads for a *fais do-do*." She smiled sadly. "Remember how everyone brought out those old tin instruments, and the music would play, and we kids would jump around between the old folks dancing on the grass and sneak sips of beer when they weren't looking?"

Surprised by her fervency, Zach only nodded.

She set the plate on a shelf, then reached for a teacup with a chunk broken off. Still holding it, she knelt and began brushing through the sharp pieces on the floor until she came up with the missing section, still fairly well intact. She looked up at him with another sad smile. "Maybe I can glue this back together."

Holding the handle between her thumb and index finger and daintily crooking her little finger the way one might at a Ritz-Carlton high tea, she gazed at the worthless cup from the grocery as if it came from a rajah's treasure chest.

Zach noticed a bead of blood.

"You cut yourself." He took her wrist and gently removed the cup from her hand. Her pain had become so visible, and he had the feeling she didn't know it, that she honestly believed she was just talking old times. He wanted to pull her close and ease that pain, and made a move to do so.

Liz immediately read his intention and was so tempted. Lord, to just sink into Zach's arms and let things be okay again. But she'd left that all behind, left *him* behind, and hurt him badly. And she couldn't even give him an explanation, at least not one she felt made sense. *I was afraid*. What kind of explanation was that?

He hadn't deserved that treatment, and she didn't deserve his comfort. It wasn't fair.

If she'd learned anything from her life, it was that being fair brought its own rewards, so she allowed herself the pleasure of his comfort for only the space of a breath, then stepped away.

"It's not that bad." She carefully placed the broken pottery triangle inside the cup, then took it from his hand and put it beside the plate. After that, she went to the refrigerator for cleaning tools—a broom, mop, and dustpan—that were stored in a space between it and the wall, thinking that Zach looked hurt by her rejection of his solace.

"Amazing," she exclaimed. "A refrigerator, an electric stove. To think Mama used to cook all our meals in that fireplace."

Zach didn't say a word.

She got busy sweeping the floor. The jars clanked, and she shoved them aside with her foot. "When Papa bought the butane stove she almost fainted with joy, but she said she still cooked her jambalaya and etouffee in the iron kettle over the open fire because they tasted better that way."

She chattered nervously to fill Zach's silence. "But I guess progress caught up with the Deverauxs, even way out here in the bayous. Can't stop it, can you? Sometimes I wish—"

Just then she heard a noise. Turning, she saw Maddie Catalon bending over inside the frame of the back door. As soon as Liz caught sight of her, Maddie straightened abruptly, one hand behind her skirt.

"Le fantôme noir done this," she said, surveying the vandalized room.

"How long have you been there?" Liz demanded.

"Ankouer come around midnight and take the opal." Maddie leaned against the door jamb, one arm beneath her small breasts, emphasizing the angles of her collar bones. She wore another sleeveless, scoop-necked dress, ankle-length and of a wispy fabric. A necklace of bone and teeth was tied around her neck, and a bright red scarf held back her hair. "Frank got in his boat early and go after it."

Liz made a disdainful noise, then briskly resumed sweeping. "Papa's not here, Maddie, and you and I are hardly best of friends, so if you don't mind . . ."

" 'Hardly best of friends,' " Maddie repeated, her usually husky voice precisely mimicking Liz's. "Who'da thought Frank and Ellie's wild swamp girl would turn into such a prissy miss?"

"What do you want?" Liz really didn't care if she got an answer. "Hand me that dustpan, will you, Zach?"

Instead of giving it over, he bent and held it in front of the pile of debris while he regarded her and Maddie. As Liz swept the shards into the pan, she wondered what he found so fascinating. She also wondered what Maddie wanted. After all—

"Didn't Papa spend the night at your place?" she asked sharply.

Maddie's smile held triumph. "All you need to know, girl, is he gone to Quadray Island."

"Quadray Island?" Zach stood up so quickly he spilled glass onto the floor. He grabbed a cigarette from his pocket, and as Liz was about to suggest he take his smoke outside, she noticed he looked kind of shaky.

"What's the deal?" she asked. "Quadray Island's a myth."

"Yeah, right, you're right." He lit up the cigarette,

took a puff and began pacing the small room, repeatedly crossing between Liz and Maddie as he spoke. "But the area where it's reputed to be is full of unpredictable eddies. Tornadoes touch down, even when they miss every place else, and it's rumored the water is poison." He stopped in front of Maddie. "Nobody goes that way. Why the hell would Frank head out there?"

"I already told you. To find Ankouer and get the opal back for Izzy." Maddie glided to stand in front of Liz. "You gotta go after him. His life, it depend on you."

"For God's sake, Maddie!" Zach barked. "Cut out this crap!"

"T'weren't Catalons who bring Ankouer to the bayous. Deverauxs brung this curse. Now Izzy is the only one left and she don't know jack about using that opal or nothing."

"I don't need to know about ridiculous superstitions, and I sure don't plan to go out and fight one," Liz replied indifferently. "I'll leave that to you."

"If it could be, I would do it. Only a Deveraux woman can tame *le fantôme*. You been running and running, Izzy, but now your duty come a'calling."

"What do you have behind your back?" Zach asked suddenly.

Maddie jerked her head to stared at him. "Nothin'. Ain't nothing. Just some papers I've been needing."

"From here?" Liz looked at Maddie suspiciously. Who could tell what was going on in that woman's head, but her movements revealed a certain secretiveness. "Did you get that from here? Let me see it."

She darted a hand around Maddie's side. Before the woman could react, Liz had snatched the item from her hand. It was an envelope, and she saw her own name written in dark black ink across the front.

"This is for me," she said. "This is Mama's handwriting."

"It tell everything about Ankouer, and Ellie knowed you'd never take it, that's why she give it to me," Maddie said. "Now let me have it back. It don't belong to you anymore. You don't deserve it."

Furious, and wanting absolutely nothing to do with anything that pertained to Ankouer, Liz let the broom clatter to the floor and stormed out of the kitchen toward and through the front door. Then swinging back her arm, she prepared to hurl the package into the water.

"Don't!" Maddie commanded.

It wasn't the power of Maddie's order that stopped Liz. It was the uncharacteristic tremor of terror in her voice. She pivoted slowly to face the woman, noticing an odd flicker to her eyes and a softening of her features as she started to speak.

"You go into great danger, Izzy. *Le fantôme noir*

come from the deep, dark, swirling chaos. Chaos he is and chaos he always be." This wasn't Maddie. The voice was soft and sweet and so achingly familiar.

Transfixed, Liz reached out her empty hand.

"You have power. You must seek it now, claim it!"

"Mama?" Liz said aloud, her voice suddenly choked.

"Turn your back on it and you are doomed. . . . *Le fantôme noir* will prevail. His evil will seep into the world. . . . Darkness will be the end. It is up to you, Izzy. You are the last Guardian."

"That's enough, Maddie!" Zach snarled.

His heated order cut through Liz's trance. She jerked backed, startled beyond belief to see her fingers caressing Maddie's face. Her other hand still clutched the envelope.

"This is just too much, Maddie," Liz said wearily. "Would you please go home?"

"Okay, okay. Only don't be throwing the package away, okay?"

Liz unclasped the envelope's metal prongs and lifted the flap. Slipping her fingers inside, she pulled out a small journal. Shaken by the fleeting instant when she'd thought she'd been listening to her mother, she brought the book to her breasts, breathing deep, hoping to smell her mama's scent, feel the hand that had once crossed the pages inside to record her thoughts.

"I'll keep it then," she said stiffly. "Now please leave."

"Okay," Maddie said. "But take heed, you. Your papa's in trouble, and you need to go to Quadray Island and help him."

"Quadray Island is a fantasy, and I'm not going anywhere." Still holding the book close, she started for the door.

"Oh, you will go. Duty call you very loud. You cannot cover your ears."

With that, Maddie slid around the corner of the house in much the same manner as the snake that had dropped from the dock.

"What was that all about?" Zach asked from the door. He phrased the question in a way that made it sound as if he didn't really care. But his shaken reaction in the kitchen hinted to Liz that he did. And very much.

"You tell me. You heard most of it."

"It was weird, that's what it was. Did you really think Maddie was your mother?"

Liz stared at him a second, then walked back in the house without answering. Weird? Oh, yes. But so sweet in the moment. So, so sweet, to touch her mother's face once more.

Zach caught up with her.

"You don't want to talk about it?"

"No, Zach. No, I don't."

He regarded her uneasily. Turning away to avoid any additional pressure from him, she carefully replaced her mother's journal in the envelope, put the package on the sideboard, and picked up the broom.

"You don't have to stay, Zach. I can manage."

He gave her another one of those piercing stares, with eyes as blue as the sky, then picked up a pail and went to the sink to fill it. "I'm staying until your father comes back," he said. "I still owe him an apology."

Later, as Zach dumped another load of broken pottery into a trash bag, he said, "Tell you what. I'll tie that tin can you came in behind my boat and we can ride back together."

Instead of replying, Liz said, "Have you seen the opal?"

"Maddie said it was— No, I haven't seen it."

"Maddie's crazy." She pointed to the center of the top shelf behind the shattered glass of the display case that topped the sideboard. "Mama always kept it there, for good luck she said, so it has to be around. Help me look, will you?"

She crouched down to search, and Zach joined her. The floor was fairly well cleared, making it easy to find a missing object if it was there. They checked between the stove and the cupboards, behind the sideboard, and even the fireplace.

"Opals are so fragile." Liz poked cautiously through the ashes. "What if we stepped on it? Or dumped it with the other trash?"

Holding back a sigh, Zach grabbed a fresh bag and began methodically emptying the original one, grumbling, "Tarantulas and opals for good luck. Most people think opals are cursed, and, hell, tarantulas are poisonous."

"Not to people," Liz replied, still peeking into corners and under cupboards. "Well, maybe some South American varieties, but not that one." She gestured toward the jar on the sideboard, and Zach felt an invisible something creep up his spine. "Besides, neither animals or objects have anything to do with luck—oh, what's this?"

"You find it?"

"Not the opal. Papa's nitroglycerin." She looked up, worry in her eyes. "Oh, Zach, he's out in that swamp without his medicine."

Chapter Five

Liz threw herself into cleaning the last of the mess in the kitchen while she worked out the problem. Maybe her father would return soon, but somehow she doubted it. After about fifteen minutes of wiping down the same surfaces, she decided to make some calls to town. She had no faith in Maddie's truthfulness, which made the woman's sly evasiveness about her father's whereabouts the night before a strong case for believing he'd actually been there. But he may have returned to Port Chatre to belatedly fulfill his promise to Liz.

Making ample use of the information service to get the numbers, she phoned every place she thought her father might go when he realized Liz wasn't at home. No results. She snapped the phone shut and shoved it back in her handbag, ignoring the worried glance from Zach that mirrored her own concerns.

Where was Papa? Out in the bayou seeking the stolen opal as Maddie proclaimed? The possibility sent a shiver down Liz's spine. He'd been acting unbalanced ever since she'd arrived at the Port, and if he was really in search of an island everyone knew didn't exist, it added fuel to her wildest misgivings. What if he *was* in the grips of insanity? She'd have to do something about it—make sure he stayed safe, get him treatment.

The inner turmoil surrounding this possibility evoked a wave of self-disgust. Her father should be her only concern, but instead she was filled with anxiety over having to explain him to her friends and associates. Was she ashamed of him, as he'd asserted?

The explanation felt all wrong. Her quivering stomach and clutching heart weren't signs of embarrassment. They signaled downright fear, a deep, inexplicable dread that seemed to come from nowhere.

"Maybe he'll realize he forgot his pills and come back for them," Zach said, breaking the long silence between them.

Liz shook her head. "He probably won't even miss them unless he has an angina attack. By then it will be too late."

"I could make a few calls; have a search and rescue team sent out."

Liz considered the offer briefly, then again shook

Connie Flynn

her head. "Papa would never forgive me. You know how swamp Cajuns feel about the authorities."

"But if . . ." As his voice trailed off, he nodded with clearly reluctant agreement. "Besides, your pa might not even have an attack."

"My point." She still felt as confused as ever. "Let me think some more, okay?"

Liz appreciated the way Zach didn't argue. Instead, he busied himself with putting the remaining jars back in the sideboard. Liz returned to wiping down the already clean counters, and even as she scoured a nonexistent spot, she knew what she had to do. Jitters in her stomach, flutters around her heart, neither of these would stop her from doing what was right. Her father came first, and she'd be damned if she'd let some nebulous terror keep her from looking out for his welfare.

She dropped the washrag in her hand, took a deep breath to calm her fear, then turned toward Zach.

"I'm going after him," she announced.

"Do what?" Zach shot back.

"Papa has to have his pills." Which was a good enough reason. Zach had no need to know of her concerns about her father's mental health.

He touched one of her arms, which she dimly realized she'd rigidly wrapped around her body.

"You haven't been in the swamp in years, *cher.* Do you even remember how to navigate?"

"How far could he have gotten?" She walked to a cupboard and opened the door, checking for non-perishable food. "We'll be back by nightfall. Morning at the latest."

"Depends on how powerful his boat is."

"It's just a fishing boat with a small motor."

"But I'll bet it's faster than the one you rented from Richard."

"I'm not taking that one!" She put a couple of cans on the floor, then added some packets of dried soups. "I'm taking the tour boat."

"The tour boat? You won't last more than a couple of hours before you run up on some cypress knee."

"I'm going, Zach, that's all there is to it." Liz had the oddest sense that the decision was out of her hands, and if she had to go, she'd just as soon get on with it. "If you're going to keep trying to talk me out of it, I'd rather you leave. But if you want to help, why don't you check the provisions on the boat. I'll need water, some crates for the food . . ."

She ticked off the fingers of one hand as she spoke. All her uncertainty had vanished, and as their eyes locked she grinned. In that instant, Zach had her pegged. She'd become one of those people who were never truly comfortable unless they had a plan. A valuable trait for a business person, but not so valuable for someone about to embark in the swamps with rusty boating skills.

"Okay, *cher*, I'll help." But letting Liz head into one of the most treacherous areas of the bayou alone went against his grain. An uncomfortable sensation wiggled inside him, a sure sign he might regret his next words. "I'm coming with you."

Liz rearranged the storage bins beneath the rows of bench seats. Plenty of gas, plenty of water, plenty of food. Matches, charcoal, even a small outdoor table grill. Because her father often took out hunting groups for trips that lasted several days, many of the provisions had already been on the boat, and Zach had insisted on doubling the quantity of food she'd selected. Looking at it all, one would think they were going out for weeks, rather than just the day.

She heard a noise and looked behind her to see him balancing one last crate on his shoulder. He pulled the front door shut and said, "We ready?"

Liz nodded. "I've checked everything. Water, fuel, food, rain gear, life jackets. But there aren't any rafts."

"Don't need 'em." Zach tilted his head toward the two cypress canoes tied to cleats on either side of the boat. "We've got the pirogues." He flashed a grin. "How quickly we forget."

"It'll come back to me."

"Like the bicycle thing? Don't kid yourself, Liz.

A mistake'll cost you more than a skinned knee. You're lucky to have me along."

A bit exasperated by his cockiness, she said, "It's not like we're boating around the world. I appreciate your offer, but how much distance could my father have covered in that small boat?"

"Enough, *cher*." The teasing smile vanished. "Enough. He knows what he's doing."

He climbed into the boat, stowed the crate in one of the storage bins, then went to the pilot's seat. A moment later, the motor sputtered to life. He reached for the shift lever, then paused, looking her over rather critically.

"Those clothes," he said, "you'll roast."

She *was* getting warm. She'd stripped off her raincoat while cleaning up the kitchen, but now found herself tugging repeatedly at the neck of the speckled sweater.

"Yeah," she said. "But I— Wait, my mother said she kept most of my old clothes."

She rushed back to the house, climbing the outside stairs to the second floor, and rummaged through her parents' closet until she found a trunk near the back. A short while later, she pulled on a cap-sleeved cotton top, then stepped into a pair of overall-type shorts with tons of pockets that might come in handy. On her way out, she went to the kitchen for her coat, in case they were still out when the sun set.

She snatched it up hurriedly, impatient with this small delay, and as she passed the sideboard, she noticed the envelope she'd taken from Maddie. Despite her impatience, she picked it up and slipped out the journal, taking in her mother's familiar script that, typically, was part French and part English. She flipped through the pages and when she neared the end, she noticed an entry made on the day her mother died.

The sun sets soon on Port Chatre. Nights get warm now and bring sweet smells. Other afternoons, I sit out on this galerie *to watch that big bright ball shine red on the water and am filled with peace. But tonight brings a different sunset.*

With it comes le fantôme noir *and my night of reckoning.*

I must safekeep the fire opal. If it falls in his hands, he will use it to walk the land like humans. But inhuman is his soul, and like the locust he will go forth, eating all who cross his path.

All my life I prepared for this night, like Maman and her maman *before her. All the way back to time begins, our women have borne this curse to guard the fire opal against Ankouer.*

When I wonder about those who die to give him strength to seek the stone, I feel a heavy sadness. I tremble, too. I tremble and am afraid.

Most folks no more believe in le fantôme. *Even*

Frank don't really believe. Ankouer be smart to make the world think this, so none prepare for him no more.

Except for me.

Will I be strong enough? Will my heart stay pure? Will I defeat the evil one? This I do not know until the hour come. My dear Frank, he is not ready to defend me, and if he fails, I stand alone. Who can defeat Ankouer alone? Not Maman, and her heart were pure as any angel.

If I die tonight, my sweet fille will hear the call to take my place. She is the last guardian. No other stands to take her place. Triumph, she must, so darkness does not fall upon the world.

Yet she be so unprepared. She turned from it so long ago. If I die like Maman, duty will look for her. Run no more can she.

I pray for Izzy on this my night of reckoning.

Oh, Mama, Liz thought, what horrific events you imagined on your last day of life, and how sweet it was to touch your face one last time. Tears lodged behind her eyes, and she was more than willing to let them flow, but they immediately faded. She hadn't cried since the night she left the bayou, and the unrelieved sorrow was nearly unbearable. The recall of the moment she'd stroked Maddie's face only added to its weight. Listening to her mother's voice and believing, oh, believing, it was actually her made Liz wonder if her mind was slipping like her father's.

She set the journal down. Perhaps madness did run through her family, a madness that reading these pages could only feed. Better to leave it here. Then later she would put it away unread as a memento of her mother.

"Liz!" Zach called from out front.

"Coming."

Instead of turning to leave, however, she continued staring at the small, prettily bound book. Although she fervently disagreed with her parents' beliefs, she'd never get a better opportunity to know her mother's heart.

A small laugh rumbled in her throat. She was being ridiculous. How could she even consider letting some silly fears stop her from learning more about her mother? This decided, she went to a cupboard and grabbed a large, plastic, food-storage bag. She'd keep the book in it to protect it from water, and maybe read it on the journey.

After tucking the journal safely in one of the larger cargo pockets of her overalls, she walked through the front door to the boat.

When she climbed aboard and draped her coat over the front passenger seat, Zach greeted her with an appreciative grin.

"Cute," he remarked. "I remember the last time you wore those."

Liz felt a bit self-conscious and looked down to see what he found so attractive.

"They're too baggy," she said. "And my legs look like they belong to a ghost."

"You've got great legs, *cher*. Trust me, I'm a connoisseur."

"I'll bet you are," she replied dryly, wanting to divert his unsettling attention. She had a feeling he was trying to travel down memory lane, a place she definitely didn't want to go. "Well, we're finally off to Fantasy Island. I feel rather inane boating to a place that doesn't exist."

"Which'll make it a lot harder to find your pa."

He eased the boat away from the dock, then gave it more gas. As soon as they'd gathered a little speed, he eased off the seat and pulled something silver out of his pocket. When he uncapped it and lifted it to his lips, Liz realized it was a flask.

Oh, great, she thought. Just great.

He recapped the flask and put it on the floor by his feet, then lit a cigarette. This hinted that he planned to stay sober for the trip, so Liz relaxed somewhat. She wiggled around in her seat, trying to get comfortable, and felt a prick from the corner of the journal, which prompted her to take it from her pocket. After she'd slipped it out of the bag, she leaned back to read.

A dog-eared page drew her attention, and she flipped to it.

"A map."

"To where?"

Liz let out a short laugh. "To Quadray Island. There are some notes about it too."

"That's a piece of luck. It'll give us an idea which way your pa went. Although, I should remember. I headed that way myself . . . once."

"Yeah," she said, a smile coming to her lips. "To bring me back a golden orchid."

"Boys do besotted things," he replied curtly as he extended a hand. "Let me see that for a sec."

Liz handed the book over, a bit miffed about his dismissal, and about bringing the incident up in the first place. Hadn't she herself decided not to discuss the past?

They were headed north into a smooth, wide waterway that allowed Zach to prop the journal on the steering wheel and read while they traveled. He'd opened the throttle full bore and wind rushed over the windshield, tearing at Liz's short hair, causing her to experience a feeling of freedom she hadn't known in a long time.

"If this map is accurate," he said after a time, "we'll have to cut off here into this cypress swamp." Liz leaned over to see the spot he tapped. "It might be tight for this big tub, and your pa'll get through easy, so that will cost us some time. But I think we can catch him before dark."

"Glad to hear you being optimistic."

"No, *cher*. Just not quite so pessimistic."

As she settled back into her seat, she noticed him scanning the opposite page, which was written in a combination of French and English and contained baleful warnings about the island. Dividing his attention between the book and the waterway ahead, he studied the information with obvious interest. Once she saw him mouth a phrase she suspected was in French and wasn't easy for him to understand.

Finally, he handed back the journal, tossed his cigarette overboard, then bent for the flask. The tour boat sped across the water as he took another drink.

Zach sighed as he put the flask down. He was getting downright schizoid around this woman. Sometimes he saw so much of Izzy in her. At those times he was torn between intense hostility at the absence of the girl he'd loved, and a craving to yank this replacement close and kiss her till she begged for more. At this precise moment, he wasn't sure which he felt.

She looked soft and cuddly now, with her hair curling into soft tendrils around her face and bare legs sticking out of those shapeless shorts. Yet intense, too, in the passionate way she'd been as a girl. Alive and eager for each experience. Feeling each one deeply. Looking almost as she had the last time he'd seen her wear those denims.

Her parents had thrown another *fais do-do* shortly before Liz disappeared. Only they hadn't been little kids anymore. As teenagers, they'd thought they were so grown up and had two-stepped and waltzed on the lawn with the adults, trying hard not to betray the heat they felt for each other.

That was no longer all there was to the girl he'd loved. That was only Izzy. A "what you see is what you get" girl, incapable of hiding her thoughts and feelings. A girl who'd touched his heart so much he'd once wanted to find her a golden orchid.

Liz Deveraux isn't Izzy. Liz Deveraux isn't Izzy. If he repeated it enough times, he might get it through his thick skull.

Man seedling, come to me.

The words intruded into his thoughts and wiped out the mantra he'd been repeating. He shivered, recalling the day he'd attempted to find the fabled Quadray Island.

On a dare. After one of the guys on his eighth-grade football team had said he was too chicken to go after the orchid that reputedly grew there. They'd been scaring each other with stories: Half-Man, a creature missing half its body who traveled by forming himself into a hoop; and the ghost of Jean Laffite, which no one bought because good old Jean was reported in every spooky nook and cranny of Louisiana.

But *le fantôme noir*. Even the name made kids tremble. A swirling mass of inky black, he was said to turn men's blood to ice, to suck up young boys, only to spit them out like icicles.

Izzy had been listening to the stories, too. When the dare came up, she looked at the other guys like they were fools and said, "Zach can do it."

So Zach, barely thirteen, and wanting so badly to impress her, had climbed into his pirogue one summer morning and headed out to fetch the orchid. He'd paddled and poled through the swamp all day until, as he let everyone think later, he'd actually found those mythic shores.

The sun was nearly down when he entered the bog near the island's reputed location. Cut grass and lily pads choked the shallow water so badly he couldn't row more than two or three feet that the vegetation wasn't grabbing at his paddle or slicing his hands and arms. Mosquitoes swarmed, biting him and raising welts that itched all the worse when he scratched them. Nothing else moved out there—not an alligator or a nutria, not even a fish surfacing for food. He hadn't seen a bird in over an hour.

But he was determined to get Izzy that orchid.

Then things got scary, real, real scary. The sky darkened, but Zach saw no clouds in the sky. The falling sun looked like a pale fuzzy moon behind the gloom. He stopped paddling, scanning the area for anything to explain it.

Fires danced on the bogs, lifting and falling, falling and lifting, or so it seemed. He knew they were just swamp gases, not spirits of the dead as some believed, because he'd learned it in fourth grade. But he could never remember will-o'-the-wisps glowing red like that.

He paddled on and on, dedicated to getting Izzy that orchid. He couldn't stand to let her see the other boys laughing at him, humiliating him, letting her know he wasn't an idol, just a damned scared thirteen-year-old boy, who still coughed and puked when he smoked cigarettes, and hadn't really laid Suzie Martin, no matter what he told the guys.

Hell, why was he doing this? She was only ten; it was not like she was a girlfriend or anything. And everyone said things about her: said she was raised to be a voodoo queen, had second sight, and you better not make her mad or she'd put a hex on you.

But all he knew was she laughed all the time and made him feel like a king.

He paddled on.

Until he heard it.

He hadn't *heard* it exactly, not with his ears. It was in his head, echoing like his conscience.

Man seedling.

Man seedling, come to me.
I need your soul.

The bog came alive with light—skimming the murky water, first as one yellow-and-red flame, then exploding into myriad fingers that surrounded his pirogue and flooded him not with heat, but with a icy chill that numbed his fingers.

Ankouer!

He grabbed the pole and stood up in that little pirogue, not nearly as afraid he'd overturn as he was that whatever talked in his mind, whatever danced on the bog, was coming to suck him up and spit him out like an icicle. He lurched and pulled, lurched and pulled, turning his little canoe almost in a circle.

The mud grabbed at his pole like it had strong bony fingers, and sometime he fell on his butt in his struggle to pull it out.

Man seedling, come to me.

Small flames bobbed around his canoe.

Worse, something inside him wanted to answer that call. But the part of him that wanted to run was stronger. This was danger, danger that wanted Izzy, and he had to get back to protect her. He knew that, knew it as well as he knew that something horrible called him. So he kept on lurching and pulling, lurching and pulling, driven by a need he didn't understand.

Then the spiders came. Tiny spiders, crawling as

with one mind around the pirogue, spinning webs that covered everything. They crept up his bare arms and legs, biting his skin, making it itch worse than the mosquitoes. He'd let out little horrified cries that scared him almost as much as the swarming spiders and the strange voice calling him. And all the while, the fires danced around him.

Somehow, he blocked it all out. He just shoved that pole in the mud and pulled and pulled, ignoring the swarm that he swore covered every inch of his skin.

At some point, he saw the lights of the Port, and he poled more furiously, running and running from the mesmerizing voice in his head, the icy fire, and the spiders that assaulted him.

Finally, the grasses thinned, and each pull propelled his little craft a greater distance. By the time he lay down the pole and picked up the paddle, the fires were gone, the voice no longer called him, and the spiders had vanished, taking their webs with them.

When he reached the dock, his parents were out looking for him with searchlights. And while he waited for their return, his grandmother wrapped him in a big blanket because he'd been shivering like crazy, even though it was one of the hottest nights of summer.

He'd never told anyone about the voice or the flames or the spiders, and when asked if he'd really found Quadray Island, he just forced a smile and refused to answer.

Man seedling, come to me.

But he'd never forgotten the flames or the voice and, damn it all, he still dreamed about spiders.

Chapter Six

Liz appreciated Zach's steady hand on the wheel. It gave her a chance to relax, and also to call Stephen before they got out of range. She didn't particularly want Zach overhearing, and since she'd put her purse in one of the storage bins, she had a perfect excuse to go to the back of the boat.

The conversation was brief, covering the stock she'd finally decided on the previous night. After business was done, Stephen perfunctorily asked how she was, then told her a little bit about the basketball playoff game he'd attended the night before with his girlfriend.

When Liz disconnected, she replaced the cell phone in her handbag, then returned it to the bin, being careful to secure the complicated latch that kept the seat benches that served as lids from flying up in a brisk wind.

When she returned to the front seat, she thought about telling Zach how glad she was he'd come, but before she could, he spoke.

"You ever go anywhere without that phone?"

"Not if I can help it."

He gave no response to her answer, and dropped back into the funk he'd entered earlier. She didn't know the reason for it, but since he appeared in no mood to talk she decided to go back to the journal. She read for quite a while, her throat thickening when she encountered a passage about how deeply her mother had loved her. Later that sentiment turned to guilt as the pages relayed the grief Liz had caused during the months she'd allowed her parents to think she was dead.

She lifted her head, staring out. A warbler sang in the distance, and a little blue heron stood on the shore. Willows and oaks rimmed the shore, interspersed with the occasional cypress and maple. She'd forgotten how beautiful the bayou was, along with why she'd left it.

All she remembered was being convinced that the swamp had killed her grandmother. Why she thought so, she could no longer say, but she'd believed it so completely that after her grandmother's funeral she'd taken her pirogue downstream to Vermillion Bay and hitchhiked north.

The dangers to a young girl traveling and trying to get along on her own were unspeakable. But everything had gone her way. At a truckstop in Arkansas, she'd met another runaway from Detroit who was headed for New Orleans to become a singer. She was about Liz's age, and she had a warm jacket she was more than happy to trade for Liz's lighter one. And other than an overly friendly man who'd offered her a ride to Little Rock that she wisely refused, she'd encountered none of the perils many runaways faced.

When she'd finally reached St. Louis, only fifteen, and with no education, she'd found a job as a live-in babysitter and housekeeper. Liz had realized right away how lucky she'd been to find Mrs. Ashton and wanted very much to please her, but even that hadn't stopped her from telling the woman she was from Arkansas.

The rest of that time was mostly a blur to her now. She remembered the homesickness, the way she'd yearned for her mother's understanding ear, for her father's big bear hug. And she'd ached so much for Zach she sometimes cried herself to sleep. But every time she'd tried to write her folks, every time she'd tried to pick up a phone to speak to Zach, her stomach rolled so badly she'd nearly lost her supper.

What if they came for her? What if they made her go back? So crazy, now, but then she'd honestly believed she'd die if she ever returned. Six months passed before she found her courage to write her parents.

She'd been horrified to learn that the girl she'd traded jackets with had drowned in the bayou and been identified as her. Despite her poor recollection of those events, the day she received that telephone call from home remained etched in her mind. So did the tremors that came to her hands the instant she heard her mother's teary voice.

"Sorry, I'm so sorry," she'd babbled, then selfishly pleaded with her folks to keep the news to themselves. Her father came on the phone, angry, saying the other girl's parents had a right to know about their daughter. "Please, please, please do it quietly," she begged. "And don't tell Zach, never Zach."

Later, Mrs. Ashton helped Liz get her GED, taught her proper grammar and even found a speech coach, whom Liz paid from her small earnings. By the time Liz finished college, majoring in economics, she never, ever said "y'all" or "ain't," and she sounded as if she'd grown up in the Northeast. She'd also developed a knack for the financial markets, which she took to Chicago. After a tearful good-bye to Mrs. Ashton and her children, she made new friends who accepted her fabricated upbringing. As time passed, and with no little amount of guilt, she deliberately fell out of touch with the family that had been so good to her.

For several years after, she still looked over her shoulder to see if anyone had followed. But no one came after her, which made her confident that her folks had kept their word. Judging by the shock the Port Chatre residents exhibited when she'd appeared at her mother's funeral, none had known she hadn't drowned in the swamp twenty years earlier.

Looking back, she failed to understand what would have been so bad about returning to the Port. True, she would have never become the person she now was. But she couldn't imagine thinking in that vein. At fifteen she'd had no clue to the direction her life would take. Neither did she remember such intense self-interest being a part of who she'd been.

She tapped the spine on the journal. What could it have been? What provoked the overwhelming fear that still plagued her whenever she thought her true background might be exposed? The deception she still practiced? Even when she'd purchased the Fortier house for her parents, she'd used a third party to hide her identity. Nothing short of her mother's death would have ever brought her back.

But the agonized outpourings on the pages of the journal in Liz's hand brought home the bitter truth of how much pain she'd caused. So many good-byes, so much heartache, so much deception, and all because of her.

Why? She had no answer.

But after all that, how had she found herself saying hello to everything she'd left behind and riding in a boat with the man she'd hurt as much or more than any other? The man who, above all, could expose the lie she'd made of her life?

"Can you read that?" Zach asked suddenly.

Glad to have her gloomy thoughts interrupted, she looked up to see him peering at the journal.

"Of course," she said. "I grew up speaking French, remember?"

"Sure do. I often envied you that."

This wasn't news to Liz. She knew Zach's parents had been punished for speaking French, like most town Cajuns of their generation, and seldom used it for fear Zach and Jed would get the same treatment.

"I'm glad to see you didn't leave that part of your past behind too." He laughed, but it wasn't a truly amused sound. "I miss your drawl, and your long hair."

"Give it a rest, will you, Zach? I've changed, okay? We've all changed." She let her gaze pointedly drop to the flask at his feet.

"Right." He redirected his eyes forward, then reached for a cigarette.

Liz returned to the journal. The entries weren't daily. At times more than a year passed before her mother wrote again, and as Liz got closer to the end, references to Ankouer appeared ever more frequently. Each time she saw that name, or its more dramatic alias, *le fantôme noir*, she felt a surge of irritation. As she continued reading, the irritation escalated to anger.

Finally she couldn't stand it anymore.

"This is ridiculous, Zach! Listen!"

He took a puff from his cigarette before giving her his attention. "Shoot."

She flipped back a few pages, then began reciting in an intentionally stagy and sonorous tone. " '*Le fantôme noir*, or Ankouer as he sometimes be called, comes from dark, cold regions. Not of this world, he covet the light, and seeks to—' " She paused. "I'm not sure of the idiom, but I suspect it means 'absorb.' Anyway . . . 'he seeks to absorb all that is good and pure about humanity. Above all, he seek the fire opal and its power to control the thoughts and deeds of men and bid them do his will. The guardian protects . . .' " She looked up. "Now really, Zach, doesn't this read like a fantasy novel? A very bad one at that."

"There are things in this world we don't understand. I'd be careful about dismissing them too easily."

Liz stared at him a second. "You believe this?"

"Believe? No. But I don't dismiss it out of hand the way you seem to."

His answer outraged her. She slammed the journal shut and sprang to her feet. "We're not kids anymore, talking about daughters who return from the tomb and other zombies. You know things like that don't exist. How can you even suggest they do?"

Zach patted her seat. "Sit down, *cher*, you're unbalancing the boat . . . or you might if you were a whole lot heavier."

Liz felt suddenly foolish. Many people believed in spirits, both evil and good. Zach wasn't so off base in expressing such thoughts, but his easy acceptance of the possibility sent a strange shiver through her body.

"All right." She reluctantly sat, put the journal on her lap and stared through the windshield.

"Our parents did believe a lot of hocus-pocus, Liz. I don't deny that, but keep in mind your ma was a healer. She delivered most of the babies born out there in that swamp. The herbs she prescribed, well, many of them are the natural basis for prescription drugs. My ma never confesses to it, but I know she goes to the voodoo shops and tries to speak to my pa and Jed." He paused a moment to stub out his cigarette. "You seem angry about these beliefs, but our parents are who they are. We can't change that."

The voice of reason, but the impetus for her anger seemed much more complex than just rejecting her parents' ways.

"I suppose you're right. It's just . . ." She reopened the book and riffled through the pages until she found the one she'd been reading from. "There's more. Like this stuff about the guardian safekeeping the opal. Listen."

Feeling another surge of outrage, she again read aloud. " '. . . by giving her life, if need be, to assure the fire stone falls not into Ankouer's malevolent grasp.' Now get this. 'In the hands of the guardian, the stone becomes the means of his defeat. . . .' Blah, blah, blah. What did I tell you?"

She closed the book again. "The whole Ankouer myth troubles me. People take it to heart. I've been afraid to say it out loud, Zach, but there's more that worries me about Papa's behavior than his just forgetting his medicine. Ever since I arrived, he's gone on and on about being the defender and having failed Mama. His burden of guilt is so heavy . . . and so undeserved. Then he became adamant that I take the opal from Port Chatre. All because of a stupid superstition." She looked away for a second. "I'm not sure what's going on, but I don't want him out here alone. He could be delusional."

Liz's admission sent Zach's hand flying for his flask. From what he'd seen of Frank, he figured the guy was hanging by a string. But hearing it from Liz's mouth? . . . He preferred not to think in that vein despite the damning evidence in his pocket that suggested Frank had opportunity to kill Jed. His strong hands provided the means. And Liz had just given a motive by suggesting that his beliefs in an evil power had driven him to madness.

"Grief does strange things," he said, forcing himself to let go of the flask without taking a drink.

"I suppose it does." She lifted her feet, propped them on the console, and slumped a bit in her chair. "I'll feel better when we find him."

"We'll find him, Liz, we'll find him."

Liz met his earnest gaze and for a moment got lost in the crystal-blue eyes she remembered so well. It felt like the old times she wanted to avoid, going over her worries with Zach. And comfortable . . . something she'd prefer not to acknowledge.

"Thanks," she said. "Talking about it helps."

"Does that mean I'm good for something?"

Liz smiled at his self-deprecation. "This doesn't sound like the Zach I remember."

"Just being humble." He laughed so contagiously she couldn't resist joining him.

Nothing had changed, but she did feel better, or would, if the sun weren't beating down on her so intensely. She hadn't been beneath rays this strong since she'd taken her folks to Florida a few years back, and her skin was already reddening. "You see any sunscreen in the bin?"

"Think so." He gestured to his left. "Try the back one."

She replaced the journal in the plastic bag, then

slid it into a pocket of her overalls and buttoned it securely before going to search the bin.

Sure enough, there it was, and she applied the lotion lavishly, but still felt hot and sticky. The water looked cool, and she eyed it with longing, then noticed the ramp gate that folded both in and out as needed. Walking to it, she pulled out the securing pins and brought it back, still folded, to lie on the deck. Next, she sat down, took off her shoes and socks, and dangled her toes in the rippling water.

Instantly, she felt less overheated.

"I don't think that's a good idea," Zach said.

"Why?"

"There're gators all over the place, and it's mating season."

Except for the wake caused by their boat and the rush of water around a floating log a short distance ahead, the river was clear as glass.

"When did you become such a worrier? We haven't seen or heard an alligator since we started out."

He made an annoyed sound, and she noticed he changed course slightly to avoid the log. Choosing to ignore his warning, she idly splashed her feet. The pirogue tied in front of the gate created small waves that washed deliciously over her ankles, and she couldn't resist leaning forward to scoop up a handful of water to dribble over her neck and arms. Heaven, pure heaven.

It was hard to think about danger when everything around her was so beautiful. Feet still in the water, she let her gaze drift to the lush shore. Suddenly she saw a flash of intense color. Holding on to the rail of the boat, she leaned farther out, this time catching the hue of dusky skin.

"Maddie," she said softly.

"What did you say?" Zach asked.

"Maddie's out there!"

"Impossible. We've covered nearly twenty miles."

"It's her, I swear!" Liz braced herself and was halfway to her feet when the log came alive with a hiss and sped toward the boat.

"Gator!" Zach exclaimed. "Hang on, Liz!"

He swerved, sending Liz reeling, but she clung tightly to the rail, staring in numb shock as the alligator rose from the water, wide jaws revealing rows of sharp jagged teeth. In the blink of an eye, the creature struck the bow of the boat. One hand still gripping the rail, Liz fell through the open gate and dangled, with her feet underwater.

The reptile rushed toward her.

She twisted to grab the rail with her other hand, and tried to walk up the side of the boat. The alligator slapped the water with its long broad head, and the ensuing wake caused her feet to slip.

The creature was so close she could smell its rotten breath, and she whirled her legs frantically in her attempt to scramble up the side of the boat, never taking her eyes from the gaping jaws closing down on her. She knew what alligators did, how they clamped their enormous snouts around a body, then rolled and rolled in the water until the victim drowned. She'd read about it, heard about it, but, dear God, she'd never thought it would happen to her.

A blur crossed her line of vision. An oar.

Zach was standing above her, swinging the oar directly at the reptile. It connected with the alligator's snout. The creature hissed, then rolled in the water, reemerging to fight again.

It was the diversion Liz needed.

Her shoulder muscles screamed as she pulled herself up the water-slick side of the boat. A moment later, she flipped over the side and clawed her way across the ramp, its ribbed surface punishing her elbows and knees almost beyond endurance.

An eternity passed, and then she was panting on the deck, every inch of her body aching. Curses and bellows filled the air, along with the sharp cracks of wood slamming against armored flesh. Liz forced herself to scoot off the gate and began pushing it back in place.

"Forget it, dammit!" Zach shouted, swinging his weapon one more time. "Get away!"

The alligator was still coming, swerving to escape

Zach's repeated blows, but keeping its glassy eyes pinned on her. All she could think was that it would crawl up after them and swallow them whole, leaving nothing of them to bury. She had to stop it. With trembling fingers, she slammed the gate in place, fumbling for one of the pins. It slipped from her hand and the gate started to fall back.

Zach screamed at her to move back, but she paid him no heed as she pushed the gate back up. Just as she nearly had the first pin inserted, the creature leaped straight out of the water, aiming for the ramp. Liz barely escaped before the gate came crashing down, and the abruptness of her movements sent her sprawling.

Easy prey.

The alligator seized the opportunity and lunged. It landed half in the boat, almost on top of her. Its long whipping tail repeatedly struck the attached pirogue, sending it into an obscene jig. Jaws of death snapped violently, heading directly for Liz's face. Half-sitting, she scooted backward, only to be stopped by the wall of the storage bench.

No escape. None. She brought her arms up to cover her face. Images flashed in front of her clenched eyes. Her mother, her father, Zach and Jed, and then, horribly, her own shredded corpse being placed in a casket. She screamed.

Then she heard footsteps in front of her. She

opened her eyes just in time to see Zach drive the oar straight into the alligator's snapping mouth. The stout cypress withstood the onslaught for mere seconds before it fractured. Broken teeth and wood splinters scattered in all directions. The alligator fell back from the boat, turning and diving, only to rise and dive again. Churning water crashed around the craft with the ominous knell of storm-tossed ocean waves.

Liz froze, bile rising in her throat as she watched the creature's spiked teeth savage the oar. Realizing with terrifying clarity that it could just as easily been her, she rose to her quivering knees. A touch on her shoulder made her jump, and a squeak escaped her half-paralyzed throat.

"Goddamit, Liz!" Zach lifted her to her feet and shook her. An instant later, he pulled her close, then pushed her away and shook her again. She was too weak to protest or resist, and when he finally pressed her to his chest, she simply allowed her head to fall on his shoulder.

"You little fool," he whispered hoarsely into her hair. "Don't you realize I couldn't stand to lose you a second time?"

Chapter Seven

"That could have been you between the gator's jaw, Liz."

He'd stopped shaking her and now had her close, so very close. His ragged breath warmed her face, and his heated, trembling body took her chill away. The boat moved slowly down the middle of the waterway, unmanned. Behind them echoed the sounds of the alligator crushing the oar.

Liz shivered, letting Zach's strong arms enclose her, letting him take care of her the way he used to, back in that sweet time before she'd felt the need to flee.

She lifted her face, wanting to taste again the honeyed flavor of his mouth. He cupped her chin, his steel-blue eyes reflecting the shade of the sky and coming to rest on her parted lips. His head dipped ever so slightly.

Liz sighed.

Zach's eyes narrowed and he stiffened. "I best get back to the wheel before we run aground." She heard the edge to his voice, felt contained fury come off him in waves.

She nodded and stepped back, then moved leadenly to the passenger seat and wrapped herself in her raincoat before collapsing.

She'd felt his horror at almost seeing her killed before his eyes, and also sensed the earlier horror he must have felt when he'd thought she'd drowned in the bayou. But she didn't want to feel it. She'd done what she'd had to do, and she refused to feel guilty because she'd failed to let him know that some other runaway had been identified as her. Absolutely refused.

Zach glanced at Liz all huddled inside her raincoat, and his mind fixated on the reality that Liz had let him believe she'd died. She hadn't let him know it wasn't true, or apparently even let her parents tell him. A cop, for Christ's sake, he'd been a cop. And now he was an investigator. He'd had the means to track her down if he had known.

She hadn't wanted to be found! Why couldn't he get that through his thick head? Everything about her proved she'd rejected her heritage, and he was a part of it. She wouldn't let him back in. After her deception, why the hell would he want back in anyway?

Until the gator showed up, he'd almost convinced himself he didn't. But the image of that bull rolling and ripping the cypress oar apart was burned into his mind's eye. Every time it popped up, he saw Liz between those jaws instead of a stick of wood.

He bent for his flask, opened it, and took a long gulp. You're drinking too much during daytime hours, he reminded himself, but took another gulp anyway, drawing deeply on his willpower to recap the bottle and return it to his pocket. The pleasant burn eased his inner trembling, and he relaxed some, allowing another thought to enter his mind.

He'd have sworn he'd seen a log ahead. Up to the moment the gator attacked, he'd been sure they were approaching a log. Alligators usually kept their bodies submerged, allowing only the bulging eyes to peek out. It was odd for one to float so high in the water. Very odd.

Still, the incident was behind them now. He had to hold that thought. Behind them, all behind them, and he didn't need another nip of vodka to make that true.

"Zach." Liz's voice was soft, imploring, but he didn't look at her. "Maddie *was* on the shore."

That made him turn. "You almost got eaten by a gator and all you talk about is Maddie Catalon?"

"She's hiding something. I know she is."

A sneer wanted to form on Zach's lips, but he tried to hold it back. "So what are you thinking,

107

that she ran more than twenty miles by land to put a curse on us? Why are you so obsessed with that woman?"

"You don't have to be sarcastic," she replied evenly. "And you know why. Everyone knows . . . knew."

"Yeah, but that doesn't mean she's out to get you. Seems the other way around, you ask me."

"She's my father's— It's not right, she took away love that belonged to my mother!"

"When're you gonna get it, Liz? Cajun men have had mistresses, since . . . well, way back when. I'd hazard a guess it didn't bother your ma as much as it bothers you."

"Oh, right! Hard-drinking womanizers, and being Cajun explains it all!"

"When did you get so stubborn?"

"Look who's calling *me* stubborn!"

Zach blew out his breath and reached down for his flask. "If it weren't for you making up your mind your father had taken off in the bayou, we wouldn't even be here. And you sure as hell wouldn't have been in danger of becoming alligator fodder. Did it ever occur to you that your pa might be off on a bender?"

Liz flinched, then eyed him levelly. "I suppose you know all about benders, don't you, Zach?"

"What?"

"You seem to like your liquor." She glanced

down at his searching hand, and he hated the way he jerked it back so fast.

"I like a drink or two, *cher*," he replied breezily. "It mellows me out, but I keep it under control."

"Sure you do."

She let out a sigh that burned a hole in his armor, but he refused to let it sting. Directing his eyes back to the waterway, he opened the throttle a bit. "Check your ma's map again, will you?"

"The journal!" She quickly undid the button of her pocket and snatched out the plastic bag. When she opened it, she let out a relieved sound. "It stayed dry. It's about all I have left of Mama. I would have been heartbroken if . . ."

"Yeah," Zach replied, more sharply than he'd intended. He'd heard the ache in her voice, and wondered if tears would follow. He understood her pain and felt a dangerous sympathy for her. She hadn't wanted to be found, he reminded himself. She didn't want his support, his caring. She'd left Port Chatre without a word—

Damnit, he had to stop wishing for something that would never be!

"Check for the turnoff to the cypress swamp, would you? If I recall right, there's a grove of maples on the western shore just before we're supposed to change course."

"Well," she replied, speaking with clearly forced light-heartedness as she opened the journal to the dog-eared page, "I can add something new to the map. 'X' marks the spot where Liz almost became a power lunch for an alligator."

Zach grabbed for a cigarette. "Not funny, Liz." Bracing the wheel between his elbows, he lit up, then goosed up their speed. "Not funny at all."

They should have sighted her father by now, Liz thought. Not long after encountering the alligator, they'd left the main waterway, and Zach had soon given up his trust in the map.

"Who knows how long ago she drew it," he commented at one point. "It could be years out of date."

Liz replaced the journal in her pocket and agreed that the map didn't appear to be much good. The tour boat had superior speed, but they'd been on the water over four hours and hadn't heard one other engine, even though they'd followed the prescribed route. They'd already found themselves in a bog so shallow, Zach had worried they'd run aground.

Somehow he'd managed to back out, and soon after, they headed up a tributary that gave fairly easy passage. It turned out to be another dead end, so here they were, turned around again, returning to the river to search once more for the turnoff.

She hadn't remembered it being this hot in May. She'd taken off the raincoat sometime back, and the sun had dried her shorts for the most part. Though she'd tried to smooth back her wind-torn hair, she was pretty certain it resembled a whisk broom.

Not that it mattered. Zach now spoke to her only for informational purposes and looked at her even less often. Unfortunately, with just twenty feet to roam, he was her only entertainment. Unless she wanted to return to the journal.

Reading it simply made her heart too heavy.

She slanted a glance in Zach's direction. He'd slipped off his windbreaker and unbuttoned his shirt, which flapped in the wind and bared his chest. How different he was from Stephen, who was long and rather rawboned, with a smooth chest that Liz suspected he shaved in conformance with the current trend. Zach's body was . . . well, it was elementally male. And big. Broad shoulders. Hard, compact, chest. Arms that looked as though they could snap a tree limb in half.

She became fascinated by how the light played on the sprinkling of golden hair that curled on his chest to spiral down toward his jeans. Had his adolescent body shown the pattern of the man to come? Had she dipped her hungry fingers in that mass and followed it down to its sexual source?

She closed her eyes, trying to recall what it had been like so long ago. She could almost feel the texture between her fingers, and very vividly remembered the sweet hot thrill of stroking him. God, how intense their love had been.

Her eyes snapped open. What was she doing? The Zach behind the wheel of that boat and the Zach she'd loved then weren't even the same person. The Zach she'd loved had been sweet, caring, and protective.

Still, the Zach sitting in the pilot's chair had done one fine job of saving her from the alligator. But he was so cynical and moody now, and he used his powerful charm to conceal a simmering anger that had exploded when she'd been attacked. She didn't have to be a psychologist to know the reason.

Why didn't he ask? The question was on his mind. It had to be. She supposed she could explain, but somehow explanations seemed useless at this late date. Leaning forward to flick a leaf off her leg, she turned toward him, and somehow the words just rushed from her mouth.

"Yesterday," she began, "at the Cormiers', it started all over again. Everyone whispering about me, a little afraid, wondering if I have powers they don't. It was almost as if I'd never left, you know. There I was again, Ellie and Frank Deveraux's wild swamp child, heiress to the guardian's throne."

She leaned forward earnestly, vaguely noticing the blank look in Zach's blue eyes. They seemed bluer now, with the sky above and the water below, and for an instant she was tempted to forget her stupid confession and just get lost in them. She wasn't even sure she was being truthful. Her reasons way back then were so complex. But what else could it be? No other explanation made sense. This she knew: the words straining to leave her lips came from the depths of her heart.

"That's all I would have been, Zach, if I stayed. Mama and *Grandmère* were teaching me the spells—not that I was any good at them—and Papa kept reminding me I'd be caring for the opal some day. And at school the same kids who wouldn't speak to me on the bus caught me behind the bleachers and asked me to tell their fortunes. I had to leave, Zach, can't you see that?"

He still had that blank look.

"Well, can't you?"

"That was a long time ago, *cher*," he said evenly, idly flicking his cigarette against an ashtray affixed to the console. "I don't understand why you're telling me this."

Now Liz stared blankly. He didn't understand? She'd just spilled out her guts, spoken words she suddenly realized she'd wanted to say to him for so long. The last time she'd felt so foolish was when she'd been a junior stockbroker at Schwab. She'd been invited to a company party, where she'd enjoyed herself thoroughly. Someone kept filling the glass in her hand, and before she knew it, she was in the middle of a group, telling an old Cajun tale about how a rabbit tricked a fox out of the contents of a honey pot, complete with colorful Cajun dialect.

Several years of speech therapy vanished in the wake of one drink too many. She'd been teased about it for weeks, with people telling her she was quite an actress. That close call made her vow to never again drink too much.

"Right." She stood up and turned away to hide her blazing cheeks. "A long time ago. I felt like talking about it, that's all."

She caught his nod from the corner of her eye.

"It's going to start getting late." His tone sounded softer but she probably was indulging in wishful thinking. "We better start looking for a good place to pull in for the night."

"I'd rather wait till we get back to the river," she protested. She wanted this trip done with. More, she wanted to get away from Zach and the feelings he brought up. "Maybe we can still catch Papa today."

"We'll have a hard time finding a good anchor spot at night." He pointed to the low-hanging sun. "Look."

Liz reluctantly agreed and started searching for a place to pull in.

"Over there?" Liz pointed to their left.

"Nah, it's marsh. Look for high ground with some oak and elm."

Soon they spotted a high point with the requisite

trees and grass. Zach eased the boat close to shore and anchored it. "We could take the grill and a kettle," he suggested. "I'll catch some crawfish and boil 'em up. How long's it been since you ate crawfish?"

"A while." She didn't add she normally avoided all things Cajun because now the idea made her mouth water.

Zach unlatched the passenger gate and let the ramp fall to shore, while Liz got out the charcoal and kettle and rummaged around for other supplies and something to go with the crustaceans. She shoved everything into one crate, while Zach gathered up the grill and a net, then put several bottles of water in a bucket.

Soon he was lighting the charcoal, and Liz was filling the kettle. By the time she began peeling potatoes and onions, Zach had taken off his shoes and socks and was rolling up his jeans, preparing to wade into the water with the net.

As she worked, Liz heard him let out an occasional "Damn," and she smiled, knowing a crawdad had just gotten away.

When she finished peeling the vegetables, she settled back, listening to the buzz and chirrups of the swamp at dusk and keeping an eye on the kettle. Now and then, Zach let out a low cheer, and after Liz had heard more than a dozen of them, he came back.

"Br'er Crawdad's all over the place out there," he said, his spirits so high Liz wondered how often he'd dipped into his flask. "Caught nearly two dozen of those suckers. A couple of 'em are over four inches long. How's the fire coming?"

No mater where his good spirits came from, they were contagious. Liz smiled and gestured to the grill. "The water's coming to a boil and I'm about to put in the vegetables. 'Course we could eat the potatoes half raw, the way we did when we were kids."

"Now she wants to go down memory lane." He said the words mildly enough, but Liz still felt their sting.

"I tried to explain," she replied weakly.

"Yeah. Forget it, *cher*. I didn't mean anything."

She started to say she was sure he did, but he put the bucket down and replaced his socks and shoes, then stood up. "I gotta go see the man."

He came back a few minutes later, looking deflated. "Those potatoes coming along?"

"They're ready for the crawdads."

He went to the bucket and examined his catch.

"Think this will be enough?" he asked so morosely it sounded as if he were about to boil his best friends. "Maybe I should have caught more."

"They're fine, Zach, just fine."

He crouched beside the kettle, poking the potatoes to see how done they were, then dipped in his back pocket.

She got up, collected some paper, and told Zach she was going to find her own potty place before it got too dark. He nodded and opened the flask. As Liz walked away she saw him take a drink.

Lord, oh Lord, it was going to be a long night.

Chapter Eight

When Liz got back, she heard water bubbling and saw Zach stirring the pot with a wooden spoon. He'd taken out plates and plastic utensils, which were stacked beside him, and had also carried the crate with the charcoal and water bottles back to the boat.

"Won't be long," he said chipperly. "Sun's setting real fast, so I got out the lantern in case it gets dark before we eat."

Putting her hands on her hips, she paused to stare at him.

"If you don't stop doing this Jekyll and Hyde thing, I don't know how we'll finish this trip."

He grinned at her, showing not a trace of remorse. "You aren't the first woman to say that." He returned to stirring the crawfish. "Wanna come over here and help me serve?"

She went to his side and bent for a plate. "Do you ever do anything to control your moodiness?"

Zach shook his head gravely. "Nope. I'm incorrigible."

Liz couldn't help smiling. "Should I be grateful Dr. Jekyll's back then?"

Zach laughed. "Liz, I doubt you've ever been grateful for anything. But I forgive you. Are you ready for this crawdad stew?"

She crouched beside him. "I'm going to shock you, Zach. By saving me from the alligator, you've earned my undying gratitude." She winked then, and stuck out her plate. "Now dish up my meal, manservant."

With the grin still on his face, Zach scooped out the crawfish, dividing them equally between them. When Liz said he'd given her too many, he should take more, they argued about it briefly, with Zach finally giving in and taking a larger portion. While they divvied up the potatoes, he nonchalantly asked, "Who's Stephen?"

"My partner. We have a small investment office."

"You are a stockbroker then. I thought so."

"Of sorts. Stephen and I work alone, not for a firm. He does an investment letter, too, but I just trade stocks, bonds, and commodities."

He chugged some catsup on his plate, then set it on the ground, while he dished up the onions. "Is that all there is between you two, a partnership?"

119

"Yes." Liz oddly felt as if she was lying. She and Stephen had been involved briefly, but there had been so little ardor, just many shared interests and a genuine respect for one another. Finally they'd agreed they made great business partners, but a romance wasn't in the cards. Shortly after, Stephen started dating a redheaded runner from the exchange floor, and for a while she was all he could talk about. Now that was ardor. Or so she'd thought at the time, while enduring hours of Stephen's copious praise of his flame-haired paragon.

"And you never married?" he went on to ask.

"No, but I know you have. Mind if I ask what happened? From what I heard at Cormier's, I assume you're single now."

He nodded. "As Richard pointed out, they all left me." His voice again took on that cynical edge. Then, in a fonder tone he continued. "But I can't complain about the first two. They gave me my kids. Zettie's the oldest, she's in college now, and my son, Chet, plays high school football. Too bad Carol's none too fond of me. If not for that, Chet and I would get along a whole lot better."

"And Zettie?" Liz cocked her head.

"Things are just fine with her. Rita's her mom, and we made our peace a long time ago." He patted his pocket. "She gave me this flask. First Christmas after we were married."

He dropped a few onions on Liz's plate. "Better

eat up afore those crawdads get cold. Sure wish we had some Jax to drink with this. It'd go down real smooth.''

Liz sipped some water from the cup she'd poured earlier and refrained from commenting that he didn't need beer on top of whatever he'd been sipping from the flask. Besides, her mind was a bit fixated on the name Zach had given his daughter.

"Zettie," she repeated. "Is that a nickname of some sort?''

He raised his eyebrows and regarded her a moment. "Yes."

"For what?''

This pause was longer. "Lizette.''

The word hung in the air as their eyes locked.

"It was Rita's idea," Zach explained hastily. "She liked the name, that's all.''

She didn't believe Zach, but no way was this a road she wanted to travel. "Three wives in nearly twenty years? You can't be that bad.''

His eyes narrowed. "I should have warned you, *cher*. I'm a real bastard.''

Liz dearly wished she hadn't blurted out the question, but she'd wanted to get away from the subject of his daughter's name, and this open exchange had revived the feeling of camaraderie they'd shared as kids. A time when she hadn't censored her thoughts before she spoke.

"It's the business," he added, breaking the awkward silence. "I was away all the time, setting up systems, working cases." He gave a bitter chuckle. "Funny, now Jed's gone, all I do is push paper and talk to pinstriped suits. Vera would've loved that."

It wasn't a stretch to assume Vera had been the latest wife, so she didn't try to confirm it. "I'm truly sorry about Jed," she said softly. "You must miss him very much."

"Yeah." He popped a crawdad in his mouth, his first, and she took that time to eat one herself, realizing she was hungrier than she thought.

"I wish Allain hadn't blabbed all over the place about the similarity between Jed's death and your ma's," he said. "It's only superficial, and I don't accept the doctor's conclusions."

"What happened?" Liz popped another tasty morsel in her mouth. "To Jed, I mean."

"He . . . he came to Bayou Chatre chasing a guy who'd escaped from the Louisiana pen. Jed was missing for nearly six months, and then he and the con washed up in Vermillion Bay handcuffed together." She saw him shudder slightly, and offered to get his windbreaker. He nodded, and she walked over for it.

"They were murdered?"

"Not according to the findings. They called it an accidental drowning."

She handed him the windbreaker and sat back down. "But you disagree."

"Yeah, I do. You know how Jed loved the water. He'd survive under almost any conditions."

He shrugged into his jacket, then went on. "The blue lips are what made me suspicious. Odd thing to happen. Usually the color fades right away, and it made me suspect poisoning. . . . It's also the reason the doc got ahold of me. Thing is, just like your ma, Jed's toxicology came up negative, only there wasn't a family history of strokes to explain it away." He put his plate down. "I'm not hungry anymore."

"Oh, Zach." Liz put her plate down, too, and touched his shoulder. "How awful it must have been for you."

"Awful doesn't describe it." He pulled out a cigarette and lit it. "What's worse is not knowing the truth. See, I think the con was connected to a drug ring working out of the backwater, and that Jed found it. Then the ringleader disposed of them both to keep anyone else from stumbling across the hideout. Trouble is, I can't prove it. I had teams comb those bayous, and nothing. Nothing at all." He got to his feet and reached for the flask. Then, apparently reconsidering, he dropped his hand. "I should have been with him, Liz. It never would've happened."

"Or maybe you both would be dead," she replied softly, standing up to join him.

She moved to comfort him, but he turned away sharply.

"Light's almost gone," he said. "We'd better wolf our meals down and get back on the boat."

Feeling helpless, Liz bent and picked up her plate.

A soft sound rose from the brush.

"What's that?" she asked in alarm.

"What?"

A soft hiss, like air slowly being let out of a tire, or—

"A snake! Dear God, I hate snakes."

"It's not a snake, Liz. They don't move much at night. Besides, I didn't hear anything."

"Snakes don't move, they slither like slime," she countered, not the least bit amused when Zach chuckled at her unintentional alliteration.

The sound came again.

"There!" Liz pointed at the bushes.

The light from the charcoal fire gleamed off a pair of eyes in the brush.

"Relax," he said reassuringly. "It's just a raccoon. Crawdad is their favorite dish. He probably wants an invite to dinner."

Liz smiled at her own foolishness, and turned to tell Zach he was right. Just then, the hiss transformed into a horrifying wail that brought up images of blood and carnage and terrible, terrible slaughter. Liz whirled to see a streak of tan and black hurling itself at her.

"Watch out!" Zach yelled.

He grabbed her arm and pulled her forward just as the racoon leaped. Its body brushed her other arm, sending crawfish and potatoes flying. Frozen to the spot, she watched in stunned shock as the animal turned around, then crouched to leap again. Its eyes held such malice, an almost human malice, and her blood froze as she realized it was deliberately attacking her.

"Let's get the hell out of here," Zach rasped, dipping to grab the lantern as he yanked Liz from her spot. The next thing she knew she was running after him. Despite their marathon speed, he somehow managed to steady her each time her trembling legs gave out.

Sometime later they emerged from the woods, finding themselves on a dirt road. Both bent over, their hands on their knees to let their heaving breath subside. Finally, Zach straightened up.

"Sure as hell hope that coon likes my cooking."

Something gurgled in Liz's throat. A laugh. And when it came out of her oxygen-starved lungs, she coughed. For a few minutes she alternated between laughing and coughing, and when she felt tears come to her eyes, she pushed them back. Damned if she'd cry over a crawfish supper when she couldn't even cry about her own mother.

Zach just waited, his breathing still quite heavy. This inanely reminded her of the ardor she'd failed to find with Stephen, and when her choking laughter finally ended, she just stared at him a minute.

The moon had risen in the dusk, a big yellow ball that bathed his tanned face and shock of wheat-toned hair. He gleamed gold against gold. Such a beautiful man, truly he was. Her ardor became physical, a rising heat low in her belly.

Zach smiled, white teeth showing in the golden haze. She took a step toward him, wondering if his skin and hair would feel as smooth as they looked in the moonlight, not quite sure what she was doing or why.

"What're you doing to these animals, *cher*, they keep attacking you?" He continued to smile. "So what do you think it is? If you're a voodoo queen, after all, tell me now."

Whatever crazy purpose she'd had in mind vanished in the shock she felt at Zach's innocent remark. She stopped short, feeling once again exposed, as much a victim to those superstitious rumors as she'd been before.

"That's silly. I'm not doing anything." Why was she defending herself? He'd only been kidding. "The raccoon must be rabid, and the alligator . . . you said yourself it's mating season. He was defending his territory. And there you go."

"Just a joke," he said, realizing Liz was getting frantic over his stupid remark. "If I really thought you were into voodoo, I wouldn't've come on this trip."

She buried her hands in her hair. It gleamed like polished ebony in the moonlight, all curly now that wind and dampness had erased the sleek form she'd molded it into, and her cheeks were rich with color that the moon turned a tawny pink. What had been on her mind when she approached him? he wondered, recalling the dreamy quality in those amber eyes.

"You're so beautiful, *cher*," he said, almost in a whisper. "No way you could be a witch."

She smiled so sweetly he could barely resist ravishing her right there on the spot. But she was still the gal who'd turned her back on him, and they were still stranded miles from nowhere.

"We'd better find shelter." He circled around to the south and pointed. "It'll get mighty cold mighty soon, and we'll have better luck finding civilization that way. We need a place to spend the night. You cold?"

He touched her bare arm and she shivered slightly. "A little."

"It'll just get worse with the sun falling."

He took his key chain from his pocket.

"You planning on driving?"

"Cute, Liz." He opened his pen knife, then began sawing through the inside placket of his shirt.

"What're you doing?"

"Leaving a marker so we can find this place again."

She let out a soft sound of comprehension, then watched as Zach cut a strip of fabric from his shirt and went to the nearest tree to tie the frayed piece around a branch.

"Come morning, this'll stand out like a beacon."

"Seems I put my trust in the right man," she said jauntily. "Lead on, great navigator."

He lit the lantern with his cigarette lighter, a tricky task at best, considering the fuel might ignite the lighter as well as the jets. When it started to glow he held it aloft with more relief than he wanted to admit.

They headed in the direction he'd suggested, keeping their eyes peeled for signs of civilization. People camped and kept cabins out here, and they were bound to come upon someone. But he gave only half his mind to the search. The other half was occupied with Liz's words of encouragement. "Great navigator." Right. If he hadn't insisted on stopping, they wouldn't be stranded on this dark and lonely road, with him scared sober by a maniacal raccoon. A fact he'd kind of like to remedy.

He reached for his flask, but caught something

funny in Liz's eyes and stopped himself in mid-reach, going for a cigarette instead.

"Anyone ever say those aren't good for you?" she asked as he lit up.

"What do you think?"

"Hundreds of times, I imagine."

"Then why waste your breath?"

"Don't know. I waste it with Papa, too. Do you know he still rolls his own? Still keeps his tobacco and papers in that wooden box we made for his birthday. One time when I took him and Mama to the Cowboy Hall of Fame, he nearly got arrested cause they thought he was smoking marijuana. Can you imagine? Papa thinks drugs are the devil's tools."

This was the most she'd talked on their trip, except for that confession about why she'd left the Port, and Zach figured she was trying to overcome her terror at being attacked not once, but twice, by swamp animals. She also had wrapped her arms tightly around her body, saying the words between chattering teeth.

"We went on so many great trips. I keep remembering our trip to Disneyland. We rode the Pirates of the Caribbean. Afterward Mama got cotton candy. She loves— loved cotton candy, and she was still laughing about the holograms while she ate it, and the wind was blowing her curls into a tangle and . . ."

She talked nonstop, giving tidbits about her adult life with her parents that both enlightened and confused him. She was confirming what the people at Ellie's wake had told him—Liz had never returned to the Port. So exactly how had she arranged all these encounters in cities as far away as Anaheim? Who had picked up the tab?

Opportunity, means, motive, and visible evidence of an unexplained source of cash. These thoughts bothered him, but what bothered him even more was he didn't want to find out who murdered his brother if it led to Liz's father. How would he live without this driving force in his life? And what would he do after Liz left Port Chatre, probably never to return?

It was totally dark now, except for the rising moon and the light cast by the lantern. On their left were the wetlands, a mass of shadowless vegetation, but the other side was dry, and he'd expected to spy some sign of people long before this.

"You're freezing, aren't you?" he asked Liz.

"Pretty much, and wishing I'd eaten more crawdads, too."

"I can't do much about your hunger, but if we don't find shelter soon, I'll fix us a bed of leaves in the underbrush." Not something that appealed to him. Bugs abounded in those leaves. Spiders, too, which came out at night to weave their sticky webs.

"There!" Liz said excitedly. He looked over to see her pointing at a tall, ominous cypress tree. "Look, Zach, lights. Over there. Look."

He didn't see a thing.

"Behind the tree!" she cried, crouching.

Zach flexed his knees until he was at Liz's eye level, and between the curtain of moss blanketing the cypress, he saw twinkling. "I'll be damned," he said. "The saints are watching out for us."

"Saints have nothing to do with it. We're just resourceful."

"Sometimes resourcefulness isn't enough."

"Sure it is." She stood up and put her hands on her hips. "So how far do you think it is?"

"Hard to tell without knowing what kind of lights those are, but we should get there by morning."

Liz's jaw dropped.

"Kidding," he said with a grin. "Just kidding."

"You have the weirdest sense of humor, Zach Fortier."

"I know, *cher*." He lifted an arm. "But I also have a warm spot here if you'd like to take advantage of it."

She rubbed her cold bare skin and regarded him a moment, clearly tempted. Then, giving in, she stepped into the shelter he offered.

"There," he said as if to a child. "Better?"

"Much."

They started forth, arm in arm, and after a distance, Liz said, "I'm glad you came along, Zach. Very glad."

"Hmm," he responded, then pressed her smaller body closer to his and kept on walking.

Chapter Nine

Christmas tree lights, Liz noticed as they got closer, the small, twinkling kind people put up for festive occasions. This meant they weren't as far away as it first seemed. She refused to admit it to Zach, but weariness was overtaking her fast. The day had held one crisis after another, and so much had happened, she'd nearly forgotten she'd just buried her mother and that her father was in Bayou Chatre without his medicine.

But now, walking silently in the warmth of Zach's arm, with only night sounds and the soft scratching of their feet upon the ground, it all came back. Had her father encountered troubles, too? Had his angina acted up? Was he even now in his boat, clutching his chest, cursing himself for leaving his nitro behind?

She reached in a pocket of her overalls and rolled

the vial between her fingers. Why had he gone on this crazy trip to a nonexistent island? Why had he forgotten his pills? Why the hell didn't he carry a cell phone?

That last thought sent a gurgle of laughter to her lips.

"What is it?" Zach asked.

"Nothing. Just a stupid thought."

"No crime in that."

Soon, a low irregular roofline came into view. Zach stopped so abruptly Liz almost stumbled. He put his hand over his eyebrows.

"Well, I'll be a . . ."

"Is it?" Liz said, realizing they were seeing a zydeco joint they'd gone to as kids. "Is it really?"

"Harris's!" they cried simultaneously.

"We're gonna eat crawfish after all, *cher*. And Harris cooks them up a whole lot better than I do."

Liz was ready to break into a run, but Zach hesitated and looked back. "I'd swear we'd gone a lot farther north than this." He shrugged. "It's been a long time. I've probably gotten the location confused."

As they reached the disreputable-looking, tin-and-mud building, Zach remembered Harris's had been a private club of sorts, where outsiders, particularly Anglo-Saxons were not welcome. He'd been a scrawny stringbean of a kid then. He, Jed, Liz, and whoever else felt like tagging along, would sneak into Harris's with badly faked IDs that the door people accepted without question to drink tap beer, and listen to the zydeco bands.

Liz had barely been a woman then, but soft and curvy, with wild curly hair that drove men just as wild thinking about running their hands through it. He'd gotten into more than one brawl with a guy who'd decided to try it out.

But this was the nineties, when all things Cajun and Creole were cool. Harris's was probably a new in spot, catering to yuppies seeking the exotic in music and food.

As they neared the door, Zach reached back to check his wallet, figuring prices had gone up, too. Beer'd hardly be twenty-five cents a glass these days and there might even be a cover charge.

A tower of a black man, with arms as thick as an ancient cypress and a face that said "Mind your manners or answer to me," blocked their way. "The password," he demanded roughly.

On the other side of the door, Zach saw people buzzing about. A basketball game was on the television—jeeze, a play-off—and the most mouthwatering smells he'd inhaled in all his blessed life wafted to his nose.

"Password," Liz whispered. "I'm starving."

Password, password. He hadn't been here in nearly ten years. Even if he could dredge up the last one he knew, it couldn't still be current. Be-

135

sides, this gargoyle scowling down at them didn't look like he understood English, let alone French.

"Tell him we know Harris," Liz urged, still whispering as if the man's ears were so far from the ground he couldn't hear them.

Zach gave her a quelling look.

"Tell him," she repeated.

"The guy's probably dead," Zach said, whispering back even though he knew it was foolish. He looked up, pasting on his best, nonthreatening smile.

"Un petit tombe dans le bois," he offered.

"What kinda fairy password is that?"

Zach shrugged. Liz let out a sad sigh. The man's face screwed up with bewilderment, making him even uglier, if that was at all possible. He turned his massive head on his equally massive neck and, giving a pretty fair imitation of Zach's bad French, bellowed, "Harris, you ever hear this 'En pettit toobay dan le boys' stuff?"

"The little tomb in the woods? That's one I ain't come across in a long time. Eight, ten years at least, for true."

Zach leaned forward, sneaking a look around the human roadblock. An aged black man, his face a mass of wrinkles below a cap of curly pure-white hair, popped his head through the throng surrounding the bar.

"Harris!" Liz cried in delight.

The old man turned and said something to an unseen person, then walked from behind the bar toward the door. The closer he got, the surer Zach was that this was Harris. The guy must be a pure immortal. Shorter, definitely shorter, but just as wiry, and Zach would bet he could still give that baseball bat he kept behind the bar a helluva swing, if need be.

"Who you be, boy?" he asked, his voice still deep and booming, sounding well able to hold a strong bass note during a jam session. "You ain't a revenuer are you? Hear tell they got hold of that there password some years back."

"Revenuer? Hell, no!" Despite the warning glare from the gargoyle, Zach stepped forward, hand extended. "It's Zach . . . Zach Fortier. Don't you remember me, Harris? Used to come here with my friends all the time when we were kids."

"Zacharie?" Harris squinted, looking up to take a closer look in the muted light. Then his wrinkled face broke into a grin. *"Oui, oui,* it is you."

Harris nodded to the bouncer, who backed away and melted into the shadows, motionless, almost like a statue that had come to life for the occasion and now wasn't needed.

Opening his arms wide, Harris enclosed Zach in a bone-crushing, good ol' boy hug. "You old troublemaker," he exclaimed, slapping Zach's back. "Good to see you, boy." Stepping back, he looked

Zach over, then patted his stomach. "Filled out a mite, ain't you?"

Resisting an urge to suck in his gut, Zach forced a chuckle. By then, Harris's eyes moved to Liz with a frank up-and-down gaze. "And who is this pretty lady, here?"

"Liz Deveraux," Zach said. "We used to come here a lot . . . back then." Abruptly, he realized that in the whole scheme of life, their time together had been very short.

"Ah, *oui*," the old man replied, peering at Liz with great interest. "The girl what came back from death. We been waiting for her."

Liz went kind of white at the remark. "It was all a misunderstanding," she said, laughing uncomfortably. She spread her arms wide. "I've been alive all this time. See?"

Zach wondered what the "waiting" part of Harris's remark was about, but his stomach was growling, his flask almost empty, and he was down to his last cigarette. He told Harris this.

"And food," Liz pleaded. "Crawdads, red beans, rice, whatever you have."

Harris wrapped an arm around each of their shoulders and guided them toward the door. "How 'bout some good 'n' spicy shrimp gumbo, as only Harris can fix it?"

"Wonderful," Liz crooned, her pink little tongue sneaking out to lick her equally pink lips.

Kissable lips, Zach thought, very kissable. And as they stepped into the warm room, alive with cheering game viewers crowding the bar, and rich with the aroma of down-home cooking, it was easy to believe he'd stepped back in time.

"Umm," Liz said, shoveling in another mouthful of gumbo. She'd forgotten how wonderful Southern cooking was, and was making up for lost time.

"Don't forget to chew," Zach said. He was slouched in a big barrel chair, sipping on a ginger ale and vodka, and even though the room was dim, she could see his eyes boring into her.

"Don't you have better things to do than examine my every move?" she asked in a mild tone. "Like watching the game?"

"Game's over," he replied. "Besides, you're better looking than the basketball players."

His attention made her a bit uncomfortable, but she was enjoying herself too much to let it get to her. Which in itself was reason to be uneasy. A woman grieving for her mother and worrying about a father with a bad heart and no medicine out in the bayou shouldn't feel this good.

But the big, red-plaid jacket Harris had found for her smelled of fresh tobacco and cypress smoke and reminded her of her father. And eating spicy gumbo and crumbly cornbread amid the mingled scents of freshly poured beer and simmering food, with a zydeco band tuning up on the floor, brought back the forgotten comforts of her girlhood.

Seize the day, she thought, taking in another piece of cornbread.

"Why aren't you eating, Zach? The food's great."

Zach gestured to the half-empty bowl in front of him. "That's my second helping, 'case you hadn't noticed."

She nodded and took another spoonful of gumbo.

"Harris always cook like this?" she asked between bites.

"Long as I remember."

"You'd think with food this good the place would be packed."

"It is. People all over when we came in." Taking another sip from his glass, he looked around. "Where'd everyone go?"

"My point. We're the only ones here. Why do you think that is?"

"It's late, it's far out, everyone went home."

She glanced down at her watch. "At nine o'clock? On a Friday night?"

"How should I know the vagaries of the restaurant business, Liz?" He took another drink from his glass. "I'm just a dumb PI, not a gourmet."

"Who happens to run one of the biggest security agencies in the country."

He put the glass down and propped his elbows on the table. "Now how do you know that?"

"Investments are my business. I look for going concerns all the time." She waved an arm around. "Like Harris's."

"You didn't answer my question."

Before this his attention had contained sexual undertones, but she heard something new now. More precisely, renewed. He'd renewed his hostility.

"It . . . It's . . . I get calls. Others wanting a going place to put their money. They ask if you're ever going public."

"Others, huh? You don't have any interest yourself."

"Oh, yes. If you ever decide, please let me know."

"That would be insider information, wouldn't it, *cher*?"

"No, no," she said with feigned cheerfulness, wishing he'd let the subject drop. "Not under certain circumstances."

"Right, there's always those circumstances." Returning to his slouch, he sipped his drink, then sipped again.

"Shouldn't you lighten up?" Liz asked.

"I've got it under control." He took out a fresh pack of cigarettes that he'd purchased from Harris, unwrapped it with overdone care, then took one out and lit it before speaking again. "You knew where I was all along, didn't you?"

She met his gaze. Direct, straight on. A shimmer

of blue escaped from his eyes into the muted light of the room. "Yes, Zach. Yes, I did. . . . I'm sorry."

He surprised her by laughing. "No big deal, *cher*, no big deal." Then he dragged from the cigarette, leaned back again, and blew a long puff of smoke to the ceiling. "I just wanted to know, is all."

"Well, now you do."

She went back to the gumbo and cornbread, but shortly after she pushed it away, having lost her appetite. The weariness she'd felt in the last leg of the hike to Harris's returned.

The band started playing, and the music was so lively it perked her up. Harris had turned the bar over to the treelike giant and joined the jammers to strum on an old, string banjo and croon throaty tunes in Acadian French. Before she knew it, her foot was tapping, her fingers drumming out the melody. There was something so elemental about Cajun and Creole music. Like the food and the smells, it took her back to the days before she'd left Louisiana and reminded her there had been much that had been good about it.

"You remember how to two-step, *cher*?"

She looked over at Zach, who was again regarding her intently, his hostility apparently gone, if his appreciative gaze was any measure.

She grinned. "I'm not sure, but I'd like to give it a try."

He took her hand and guided her out on the

dance floor. She followed his lead, letting his expertise make up for her rustiness.

"Now, *this* is like riding a bicycle," he said, as the pattern of the steps came back to her.

"And a lot more fun."

They finished that dance and entered the next one, alone on the floor. Harris watched them from the stage, grinning from ear to ear, and after two or three lively songs, the next one slowed into a haunting French melody about a beautiful woman.

Zach pulled her close, placing her right hand over his heart. His shirt hung open again, and the firm steel of his muscles gave her a shock she would have preferred not to identify. But she knew what it was, and a barely audible sigh left her lips. When Zach's mouth turned up, she was almost certain he'd heard.

Although the lights had already been low, they seemed dimmer now, and she felt almost as if they were moving together to the music of an invisible band. He gently pressed her head against his shoulders, holding her close, and led her into a waltz of sorts. It felt right being in Zach's arms, safe again in a way she hadn't felt since they'd explored the bayous together. She felt one with him, moving as he moved, dipping as he dipped, their thighs and hips and bellies touching and parting as they rocked and swayed to the music.

He stroked her hair, lightly, just grazing it, yet

his touch emanated a current that flowed into her scalp, down her spine, ending in a crackling white-hot ball that lodged low in her body, bringing up a languid yearning that forced another sigh from her lips.

"What do the words of the song say?" he asked.

"Roughly translated?"

He nodded, and she began to sing along in English.

" 'Sweet Lorilee, you smell of honeysuckle' "— her voice was childlike and slightly off-key, a delight to Zach's ears—" 'but your beauty is greater, far greater, oh, greater. Sweet Lorilee, I miss you so.' "

As the lyrics unfolded, Zach began to wish he hadn't asked.

" 'One black morning I get up . . . and you are . . . gone.' " Her voice fell behind the band. " 'Sweet Lorilee, why did . . . you go? I . . . loved you so.' "

"That's good enough, Liz." He pulled her closer, aching from the meaning of the song, aching from wanting her. A feather in his arms, that's what she felt like. She sighed again, and Zach went instantly hard. Her pelvis brushed against his, and by her responsive shiver, he realized she knew the effect she was having. He barely contained his groan, then found he wasn't in a hurry anyway. So sweet, the pain of holding her this way, unable to do anything but touch and want. And he did want her, no matter how she'd hurt him, no matter how she'd changed. God help him, he wanted her.

"Back there on the road, *cher*," he whispered, his lips a hair's breadth from her silky cheek, "when you were standing in the road, your hair tossed by the wind, all curly and wild, your eyes sparkling in the moonlight . . ."

"Hmm?" She snuggled closer, which put his lips in contact with her skin. She smelled so good, sweeter than Lorilee of the sad, sad song. A light mixture of rose and gardenia mingled with the musky smoke and cypress scent of Harris's beat-up old jacket. Like the bayou, like Louisiana in bloom, and Lord, how much he wanted her.

"You looked how you did when we'd paddle my old pirogue through the backwaters. Things have changed, I understand that, but back there . . ."

He felt her stiffen, knew he should curb his vodka-loosened tongue right now.

". . . back there, you looked like Izzy again."

She arched her neck to meet his eyes. "But I'm not Izzy," she said firmly. "I don't want to be Izzy. She's gone and she's never coming back. Why can't people understand that?"

She wasn't angry, just very stern, and while her reaction didn't surprise him, he still felt a flash of rage.

"I can see that," he said. "Izzy was warm and caring. Izzy . . . Izzy would never have let me think she died. Izzy wouldn't have left me at all." He let go of her, his anger mounting to fury. He wanted to hurt her, make her ache the way he had for years because of her omission. "You can't even cry at your mother's funeral, lady, and you take business calls at her wake. I don't know who you are, but you're sure not Izzy. It was my mistake thinking you were, one I won't make again."

Liz's arms dropped helplessly to her side. "Zach—"

But he spun and headed for the long wooden bar, leaving Liz in the center of the floor. The music stopped mid-song.

"You not gonna dance no more?" Harris called from the stage.

"No," Liz said, feeling like she'd just been through a blitz.

"Too bad, too bad. You two look good together."

Zach's snort of laughter could be heard across the room.

"Looks can be deceiving," Liz replied, grateful that the darkness hid her burning cheeks.

"For true, missy, that sure be for true. And a body gotta be careful. Fool's gold glitters, the ol' shellfish, he got the pearl, huh?"

The old man was telling her she was misjudging Zach, but she knew who she was now. And who she wasn't. Zach was all wrong for her, and letting him in her life could—no, it *would*—expose her. It was too late to look back, because Izzy Deveraux really was dead. She'd died the day Liz left Port Chatre.

Chapter Ten

"No, no, *cher*, Izzy be much alive."

Liz tilted her head. Had Harris really said that? She'd rejected her mystical upbringing—it had caused her so much pain. But maybe fate did sometimes intervene. Was all of this—her mother's death, her return to Port Chatre, her father's disappearance, and her quest with Zach—simply a means to finally put her past to rest?

It was all a bit mind-boggling, so she forced a hollow laugh. "Good words for a song, Harris. Why don't you play it for me?" That said, she returned to her table.

Harris let out a low chuckle, then went back to strumming his banjo with the band.

Liz fidgeted in her chair for a while, still feeling a bit uneasy about the old man's uncanny remark, and also unable to tear her gaze from Zach. He was slumped over a drink, staring at nothing in particular. Finally, she got up and went to sit beside him.

"I know I hurt you, Zach. I'm sorry."

He didn't look at her, but he let out a bitter chuckle. "Hurt? Hurt doesn't begin to describe it." He turned toward her then, his blue eyes full of ice and fury. "I asked you to be my wife! And you said, yes! Then you run out on me?"

She touched his arm and he jerked it away. "We were just kids, too young to make that decision."

"Yeah, well I wasn't. I knew what I wanted and it was you." He leaned forward suddenly, his face coming within inches of hers, the edge leaving his voice. "You remember the first time we made love? Beneath the bleachers, after the game. Magnolia blossoms in the air, and you so soft and sweet in my arms. God, I knew then I'd never leave you, and I vowed I never would. Why did you leave me? Why did you let me think you died?" He let out a scornful laugh. "Hell, you did die. You aren't the same girl I loved."

His voice had broken several times, and Liz realized what his words were costing him, but she was too caught up in his unfair accusations to really care.

"I'm sorry, okay? Sorry, sorry, sorry. But I'm also damned sick of this guilt trip you're laying on me. I am who I am, Zach, and you're not so perfect yourself." Then a memory, one never completely lost, flooded back to her. "And you did leave me. You did. After *Grandmère's* funeral, I begged you to take me away. You remember what you said?" She felt her face twisting with a fury she hadn't known in years. "You said Richard would take your place in the football game, and you couldn't risk it because the coach was about to choose a captain. So stop trying to make *me* feel guilty!"

"You were nutty that night, talking about *le fantôme noir* and other things you turn your nose up at now! I tried to talk you out of it, but you didn't listen."

"I talked about what? That's absurd!"

"Absurd?" Zach snorted, spinning to face the bar and slamming down his fist. "Hey, gargoyle," he shouted, "I need this damn glass filled!"

The doorman had been drying beer glasses, which looked ridiculously small in his hands, and now he put down the towel and stormed to stand in front of Zach.

"What did you say, man?"

Zach glared up at him. "I said fill this damn glass."

"You called me something."

"Oh that. I called you a gargoyle."

"Zach," Liz cautioned.

He put out a hand to warn her off. "You've got the ugliest face I've seen in decades. Know what that means, decades? Maybe you don't even know what gargoyle means."

"I know. I also know you already had too much." The man reached for Zach's empty glass.

Fast as a striking snake, Zach's hand shot out to stop him. "I said fill it!"

Suddenly, the man had Zach by his collar. "Look, creep," he snarled. "Maybe you're a friend of Harris's, okay. That don't give you the right to—"

Liz swung desperately toward the stage, hoping Harris was watching. She saw that he'd put down his banjo, and was signaling the other players to go on without him. He came down from the stage, amazingly agile for a man his age, and rushed toward the bar.

He arrived just as Zach's fist was about to deliver a blow that Liz figured would do as much good as punching the side of a barn.

"Hold on," Harris said quietly, circling his fingers around Zach's biceps. The giant let go of his collar, and Zach swiveled on the stool, taking his clenched fist with him. Just as he was about to let it land, he saw who had him.

"Shit," he said. "Sorry, man." He looked back at the giant behind the bar. "You, too. I take it back. You don't have the ugliest face I've seen. I've seen one or two uglier."

The giant's face twisted in rage, confirming

Zach's insult in Liz's opinion, but that still didn't excuse what he'd said.

"I will take care of this *bouffon*, Samuel," Harris said. "I apologize for my friend. He drinks too much. Come on, Zacharie, time you sleep."

"Whadya call me?" Zach asked blurrily. "Whad he call me, Liz?"

"A fool," she said sharply, "a fool. Which is better than you deserve."

"You called me a fool?"

Harris only shrugged.

Zach blew out his breath. "Okay, okay, mebbe, just mebbe, I have had too much."

"*Oui, mon ami,* you have for true. Come sleep now."

The steam went out of Zach. "Okay, okay." He slid wearily from the stool, then looked sadly at Liz. "You could'a phoned, you know, or even wrote a letter."

His eyes bled with pain, and Liz felt the sharp prick of all-too-familiar guilt. She'd caused his agony, and with the death of her mother so fresh in her mind, she understood it better than she wanted to. "We'll talk again," she said softly. "Tomorrow. All right?"

"Guess so." With that, he straightened himself with as much dignity as possible in his drunken state and followed Harris to a row of booths against the wall. The older man settled him there and disappeared for a moment to return with a blanket. Lifting cushions from the barrel chairs as he moved, he placed them on the bench of the booth. Then, gently, almost like a father, he helped Zach recline and covered him with the blanket.

After that, he climbed back on the bandstand and launched into another love song with his whisky-thick voice. Liz returned to the table, listening to the sad music and aching for Zach. What happened to the optimistic boy she'd loved as a girl? His future had been so bright, and he'd lived up to it as far as she could see. But she was also certain his dream for that future hadn't included three ex-wives, a son whom he couldn't get close to, and a brother whose life was cut short by murder.

Some time later, Harris again put down his instrument and went to the bar. She saw him fill a small mason jar with a dark liquid.

The barrel chair creaked and moaned when he pulled it out to sink into the soft cushion. "Sounds like my old bones," he said, putting the glass down in front of Liz. "Drink, *cher*. It make you feel better."

"I really need to go to bed." She propped her elbows on the table so she could cradle her chin in her hands. Her eyelids felt heavy, and so did her heart.

"I fix one in the booth soon, but it be hard sleeping. The drink, it help. You get that warm stuff in your belly, you nod off like *le bébé*, yes?"

His dark, wrinkled face held such understanding. And those deep-set, round eyes reflected decades of experience. He'd seen it all, done it all, forgiven it all. If he said the drink would help, she believed him.

She sipped. "Blackberry brandy, umm, I always did have a taste for blackberry brandy."

"It taste like what you want it to," he replied.

"Yes," she said, having no idea what he meant. She took another sip.

The band resumed playing without him, and Liz continued sipping, sitting with Harris in companionable silence. Relaxation seeped through her body, and she soon discovered she wasn't sleepy anymore. Sleep would come, if she wanted, she was sure of that, but her body and heart didn't ache anymore. After a while, she realized she'd almost drained her glass.

"Could I have another?" she asked, surprised at how much she wanted it.

"One's enough, Izzy." He hadn't called her that earlier, but she found she didn't mind. It seemed right coming from Harris. He looked taller now, his skin firmer, his eyes a bit brighter, as if the passing of the night had made him younger. Leaning forward, he took her hand.

"You must listen carefully."

She widened her eyes in silent agreement.

"You go into darkness, girl. The time of *le fantôme* is come. He have the power now, the fire opal be in his hands. Your papa, he want to make it right, but he have no guardian by his side, him."

Something told her his words were odd, but Liz paid it no heed and simply nodded. Right. She understood. The opal had to have a guardian. "Go on."

"You is a woman now, but the heart of you got left when you ran from the bayou."

He pressed an object in her hand. She looked down and saw a *gris-gris* bag. An especially nice one made of chamois instead of the usual flannel. Her mother had made charms like these for the people who came to her for mystical advice on getting their hearts' desires.

Liz raised her eyes to Harris in mute question.

"It be an evil thing inside," he said, "but some of the time it take evil to fight evil. I put with it a stone and a powder that will keep it under your power—the two to keep the one at bay. This will protect you for now, *cher*, but it be not enough in the end. It take another kind of strength to fire up the opal and defeat Ankouer. You find it in your heart, the part that got left behind with Izzy. Look for what Izzy knew. It is in the book your *maman* wrote. Study it, and remember who you are. Other-the-wise, we all go back to the dark—man, woman, child, all fall into dark. We, us, everyone, need you. Mind what I say."

The music still played, and the cells in her body felt like lead, and she doubted she could move them if she tried. She didn't feel like trying. It was a good feeling, really, rather like the aftermath of a massage . . . or of incredible sex.

"Yes," she said dreamily, his every word making perfect sense although, in fact, none of it made sense.

"Good on you," he answered. "And for the last. The man you run from, him, he is your defender. Trust him, 'cause he is a good man, and when the battle time come, he stand by your side. Be good to him—he love you for true."

She felt, rather than saw, Harris stand, and when he moved away, she continued sitting in her chair, caring about nothing, worrying about nothing, just sitting. The next thing she knew, Harris was taking her arms and lifting her from the chair.

"Come, Izzy, sleep now."

"Where's Zach?" she asked groggily, wondering how everything had changed so fast. She'd been talking to Harris just a minute ago, but now the band was gone. The room was completely dark except for a glowing light above the liquor cabinet behind the bar.

"Gone sleepy time." Harris nodded to a blanket-covered heap on a bench of one of the booths. "Just like you soon to be."

Right, she remembered hazily. Zach had argued with the gargoyle. The man's ugly face popped in her mind and she giggled. Zach might have been drunk, but it hadn't hurt his eyesight any. Harris smiled, but didn't ask why she'd laughed as he led her to another booth, where he'd already placed cushions from the chair. "Lay you down. Morning come soon. Old *soleil*, he will be rising. You got toil ahead, *cher*, so rest now."

He helped her into the booth, then draped a big scratchy blanket over her. As she tucked her hands beneath her head, she turned her droopy eyes up to him.

"How come you Frenchies hardly ever call a woman by her given name?"

"It be much too dangerous."

She was too tired to convey her question by anything but raised eyebrows, but he got it anyway.

"If a man make a mistake during that loving time, why, *cher*, he'd'a be sleeping with that old dog till his hair turn white as mine."

Then he chuckled and walked away.

Liz was fast asleep before the echo of his chuckle faded, but she had one last thought before drifting off. Zach often called her Liz. That must mean something.

*   *   *

"Exactly where you tied it," Liz said when she spied the shirt scrap tied around the tree. "That was smart thinking."

"Sometimes the brain works," Zach replied, and she knew it was an oblique apology for last night. She sighed. It wasn't as if she'd never witnessed that kind of behavior before. Although her father often drank excessively, he rarely lost his temper. But she'd been there once or twice when he had, and he'd acted very much the same as Zach. Maybe worse.

"You're lucky Harris showed up before the giant tossed you all the way back to the Port."

"Gargoyle," Zach muttered.

"That pretty well says it." She laughed.

So did Zach. "I'd probably be looking worse than him if he'd gotten hold of me."

"Un-huh." He slanted her a glance of mock offense, and Liz laughed again. They shared a moment of warmth that felt good after the argument, and for a brief time she just smiled up at him.

Zach broke it short, saying in a gruff voice, "Time to check out the attack site."

Liz kept pace with him as he turned into the thick stand of brush and trees. She felt good this morning despite the lack of sleep, and she'd had a lovely dream she couldn't quite remember, except that it included Harris. The man had awakened them shortly after dawn, with Zach looking a little worse for the wear. But Harris produced a razor and plenty of hot water. By the time they sat down to a breakfast guaranteed to put ten pounds on Liz's hips, Zach showed no signs he'd downed more vodka than she cared to think about.

When they approached the clearing where the raccoon had attacked, Zach put out his arm.

"Hold on." He stepped between the trees. She wasn't exactly uneasy, standing in the cool shadows without him, but she dearly wished he'd hurry.

"Is the raccoon gone?" she asked when he returned.

"Not exactly, but it isn't a danger anymore."

Liz cocked her head. "You sure?"

"Yep, dead as a doornail." He motioned for her to come forward and started walking to the boat.

"How?"

Zach shrugged. "All that matters is he didn't do much harm. He did get into the storage bin, scattered stuff all over the place, and—well, you'll see for yourself."

He leaned forward, grabbed the rail of the boat, and swung his body over it. Then he turned and stuck out his hand. Liz took it and used his lift to vault up.

"Why didn't we use the ramp?" she asked.

Zach inclined his head in that direction.

The raccoon. Dead, all right. Rolled on its back with its small, handlike paws curled up, and its dark round eyes staring through its mask at the sky, it now seemed sad and harmless.

"Who knows what kind of disease that crazy thing was carrying," Zach said. "I'll get rid of it as soon as we clean up the boat."

"You think it had rabies?"

"I dunno. All that matters is it can't hurt us now."

Liz nodded, gazing around the ravaged boat. All the bins had been opened, their contents scattered. Oddly, it looked almost like the animal had been searching for something, because the location of the tossed objects on this side of the craft wasn't random, as might be expected from a rabid creature.

Liz leaned to check the other side and saw the same loose organization. "It missed a bin," she said suddenly. She rounded the benches, stepping over clusters of charcoal to avoid getting too close to the ramp. "It's the one I stored my purse in."

She bent and examined the site. The vinyl had been shredded by sharp little claws, and frantic scratches marked the aluminum side wall around the latch.

"For some reason it couldn't get in this one," she said in bemusement, still bent over and staring.

Zach made his way around. Charcoal dust was already getting on their shoes, leaving tracks on the wooden deck. "No wonder. You completely secured the latch. No one does that anymore, except in a storm."

"Lucky. My cell phone's in there, and it could come in handy later."

A visible shiver ran through Zach's body, and he stared north for an instant. "I hope we don't need it," he replied. "But I'm worried about the weather patterns. It's an eerie place we're headed to."

Liz recalled what he'd said about unpredictable water and weather when Maddie first mentioned Quadray Island, but thought he was lapsing into over-caution.

"Heavens, Zach. The day's as clear a one as I've ever seen."

"Never pays attention to a thing I say," Zach said, turning his eyes to heaven.

Liz smiled at him, fascinated by how fiercely masculine he looked standing above her. A mild breeze rippled his hair like a field of wheat, and his blue eyes glowed against his tanned skin. He was all muscle and sinew, and she remembered then how close he'd come to kissing her on the dance floor, how thrilled she'd been at the prospect.

What if he hadn't frightened her by talking about her girlhood self? What would she have felt? Would she have let him enter her life, putting her in the agonizing position of leaving him again to prevent her illusionary self from shattering into a million pieces?

. . . he loves you, for true.

Harris's voice, as clear as if he stood in front of her. Liz had an urge to shake her head. She didn't recall Harris saying those words, and they spoke of a sentiment she preferred not to dwell on.

Then why did they warm her heart?

She cleared her throat and straightened up. "First thing, I need to clean up all this charcoal. It's making a mess of the deck. Where's the bag?"

"In shreds."

"Okay, I guess I'll have to empty a crate. You take care of the raccoon."

"Sure, give me the easy job."

He picked up one of the less-shredded tarps, then searched for a grappling hook, which he ended up finding wedged against the side of the boat.

"Almost as if the raccoon was hunting for something," Liz said, still troubled by this unlikely organization.

"Sure, Liz. Food."

She turned toward the shore. "Then why didn't it eat our dinners?"

The plate Zach had left on the ground was untouched, and the kettle still sat upright on the grill. Even the remains from Liz's meal hadn't been eaten.

"Like I said, it was probably sick. Which is why I want it out of here." He shrugged, but Liz thought his nonchalance seemed feigned.

He dropped the tarp over the raccoon, then rolled it down the ramp by pushing it with a foot. When he reached the bottom, he used the grappling hook to shove it to one side.

"You plan on giving it a Christian burial?" Liz asked.

"I'm going to burn it." He came back to the ramp and picked up a gallon of gas. "I'd just as soon make sure it doesn't spread something catchy. There a shovel around here?"

Liz scanned the boat and spotted a small camp shovel hanging from the gunwale. Buried in the charcoal she'd been picking up, she pointed a blackened finger at it. He lifted the shovel, then returned to shore. In seconds, she heard the scraping of the carcass being dragged across the ground.

She resumed scooping up charcoal, using pieces from a roll of paper towels to drop them into a garbage bag.

Afterward, she found some rags, which she wet down in the bayou and used to mop up the deck. While she worked, the shovel scuffed at the dirt on the shore below. By the time she was ready to pack the other items into the storage bin, she smelled gasoline fumes.

"Any matches left?"

"Yep." She'd found them spilled inside the crate that once held the charcoal, and had already put them back into their box, which she now handed over the rail to Zach. As he started to turn away, she spotted something flying from the brush.

"Zach!" she yelled.

"What the—" He whirled, then stopped dead still.

A pack of raccoons surrounded the shrouded corpse.

Chapter Eleven

"**G**it coons!" Zach bellowed.

"Come on in the boat," Liz implored, terrified the raccoons would attack him. "Please."

The pack clawed furiously at the tarp. At Zach's shout, one of them stopped clawing and lifted its head to regard them with intense hostility.

"Git!" Zach roared again.

The creature ignored him and returned to its task. The animals had now uncovered a paw belonging to the dead raccoon, obviously preparing to drag it away.

"Please, please get on the boat," Liz begged.

Finally, Zach spun for the ramp and raced up it to the bow of the boat, where he pulled a flare gun from beneath the console. He whirled back to point the gun at the raccoons.

It discharged with a crack, ejecting a flash of red

that streaked toward the pack and the gasoline-soaked tarp. As a group they fixed their eyes on the whir of light. As it descended, the flare nicked one of the raccoon's flank. It shrieked, causing the others to spring for the brush.

The scent of burned hair rose from the struck animal's smoldering coat. With more pained shrieks, it thrashed around in the dirt, then flipped to its feet and took off after the rest. With a whoosh of heat and light, the gas ignited. The tarp went up in flames.

"Well, that's that," Zach said calmly. A muscle twitched in his jaw as he bent to put the flare gun away. "Sure glad this baby was loaded."

Still speechless, Liz watched him sit down and start the engine. "Let's get out of here," he said. "it's been wet enough that the fire'll burn itself out."

"No argument from me." Liz walked forward and sat beside him. "Have you ever seen anything like that?"

"Nope."

"I was afraid not."

He steered the boat into deeper water. She could see him itching to give the craft more speed, and as soon as they reached the middle of the bayou, he gave in to the impulse.

"Something really weird happened back there," he said.

"There's a logical"—acrid smoke blew from the land and a cough broke her reply—"explanation, I'm sure"—another cough—"there is. We simply . . . don't know what . . . it is . . . yet."

Zach looked back at the receding shore, prompting her to do the same. The blaze had ebbed, but a thick cloud spiraled up, carrying the stench of burning hair and flesh. The raccoon pack stood at the water's edge and followed their retreat with beady eyes.

Liz covered her nose and throat. "Hurry, Zach."

"Amen."

He punched up the speed even more, then bent for his flask. Liz suddenly wished she also had a convenient way to ease her fear.

Even after the burning raccoon and its caretakers were many miles behind them, she and Zach spoke no more of it. Deeply reluctant to explore the incident, Liz busied herself putting the rest of the items back in the bins. When she finally sat back down, she made a guess that Zach didn't want to talk about it either.

The seat felt hard and uncomfortable, and she was getting stiff. As she lifted her legs to prop them on the console, she felt the journal shift in her pocket.

When she'd left Harris's that morning to walk back up the road with Zach, the journal had been a large presence in her mind. Without knowing why, she'd felt compelled to read it. But the wreckage on the boat and the appearance of the aberrant raccoons had made her forget.

Now was as good a time as any to return to it. She pulled out the bag she stored it in, and saw it contained a new item. Turning the plastic bag upside down, she let both of them drop to her lap.

"Where did this come from?" she idly asked aloud.

Zach looked at her in question.

"This *gris-gris* bag. It wasn't here yesterday."

Zach's laugh carried an odd ring. "Just what we need. A charm to keep us safe."

Somehow she thought he believed it, if just a little, and she herself was very curious about what the little bag held. Small enough to stick in a pocket or a purse, it still felt heavier than she remembered them to be. She loosened the drawstring.

"You don't know how you got it?" Zach leaned back in his seat and reached for a cigarette.

"No." She had an image of a wrinkled black hand pressing it into hers, but it refused to come into focus. Neither did the contents of the bag. Black inside there, very black, due to a larger object blocking the light.

She tweezered her fingers around it and tugged.

The piece slipped from her grasp when it was halfway out and lodged there, its two outstretched arms hanging over the opening. A small needle protruded from the space between the arms.

"Ugh!" Liz gaped at the thing in horror. A voodoo doll, painted entirely black and staring at her with malicious round red eyes.

Zach jerked his head and uttered an equally disgusted sound. "Throw it overboard, Liz!"

She took it between her thumb and index finger, preparing to do just that, but as she slipped it out, she got the oddest feeling it was there to do her will. "In a second," she said, leaning to put it on the deck between their seats. "I want to see what else is in here."

"Not more black magic, I hope." He puffed quickly on his cigarette, then turned away.

Liz shook the remaining contents of the bag on top of the journal, hoping she wouldn't find them to be of the same ilk. A small green stone and a cellophane packet appeared.

"Green chalcedony. And what's this?"

She picked up the packet, pulled the folded edge apart and peered inside. A sweet and pleasing fragrance reached her nose. "Rose petal dust. Two to keep the one at bay."

"What?"

"Something Mama used to say. If someone is in danger, you give them a malevolent object along with two benevolent ones that control it. I'm surprised I remember after so long, but it almost feels like I just heard that phrase." She put down the packet and picked up the small green stone. "And I also remember what this gem is called." She dropped the stone into the chamois bag, then did the same with the packet. Finally, feeling irritatingly nervous about it, she gingerly lifted the voodoo doll from the deck and started to put it away.

"Aren't you getting rid of that creepy thing?" Zach asked, puffing tensely on his brightly burning cigarette.

"No. I don't think so. It came with the bag and having it reminds me of Mama."

Getting the doll back in was a struggle. The needle continually snagged on the fabric as she pushed it through the opening. She reached to pull the needle out.

"Don't!" Zach said sharply.

She pivoted toward him in surprise.

"If you have to keep it, at least let it remain wounded."

Liz laughed. "I guess you can take the boy out of the swamp," she teased, "but you can't take—"

"—the swamp out of the boy," Zach finished, smiling and keeping his voice light, but he stubbed out his cigarette and reached for another.

Leaving the needle in place, Liz worked the bag around it and finally managed to get the doll inside.

Giving a pleased sigh, she pulled the drawstring tight, then placed the *gris-gris* back in the plastic bag.

"Satisfied?" she asked, grinning again.

Zach looked at her wryly. "Call me superstitious," he said, "but I'd hazard a guess your ma and her kind understand these things better than we do. They'd probably also have answers for aggressive alligators and deranged raccoons that run around in broad daylight."

"Probably, Zach." She patted the journal. "And I'll bet the answers are in here."

"You've been dying to read again, haven't you?"

Liz nodded.

"If you find anything out, let me know."

"Sure thing."

Liz opened the book on her lap and flipped to the page where she'd left off.

I feel le fantôme noir *stir deep in the bayou. He found a poor soul to swallow, maybe more.*

How this unfortunate person or persons happened on Quadray Island, I know not, but I see the fire opal spark and ebb and know it is disturbed by Ankouer's new wakening.

His power grows from this milk of human warmth. Soon the cold, cold bodies wash up to rip another loved one's heart to shreds. I weep for them, but in my sorrow I cannot forget my duty.

Here her misery seemed to eclipse even the grief she'd felt when she'd thought Liz had died. Liz looked up, once more struck by how much pain this mythic being had given her mother. Such a burden, and none of it was real, no realer than the gruesome figure inside the chamois bag. Throat thick, she resumed reading.

If I should fail, it falls to Izzy to guard the opal, so I write these warnings to smooth her way.

Liz rubbed her arms, suddenly cold, although the day was warm, then read on. The warnings contained a lot of nonsense that never failed to anger her. According to her mother, once Ankouer had bled the life from a human sacrifice, he was able to control the thoughts of men, often appearing as their ghostlike forms in odd and sundry places. Other times seducing them to do his will.

And, as the book had said before, Ankouer desperately sought the fire opal, which would allow him to permanently take over a person's body. Once he'd done this, he would proceed to build an empire and incite warfare throughout the world. But only if he defeated the guardian.

Sighing, Liz put down the book, but even as she closed it, she felt a call to continue reading. After a moment's hesitation, she opened it again. The pages fluttered in the blowing wind coming over the windshield, and when she finally flattened them, she found herself looking at a quatrain written completely in English, which hinted that her mother had copied it from somewhere else. Quite beautiful, it contained the saying Liz had mentioned to Zach not long before.

THE KEY

> *Beasts lay panting on the trail.*
> *The two keep the one at bay.*
> *When two join as one,*
> *The soft overpower the strong.*

"Listen, Zach," she said, reading it to him.

"What the hell does it mean?"

"I've no idea. It's as incomprehensible as an I Ching verse."

"Not unlike the stuff happening out here," he muttered.

Liz chose not to respond. She had a feeling he hadn't expected her to, anyway. Fingers of apprehension crawled along her skin. The incidents had started out easy enough to explain. A bull alligator regarding the boat as a rival might see her dangling bare legs as an area of vulnerability. Even the mad raccoon attack of last night could be rationalized away. But an entire pack of raccoons coming for their dead companion in broad daylight, then showing no fear of a shouting man? This was moving into the realm of the totally eerie.

So was the frequency of these events. She'd lived in the bayou fifteen years before leaving and had never encountered any such incidents.

"Zach," she asked, "anything like this ever happen to you before?"

"No," he said tersely.

"That's what I thought."

She shut the journal. Maybe she'd read it later. Or maybe sooner.

At the sound of the closing book, Zach turned to her. "We need to talk."

"About what?" Her expression made him think she was steeling herself for a rehash of their argument the night before. He figured what he really had in mind would disturb her a whole lot more.

"About heading back."

She touched the breast pocket of her overalls, emphasizing the cylindrical shape of her father's pill vial. "How much farther before we reach the main waterway?"

"Ten or twelve miles, barring any dead ends."

"Oh, not far," she said with clearly forced brightness. "We'll make it there in less than half an hour. It's not even noon, so we still have all afternoon to search for him."

"For all we know, your pa's already gone home."

174

"If he's home, he's safe. But if he's out here, he's not."

Zach glanced out the windshield, and changed course to avoid a current that hinted at a submerged tree. "I'm not sure we're so safe out here ourselves."

He expected a retort laced with sarcasm. Instead, she remained silent, rubbing the pill bottle and turning to look nervously in the direction from which they'd come.

"We've got this big boat," she said after the pause had grown in length. "And he's in a small one." She leaned forward, speaking fervently, and he wasn't sure who she wanted to convince, him or herself. "Please, Zach. Just until midafternoon. If we haven't found him by then, we'll go back to the river. That would get us home before dark."

"You *have* been away a while."

"So?"

"So . . . the correct turnoff's supposed to be a cypress swamp. They aren't so easy to navigate."

"You'll get us through. I trust you."

Zach crumpled like an empty cigarette pack. Christ almighty, a woman in distress. Even now, knowing where his former stupidity had led, he couldn't resist.

"All right," he replied reluctantly, reaching for the Winstons he'd bought from Harris. Before pulling them out, he looked down at his watch. "Until two-thirty. Then we turn back. Agreed?"

"Agreed." She picked up the book again, lost to him for the time being.

Although she didn't seem upset with him, he wished he could take away the harsh words he'd spit out in his drunken haze. Hell, he'd promised himself he'd cut back, but since embarking on this trip he could hardly keep his hands off his flask. Or off Liz.

That didn't justify the way he'd jumped all over her. Still, he found it difficult to believe she'd so thoroughly forgotten what she'd told him the night she'd begged him to take her away that she accused him of abandoning her. He'd always been there when she needed him. Hadn't he listened without scoffing to her fantastic tale of *le fantôme* coming for her grandmother? And if he'd even half believed she would really leave, he would have taken her.

So what was up with her denial? Could she honestly think she'd never told him that story? He glanced at her, saw she was still absorbed in her mother's writing, and suspected that if she'd truly forgotten, the contents of the book might very well revive the memory not only of their conversation that night, but of her entire heritage. If that happened, she'd need him, because he sensed Liz Deveraux was a woman who didn't face her self-deception well.

The possibility quickened his heart, and if not for his sinking feeling that their journey was leading them into trouble they weren't prepared to handle, he might have felt a burst of joy.

A while later he glanced at Liz again. "I'm going to need your help navigating the cypress knees soon."

They'd just passed a shore with a cluster of maple trees that resembled the ones drawn on the map. But so had several other locations, and he didn't feel much hope as he turned from the river.

Liz appeared a bit dazed as she lifted her head from the book. "I need a break anyway."

She rubbed her arms, and he noticed she had goose bumps. Somewhat odd, since a while back he'd unbuttoned his shirt and rolled up the sleeves to get cooler.

"This part is all about Ankouer. She says he's alone, suffering something akin to sensory deprivation, and that he badly longs for the joys of human life." Her voice took on a mocking tone. "But he fears love, which he also knows is his only salvation. Can you believe it, after all she's said about his evil heart, she's suddenly sympathetic?"

"I don't pretend to understand Cajun lore," he replied, a bit uneasy over her agitation. "My folks took us to mass on Sunday, but that's as close as I ever got to mysticism. They never talked about the old legends."

"According to the journal, hardly anyone does these days." She let out a sound halfway between a sob and a cough, then put the book back in the bag and returned it to her pocket. "I've been reading too much. She has a way of making it all seem real."

The reason for her chills. Good thing he'd interrupted her. Strangely, and despite his earlier anticipation that reading the book might jar her memory, he preferred not to hear more. True, he hadn't been raised amid dark legends, but this discussion refreshed his recall of the journey in his pirogue, and he was beginning to shiver just like her.

"When are those knees coming up?" Her question broke his train of thought.

"Soon enough, *cher*. Soon enough."

"What time is it?" Liz asked, simultaneously taking in the sky and checking her watch. "Two o'clock!" she exclaimed, answering her own question. "Why's it so dark?"

She plucked at her thin top, which stuck to her skin in the suffocatingly thick air, then pointed behind them. "Over there the sky's as blue as it can be."

"We're in the shade," Zach replied. "The sun can't get through."

"I know shade when I see it. This is different."

They were deep in a cypress swamp, stopped beneath towering trees in a water-choking sea of fallen moss and grass.

Zach peered up through the leafy canopy. He'd been worried they'd taken another wrong turn, and wished like hell they'd used Cormier's smaller boat. This tug of Frank's needed room, and if he'd read the signs of the sloping shore correctly, the channel would narrow even more before they passed through it.

And Liz had to take this moment to point out the dark sky that only served to revive his chilling memory of that long-ago journey.

"Hmm," he said, carefully maintaining his facade of nonchalance. "A storm front. It'll probably pass, but let's concentrate on getting through here in case it doesn't."

Cypress knees jutted up all over, like bones in some ceremonial burial ground, some of them taller than he was. Now and then he spotted the round protuberant eyes of a submerged alligator, but otherwise there was no sign of life. All was so quiet their voices split the air each time they spoke. Too quiet, he thought, way too quiet.

He wished Liz had taken his advice. What were they doing out in this wild terrain? They'd once known this swamp like the backs of their hands. But they weren't kids anymore, and this was still a corner of the bayou that even then had scared the hell out of him.

Chapter Twelve

Zach opened the throttle just slightly and started slowly forward. "Check the clearance on the port side, will you?"

"Port? I've forgotten which side that is."

"Left, if you're facing front."

"Oh, left, right." She laughed nervously, then did as he asked and stood there gazing down. "All clear."

Zach applied a little more gas. Ahead, was an even narrower passage. "You think we can make that?" Liz asked. "Maybe we should turn around and try a different route."

"We'll never get out by dark. If your ma's map is right, that narrow spot's supposed to lead into a channel that goes back to the river."

"Watch out, Zach, there's a small knee over here." He corrected to starboard until she said, "Clear."

Two o'clock, Liz thought. But she'd agreed. Once they were out of here, they'd turn back. Everything Zach said rang true. Her father had probably returned to the cabin even as they were navigating this treacherous swamp. Trouble was, she didn't want to go back, and she failed to understand her own stubbornness. How unlike her. If she knew anything, it was how to cut her losses.

A chill ran down her spine, along with the oddest sense that this journey was out of their hands. She had felt that even as they'd embarked, but the farther they went, the stronger the feeling got. What if they couldn't turn back now, no matter how hard they tried?

This line of thinking scared her, so she forced her attention back to checking for obstacles. They twisted through the morass of cypress knees for quite some time, with Liz occasionally giving warning and Zach making corrections. Soon they reached a cramped bottleneck that led to a wider passage.

"Stay alert," Zach said, standing up to see clearly. He slowed the boat to a crawl. The way looked quite clear, so Liz let up her guard and looked over her shoulder at the dark, forbidding swamp they were finally leaving behind. Not a place she wanted to be trapped in when the sun went down.

When she turned back, the port-side bow was nearly on top of a knee. "Watch out, Zach!"

He veered sharply, but too late. The crunch of

metal colliding with wood mingled with the whir of sudden acceleration. Despite Zach's efforts, the boat came to an abrupt halt. Steadying herself with the rail, Liz looked forward to see what had happened.

The bow was wedged between two enormous cypress knees.

"Oh, Zach!" she cried. "I'm sorry, I'm so sorry. I could have sworn this side was clear."

"It's okay," he replied gruffly, nodding toward the knee on his side. "I didn't see this one either. These suckers came out of nowhere."

"Can you get us out?"

Rather than answering, Zach put the boat in reverse, cautiously applying the gas. The hum of rising rpms wasn't reassuring, especially since the boat didn't budge. Zach looked over his shoulder and Liz followed suit. She realized their predicament even before Zach spoke.

"If we do jerk free," he said, taking his foot off the gas pedal, "we'll end up crashing into those knees behind us."

Liz nodded. Cypress trees were everywhere, blocking out the pale sun and thrusting their bony roots up through the water. Scum rippled in a love dance with the fallen moss, and the roaring engine must have awakened the sleepy swamp. Catcalls, chitters, caws, and cheeps rose from every corner.

Liz had a chilling feeling the animals were laughing.

"So what's the plan, *el capitan*?" she asked shakily. "I pray it doesn't include spending the night here."

"You think that cell phone will work?"

Her explosion of relief came out as a laugh. "Now why didn't that occur to me?"

"Why indeed?" Zach teased. "I think of that thing as your third arm."

"Don't be ungrateful," she said jauntily, leaving the gunwale to retrieve her bag. "You'll soon owe your life to my phone."

Zach chuckled, and when Liz came back with the phone, his face no longer looked tense. "Nine-one-one?" she asked.

"This all is sure an emergency isn't it?" He leaned back leisurely and lit a cigarette.

A mass of static reached her ear. Her heart sank, then rose again when she heard a click.

"You are out of range," stated a raspy, funereal voice. "There is no help." A malevolent laugh followed.

Liz gasped and her fingers trembled so violently she dropped the phone.

"What?" Zach said, bending over to pick it up.

He put it briefly to his ear, then pushed the "off" button, his face white beneath his tan. Liz collapsed in the passenger seat and buried her face in her shaking hands.

A long while later, Zach spoke.

"We've been skirting around this, Liz," he said. "But something extraordinary is happening out here. I don't think we can ignore it anymore."

Liz straightened up, still trying to get a hold on herself. When she answered him, she didn't trust her voice.

"You may be right. But scaring ourselves with spooky stories like we did as children won't make things any better." Adopting a tone she hoped conveyed a skepticism she no longer quite felt, she added, "Our energy will be better spent trying to devise a way out of here."

Zach reached for his flask, opened it, and took a swallow.

"Try to stay sober until we do," Liz said, more irritably than she'd intended.

He gave her a hard stare. "You might try a drop yourself, *cher*, loosen up that tight ass of yours."

She let out a long sigh. "Look. We're in this together, so let's not turn on each other."

"Then stay off my back. I'm only trying to warm up before I jump in the drink—no pun intended."

Her expression must have conveyed her confusion.

"I'm going to have to go in the water and pull us out."

Her gaze flew involuntarily to the scummy, root-clogged swamp. "In that sewer? Isn't there another way?"

He raised his eyebrows as if waiting for a suggestion.

Liz flopped her arms helplessly to her side. "What can I do to help?"

"Push off with a pirogue pole." He stubbed out his cigarette and stood up, heading aft down the starboard row of benches. "Check the bins, would you? Look for rope, rubber boots, and a knife—a good, sturdy gutting knife will do. I'm going to see if the water's shallow enough for my plan to work."

Liz hopped up, nearly tripping in her haste. She didn't know why she'd chosen that moment to criticize Zach for drinking so much. Tension, she supposed, and a need to blame someone, anyone, for this mess. Ultimately the blame rested on her shoulders. Not only had she failed to warn Zach of the danger, he wouldn't have encountered it if not for her.

"Bingo," she heard him say. "We're in business."

She looked up to see him holding a pole. He wore a confident smile that reassured her. He'd get them out soon, before the storm exploded, before the sun set, before— She was frightening herself again, so she hastily went back to her search.

"Boots," she said soon after, tossing a large-size pair to Zach.

He picked them up and continued looking through the other bins. He found rope, and Liz discovered tackle boxes in the last bin, which held several gutting knives.

"What's the knife for, Zach?"

"From the way the engine lugged, I'd guess there are roots clogging the propeller."

Zach unbuttoned his shirt and shrugged out of it. A line of perspiration had formed between his pectoral muscles and drifted lazily down his chest, weaving through the sprinkling of golden hair toward the waistline of his jeans. Liz watched the trickle with fascination. Heat ignited in her belly, rising up her body as slowly as the moisture spiraled down Zach's. The sensation was so strong it took away her jitters.

Flustered, she stepped forward and relieved Zach of his shirt.

"Here," she said huskily, dabbing his chest with the sleeve. As her ministrations reached his buckle he took her hand.

"Not now, *cher*," he said with a lazy grin. "Later maybe."

She jerked away and stiffly hung the shirt on the back of his seat. "I was just helping."

"I thought proper Midwestern ladies turned their backs when men undressed," he drawled, unbuckling his belt. "But if you insist on helping, why you can . . . untie my shoes." His hands went to the button of his jeans. "It'll make it easier to get these off."

She grimaced. He was teasing, but hitting way too close to home. She bent to pull loose the laces of his shoes . . . one by one, much slower than needed. What on earth was she doing? She *should* turn her back. But he was already slipping down the jeans, and hooking his thumbs under the elastic of his briefs.

Abruptly, she straightened and turned away. "That's enough, Zach."

"A man has to amuse himself in a tight situation," he replied easily. "Tension is the enemy."

A scraping sound told her he'd kicked off his shoes. A rustle signaled the final peeling of jeans and briefs. "Couldn't you at least leave on your shorts?"

"You want me to endure jock itch so you can protect your modesty? What a selfish woman."

Soon the chair squeaked, and the muted chug of stretching rubber told her he was putting on the boots. Knowing that the pilot's seat would shield him from full view, she risked a look. She was behaving foolishly. It wasn't as if she was a blushing virgin, and Zach hadn't exactly displayed intentions of ravaging her. But the glimpse of his unclad body sparked memories. And she knew this time would not be filled with excited, inept fumbles. They were adults now, both undoubtedly skilled enough to create exquisite pleasure.

A pleasure that would ultimately bond them, shattering the life she'd built if she didn't put a stop to it right now. Resolutely, she squared her shoulders.

"Okay," she said briskly, "what do you need me to do?"

"Other than—" Zach felt an unexpected pang of loss. One look at Liz's face told him she'd quenched the heat he'd seen there just seconds before. He swallowed his disappointment and matched her tone. "I'll tie the rope to the back. Each time I pull, you push off with the pole."

He picked up the knife and coil of rope, then stood, feeling extremely self-conscious. He probably looked ridiculous standing stark naked in the knee-high wading boots and revealing the thickening torso he worked so hard to keep in check.

Her eyes widened, but she didn't appear startled, although her quick scan of his nude body was clearly involuntarily. She blinked several times in rapid succession, then met his gaze. Her tongue emerged from her mouth and skimmed her upper lip. Zach stiffened and lifted, with nothing to conceal his state from Liz. A part of him wanted to hide behind the chair, but another part wanted her to know how much he desired her.

Not that they could take an interlude in this tight

situation, and even if they did . . . well, after that, he'd want her forever, and Liz wasn't a forever girl. At least not for him. She'd made it painfully obvious the night before how badly she wanted to avoid her past . . . and anyone connected to it. Still, the fascinated expression on her face remained irresistible.

Liz felt a catch in her breath. He was heartbreakingly, magnificently male. His hair framed a face of rugged angles and strong shadows. His golden skin covered hard, sculpted muscles that flexed ever so slightly as he shifted his body to accommodate the subtle sway of the boat. A narrow streak of white broke his tan at the hips like a loincloth, and the black boots covered his legs to his knees. He looked like a Celtic warrior, with the rope hanging from his wrist, the knife in his hand, and the wide scar marking the inside of his left biceps. His swiftly growing erection only added to the image of unrelenting masculinity.

Liz couldn't tear her eyes away.

"Kiss me, *cher*," he said thickly. "For luck."

She knew it was another joke, meant to ease the tension, but she floated forward, almost as if under another's volition. A shocked expression crossed his face as she slipped her arms around his neck, but she ignored it and claimed his lips. They parted for her, and he breathed a low, hungry moan.

In keeping with the image she'd just had, he covered her mouth with a hard kiss. A warrior's kiss, the kiss of a man who fears he'll lose what he loves.

Her heart swelled, filling her with longing she couldn't deny, rekindling the love she'd once felt for him. Without meaning to, she sagged against him, bringing him flush against her belly. She felt him flex, fully hard now, asking for her, begging for her, and she synchronized her dancing tongue with the throb of his erection.

The boat rocked beneath their feet, the trees swayed above their heads, and the swamp creatures scurried and cried, creating a wild backdrop to the storm within her.

Let this take us where it will, she thought. Let me have him. I'll face what that might bring. She trembled, aching for him to fill her, aching to have him, needing to have him, wanting him so much she could cry.

Then his hands were on her arms, rough hemp brushing her cheek, a hard object she guessed to be the hilt of the knife pressing against her skin.

"Whoa, *cher* . . ." His voice was ragged. "I need to conserve my strength for the adventure ahead."

Liz opened her eyes. Weak-legged, she sank onto the nearest bench and moaned. She wanted to ignore Zach's warning, rip the rope and knife away, pull him down and spread open for him. But she saw his engorgement, and knew his act had cost him, too. It shamed her that he'd remained responsible even when she was about to throw caution away.

"Then use that sexual energy to get us out of here, because when you're done, there's no escaping me." She managed to produce a half-smile. "By the looks of you, Superman couldn't do a better job."

He threw back his head and laughed. "That will keep me going." Then he started for the back of the boat and tied the rope to the stern rail. "Get that pole, Liz. I'm about to become the man of steel."

Without further hesitation, he jumped into the filthy water to attack the roots clogging the motor.

"Okay," he hollered, when the propeller was finally cleared. "When I say pull, you push off the cypress knees with the pole. Got it?"

"Yes." Liz's face was tense, but she climbed on the bow and propped the pole on one side of the roots. Looking over her shoulder, she waited for Zach's instructions.

He waded through the water, brushing back heavy sheets of moss until he was far enough away to provide the needed lift and also to prevent the rope from pulling him under if and when the boat broke free.

Fearing that revulsion would send his gut heaving, he did his best to avoid gazing on the rotting vegetation floating around him. The cool water gave blessed relief to his aching balls.

How could he have let their kiss get so out of

hand? He'd come close to forgetting they were caught in an extremely remote area of the swamp, where they could end up skeletons before help stumbled on them. A gruesome image of Jed's mutilated body came up with that thought.

Jed and Izzy. Their names seemed to arise together. Losing her had been the single tragedy of his young life, one he'd barely overcome even into adulthood. Jed's death had pushed him to the edge. When he'd walked onto the Cormier *galerie* to find the girl he'd mourned for most of his life very much alive, the shock had almost sent him tumbling over the precipice.

He was still seeking balance. What else explained his heebie-jeebies? His rational mind rejected the concept, but he'd swear those cypress knees had jumped from the water. He'd wager his flask they hadn't been there the moment before.

Wading through chest-high water filled with God-knew-what required more courage than he'd needed the day the bullet creased his arm and he'd forced himself to pursue the shooter anyway. He'd always hated the unknown, the unseen, and this was it.

Le fantôme noir.

As he'd told Liz, stories of Ankouer weren't told in his home. His parents denied the old legends, but still did superstitious acts. Silly things—salt over the shoulder, knocking on wood, not walking under ladders. From these acts, and many more, he'd recognized their subtle fear that the lore of their childhoods might be true. At this moment, he wasn't so sure he didn't share their fear.

He'd testify under oath he'd been approaching a log before that bull alligator charged, and he'd never seen raccoons behave so crazy. Then the cypress roots. Now here he was, subliminally praying he didn't fall into a league-deep sinkhole that couldn't possibly exist in a swamp. Liz was probably right in refusing to explore these odd occurrences.

He shuddered at the unexpected brush from a passing fish, which convinced him all the more.

Finally well in front of the boat, booted feet still on the solid if squishy ground, he turned, pulling the rope over his shoulder. Belatedly, he realized he'd forgotten about rope burns. He'd take his chances, but if dislodging the boat required too many pulls, the burns could stop him from continuing.

He trudged back to the boat. "See if you can find a pad or something to protect my skin from the rope."

Liz flipped open the bins, and leaned over the rail a minute or so later with a large hot pad in her hand. "Think this'll work?"

"Absolutely." He took the pad, reassured by touching her hand.

When he was again in position to pull, he

shouted, then tugged for all he was worth. Nothing happened.

"Pull!" he yelled again.

This time he felt a shift.

"Are we loose?" he asked.

"Not quite."

He took a moment to catch his breath.

"Pull!"

No results.

He went through the process more than a dozen times, producing occasional small movements that still failed to free the boat. His legs and shoulders ached. His lungs burned. Moss, scum, and scraps of lily pads clung to every conceivable inch of his skin.

"Pull!" he shouted again, crouching to jump and provide added thrust.

He heard something scrape. The tension on his rope eased. "Are we free?"

"Almost."

"Okay, let's try again."

He prayed this would do it. Despite the tightened straps around his calves, water seeped into his boots. Soon the weight would keep him from jumping, and he didn't relish standing barefoot in the swamp. With his fingers mentally crossed, he leaped again, putting all his weight behind the pull.

"You did it!" Liz cried. "It's free!"

She ran to the end of the boat, holding a blanket,

and leaned over, a glowing smile on her face. "Come on in, Zach Fortier, you superman of steel, you. I've got something soft and warm for you."

Amen. Did she ever.

Chapter Thirteen

By the time he pulled himself over the edge of the boat, Zach was done in. He sat on the deck, head and shoulders slumped over his knees, his muscles quivering, his breath coming in gulps.

Liz draped the blanket over his shoulders, pulled the boots off his feet. After dumping the water inside them overboard, she began brushing away debris with a towel.

"You did it," she said again and again. "You did it. I was so afraid we'd never get loose."

"We still have to get through the channel," he replied hoarsely.

"I know." She got up and went to the bins, coming back with a gallon of water. "Are you up to standing?"

When he nodded, she pointed at the jug in her hand. "Thought you might like a shower."

"Best idea I've heard all day." He pushed against the bench, and found himself a bit shaky in the legs, so he moved to support himself with the outer rail and waited while Liz climbed onto his vacated spot. She handed him a cloth and a minute later water fell slowly on his head.

The jug had been warmed by the sun and the water felt like heaven as it ran down his neck, chest, hips, and legs. It trickled between his toes, then slowly ran toward the side channel that drained the deck. As she poured, he scrubbed the filth from his skin, discovering he couldn't remove it fast enough. Finally, he began to feel clean again, and Liz returned to his awareness. He couldn't recall how long it'd been since someone had done such a simple service for him. His mother, he supposed, when he was a tyke in the tub. But not from the hands of any other woman.

He looked up to see her gaze fixed firmly on the "V" of his legs. No concealing what his body wanted.

She raised her head and wordlessly stepped down from the bench. Another towel had somehow materialized in her hands, and she gently rubbed his hair dry, then smoothed it down. Next she moved onto his body, at times rubbing briskly, at other times brushing him with tantalizing lightness.

He throbbed from waist to knees, all because of one hungry spot that begged to bury itself in her.

Glorious electric shivers tortured each nerve in his body, but he waited to see what she'd do next.

When she knelt to dry his feet, he groaned. She seemed not to notice and carefully dabbed at each toe before lifting her head. Again she caught his eyes, and hers looked exactly like the cat stone they'd always reminded him of. He groaned again, and tightened his hold on the rail.

She nodded as though he'd asked a question, then dipped her head. Her hot tongue caressed his inflamed tip.

"God, Liz," he groaned.

Then his legs buckled.

Liz shot to her feet.

"Oh, *cher*, no."

But she remained silent. Draping him in the blanket again, she pushed him onto the bench and slipped between his legs. As she took him in her mouth again, he couldn't hold back sounds of anguished ecstasy. He'd dreamed of kissing her, holding her, pleasuring her until cries like the ones he now uttered left her throat, but his wildest dreams had never contained the pleasure she was giving him. This was crazy. The sun was falling fast, night would arrive, but he didn't care . . . didn't care . . . not right now while Liz's mouth and tongue were . . .

Liz had no idea why she was doing this. Danger surrounded them, the cloudy sky grew thicker, but as she grazed her teeth along the length of Zach, shivering with delight when a moan erupted from his throat, she was only certain she'd waited for this moment all her life.

This man belonged to her, with all his strength and weaknesses. He was hers to pleasure and be pleasured by, and she never wanted to stop. There *was* no stopping now. This time had been coming from the instant they had met on the Cormier veranda, and she'd see it to its fulfilling end.

His fingers were in her hair, flexing and relaxing, as excited trembles shook his legs to rumble through her body. Then he slipped his hands beneath her arms and lifted her.

"Please, Liz," he moaned, "let me hold you . . . please."

His eyes had turned to lapis blue, tortured and full of hunger. She loved seeing him like this, wanting her so badly he ached. An ache she shared. She was hot and wet with needing him, and needed no encouragement. Her hand moved to the metal buttons of her overalls as she prepared to rip them open. But then she paused. Under the stare of his ravenous eyes, she felt cruelly wanton. She unlatched one button with teasing hesitancy and let the strap fall forward.

Licking her lips, she attended to the other, letting the garment slide slowly over her hips to pool on the deck, then bent to untie her shoes.

"If you don't get over here, *cher*," he rasped, "I'm coming for you."

A husky laugh left her lips, and she licked them once more before starting on her panties. His eyes pleaded, pleaded with her to hurry.

Suddenly, her game had gone on too long. Trembling from head to toe, she jerked off her underwear and almost flew to straddle him. When she spread across him, opening for him, welcoming him, he entered her with one sharp upward thrust. Their cries of bliss simultaneously exploded in the air. Their lips met in a kiss so powerful it shook Liz's soul.

Zach shuddered as he claimed Liz's mouth. God, she was so hot and sweet and hungry for him. Beyond anything he'd hoped for. And he knew then why his wives had left him. He'd cheated them. They'd only been poor imitations of the woman in his arms and somehow they'd known that. He'd never loved them, never loved anyone but little Izzy Deveraux, who'd grown into a passionate woman who fired him up in a way the child-woman never had.

Though he was on the verge of explosion, he wanted this to last, but Liz moved into swift little frantic strokes that forecasted a prompt ending. He broke their kiss and brushed his lips against her ear.

"Whoa . . ." He took hold of her smooth round

hips and stopped her. "Whoa, Liz. Let's take our time."

Such torture, holding back, such exquisite pain, but he lifted her hips into slow, even strokes to which she surrendered. Soon she began rotating with controlled movements so tantalizing they swept all thought from his mind.

Then it was too late, too late to hold back, and they moved again into frantic movements that rocked the boat. It swayed with them, swayed with every loving stroke, and the wild things in the swamp came alive with sound, and the storm clouds emitted a roll of thunder, echoing their pleasure cries and ragged breaths until finally, too soon, yet not soon enough, they reached a crescendo that drowned out everything except the ecstasy they shared.

She had collapsed on him like a soft rag doll, and Zach held her tenderly, loving the sound of her uneven breathing, loving the warmth and the smell of her.

The swamp things still called, and the thunder had gotten closer. Dusk was coming and this dark place would soon get even darker.

"I hate to sound like the guy who won't spend the night," he said softly, "but I don't think we should linger."

He dropped a kiss on her neck as she slowly

lifted her head, her golden eyes looking slightly glazed. "Hmm . . . ?"

"In case you've forgotten, we're still in the swamp."

"Oh! Oh!" She shot up, still straddling him and looked around. "We do pick our places, don't we?"

This time he kissed her mouth. "It was worth it. You are . . . well, there aren't any words."

"I have some. About you, that is. You're incredible. That was incredible."

"Yeah. Yeah, it was."

Reluctantly, he lifted her with a pat on the rump. "Dress, woman," he said, searching the boat. "By the way, where are my clothes?"

Liz stood up, feeling the pain of separation as she pointed to the place where she'd stacked them. She was filled with the afterglow of marvelous sex, and though the fear that he'd move into her life and expose her deception niggled at her, she refused to let herself think about it.

Besides, Zach had given her something else to focus on. They had to head out. The stirring of the sleepy swamp had escalated and the discordant calls sent shivers down her spine. She hurried to dress.

By the time she was done, Zach was in the pilot's seat, putting on his socks and shoes. She supposed he was still cold, as evidenced by the way he buttoned his windbreaker to his neck. Probably starving, too.

"You need to eat," she said. "You've burned tons of carbohydrates."

He chuckled. "Sure did."

"Not that," she replied in mock exasperation. "By pulling the boat."

His stomach growled as if on cue and they both laughed. Then Zach turned on the key and pushed the ignition button. Liz turned to the storage bins.

The rumble of engine beneath her feet soothed her jitters as she searched for something that would go down quick. She settled on a hunk of hard cheese and a bottle of spicy sausages, then grabbed a knife and some plates and moved forward.

Zach had picked up his flask, which he put away as she approached.

"Eat something," Liz instructed.

She handed him a plate, and though the sun still descended and the sky still rumbled, they took that interlude to fill their bellies as they'd just filled their bodies.

Finally, after they'd consumed all the cheese and half the jar of sausages, Zach presented some wrapped, candy-striped mints from his jacket pocket. Liz took one, remarking that it would abate the garlic from the sausage, and Zach lit up, smoking the cigarette slowly and finding himself unable to keep his mind on the present. There'd been another day when he and Liz had shared cheese and sausage.

He'd been almost fourteen and in his first year of high school. Liz had been ten, and they'd sat side by side on the bench of her pa's boat, fishing poles hanging over the edge, eating as voraciously as they had just now.

"You have the gift, Izzy, you know you do." He'd been trying hard to convince her to tell him if he'd make the high school varsity football team.

Liz leaned forward to pluck up a sausage, her catlike eyes filled with excited anticipation. "I ain't in no hurry to use it. *Maman* say I to take my sweet ol' time. Yesterday, she showed me the way to grind herbs to make medicine. She give some of that stuff to Missy Martin and that baby just pop out so easy like, no screamin' and hollerin'. It's a miracle, them things she does. A miracle, for true. I want to be able to do them someday."

"You will." He touched her arm, all berry brown from the sun. "I know you will. But this is now, so tell me if I'll make the team."

She laughed and playfully slapped his arm. "That's all you want me for, I swear."

"Not true." He laughed, too. "Who else'd show me the best fishing and frogging spots?"

She slapped him again. "One of these days!"

He leaned forward then, cupping her young face. The other guys called him a cradle robber for hanging out with her. But it wasn't like that between him and Izzy. She was his buddy, she was part of him, and he knew with certainty where it would eventually lead.

"One of these days, *cher*, you'll grow up, and I'm gonna marry you."

"Pooh! Y'all'll grow up, too, and forget all about me."

"That'll never happen. I promise."

"Cross your heart?"

Cross my heart and hope to die. That's what he'd answered. And when he'd thought she'd died instead, he almost had, too. But that had been years ago, so he turned toward Liz and said, "Let's navigate, *cher*."

Liz took her position on the left side of the boat while he moved the craft forward.

"The knees seem thinner," she remarked. "Isn't the power of imagination a mystery?"

"I agreed not to talk about it," he replied. "But don't go on with that imagination stuff or I'll be tempted to break that agreement."

She looked at him levelly for an instant, a flicker of fear in her eyes, then said, "All clear on this side."

"Clear ahead, too. Looks like we're out of here!"

Liz whooped, leaning over to kiss Zach on the cheek.

"I like this side of you. Maybe we should get trapped in a cypress swamp more often."

"Very funny." But she still beamed from ear to ear as she perched on the copilot's chair. "Home, we go. I'll kill Papa if he's already there after what we've been through."

"Better brew your poison. It's my guess he is."

The channel had opened onto a wide passage, and while the sky above was still a curiously dark contrast to the blue horizon, the water was free flowing and getting deeper, allowing Zach to increase the speed. "We should arrive at your destination in approximately two hours, miss," he said with comic formality, hoping to establish a light mood in which to open his next subject. "You think you can spare some time to talk about what happened?"

Her eyes widened. "In what regard?"

He restrained an urge to mimic her stiff response. "The part where we got it on, bumped bodies, did it, fu—"

"I get your message, Zach."

"My message be damned. I have a question. Did you like it?"

"Did I . . . *like* it?" she repeated incredulously. "What do you think?"

"Enough to take up where we left off so long ago?"

She looked away, her cheeks flushing. He'd touched a nerve. He'd known it, feared it.

Her shoulders squared slightly when she turned to face him. "Part of me does, but I'm—"

"You remember the first time I asked you to marry me? You recall that day?"

She gave him a slow nod, and Zach wasn't sure, but he thought he saw a sheen on the surface of her eyes.

"I meant it, and have never changed my mind. I don't want a one-night stand. I want love, commitment, marriage. I want it all, Liz. With you . . . no one else, just you."

"No, not me." She shook her head and clenched her hands into tight knots. "You want it with Izzy." She climbed to her feet in agitation and stared down at him. "I'm not *her*, Zach, can't you see that? You don't even know who I am! You're in love with a memory of a child who doesn't exist anymore!"

Zach looked up, mildly shocked by her vehemence. With her top stained from last night's gumbo, her hair a mass of untamed curls, her eyes on fire with young Izzy's passion, as heartfelt words streamed from her mouth, he thought she'd never looked more like her young self.

"Yes, she does, *cher*," he answered softly. "She's standing in front of me. And she's a woman now."

Just then, Liz tilted. His view of her was suddenly cockeyed and jerky. The wheel spun in his hands.

"Omigod!" she whispered.

Even as she said it, Zach realized he'd lost control of the boat.

Chapter Fourteen

Zach jerked his attention back to the console. The wheel vibrated crazily, and he strained to regain control, but it was like grabbing a spinning gyroscope. Then the boat itself was spinning, dipping and rising, and throwing him out of his seat.

Everything happened at once. Liz stumbled down the deck, still on her feet. Zach's head hit the console, momentarily disorienting him. The next thing he knew the boat was going over.

Mother of God, they were going to capsize! He dove for Liz's legs, determined they stay together at all cost, but she'd been thrown too far away. Rising to his knees, he inched in her direction. Each time he thought he had her, she slipped away. As the boat yawed to one side, he made a last lunge that proved to be too late. She tumbled over the railing and into the water.

"Liz! Liz!" he shouted, rolling as the boat righted itself. "Liz!"

He reached for the rail, staring down into a dizzying vortex. Her head bobbed in the water, rising, sinking, rising again.

"Zach!" she screamed, reaching for him. He turned to grab a life preserver, but they were gone. The raccoons must have thrown them overboard. So much had been lost, he'd never thought to check.

He whirled back to the rail and leaned over with outstretched hands. "Liz! Grab hold!"

She was already too far away, her calls for help nearly lost in the turbine roar of the spinning water. Unless he went after her, she'd drown. A pirogue! A pirogue could stay afloat. He rushed to the forward cleat of the one on her side and started untying the securing rope.

The boat dipped again. Staggering, he grabbed for safety, but his hands came up empty. He flew over the rail, tumbling, tumbling, tumbling toward the maelstrom and losing sight of Liz's bobbing head as the murky waters raced to meet him.

He landed with a splash that instantly merged with the churning water, Liz's safety foremost in his mind. Liz . . .

In seconds, water rushed his mouth and washed up his nose, choking him, while the pirouetting boat loomed above. Liquid fingers snatched at his legs and arms with firm, insistent pressure. His soaked

windbreaker made it all the worse, but he didn't
have the strength to slip out of it.

The tour boat spun closer.

His eyes burned so much he could hardly see,
and he had the oddest feeling this was it. His life
was over, and he'd spent it working too hard, par-
tying too hard, drinking too much, never really
knowing his children, never really loving his
wives . . . never having the love of Liz Deveraux.

The boat was on him now. Soon the force of the
whirlpool would bring it down on his head, splitting his skull, knocking him helplessly unconscious
to sink below the waves. He numbly wondered if
his body would drift ashore like Jed's, nipped by
fish and alligators, barely recognizable, but still re-
quiring identification from his poor, poor mother,
who'd already suffered so much.

Through his disjointed thoughts came a dim realization. His flailing arm had struck something hard,
something not of metal. Still battling the vortex, he
forced himself to open his stinging eyes.

The pirogue he'd half untied had broken loose
and now skipped beside him, overturned, but still
floating. He plunged his hand in the water, coming
up to grab the under edge, then held tight and
strained until he had an arm over the hull. Next, a
leg. The rough cypress surface scraped his hand,
and his muscles screamed, but he ignored them,
and inch by painful inch he managed to lever up

until, panting and gasping for breath, he finally lay on his stomach. The pirogue rose and fell, but he held tight.

Soon—unless he was kidding himself—he sensed an ebbing of the whirlpool. He lifted his head to look for Liz, but didn't see her. His shoulders slumped, along with his hopes. He dropped his head onto the canoe. Give it up, he thought. Give it up.

No! He wouldn't lose her again, even if he had to bring her back from the dead. He craned his aching neck. Just as he'd almost lost hope again, he saw a thrashing arm. He slipped into the water, clinging once more to the underside of the canoe and prayed the churning water wouldn't swoop him away.

Mercifully, his assessment had been right. The power of the whirlpool was weakening, and he was able to guide the craft in the direction where he'd last seen Liz.

He called her name, though his voice was little more than a croak. Called it again. Again. And once again, until he forced a final decibel from his exhausted lungs.

"Zach? Help! I'm here!"

She repeated his name, following it with a gurgling cough.

Keep saying my name, keep coughing, he silently urged as he headed for her, guided only by her feeble sounds and occasional appearance above the waves. The water surged and dipped, and at times he lost sight of her. Once she went under for so long he thought she'd drowned. But after an endless moment, her black hair emerged above the surface. He narrowed the space between them in fits and starts, until finally . . .

A tired, triumphant grin crossed his face.

He had her under an arm, pulling her from the watery grave. He had her, alive, warm, breathing. He'd ripped her away from death, just as he'd vowed, and he would have wept for joy if she weren't clawing at him so fiercely he could barely inhale.

Liz scrambled to climb up Zach's body. Holding on, holding tight. She coughed and gagged and let out terrified squeaking sounds. Every cell in her body screamed to eject the brackish water in her stomach and lungs.

"Shh, shh, *cher*. I got you."

And he did have her. His strong arm held tight even as he fought off both the currents and her attempts to save herself.

"Shh, shh . . ."

Somewhere, despite her sheer animal terror, she found a scrap of common sense. And trust. She trusted Zach to hold on, which gave her enough courage to stop fighting for her life.

"That's the way," he said, pulling her against him.

She let her head flop on his shoulder and was soon able to comprehend where they were. Zach held on to the pirogue, which supported them as they traveled in a ceaseless circle. Except for the churning water, there was silence all around.

Then a crash of thunder broke the stillness. Liz jerked, clawed for Zach's neck.

"Liz. Ease up. We'll both go under."

Letting out a mewing sound, she bobbed her head and loosened her hold. But when he relaxed the arm he had around her, it was all she could do not to grab tighter.

"I'm going to push you up. You have to help."

She could hear the effort talking cost him. He'd fought these currents to get to her and must be as exhausted as she was. Although her every instinct protested, she unlaced her death grip on him and put a hand on the canoe. Slowly, tentatively, she put the other one next to it, supported only by the arm Zach had around her waist.

"Hold tight." He slid his hand to her bottom.

When he shoved, the bucking canoe fought back. Her fingers recoiled against the rough surface, and she lost her grip. A helpless shriek escaped her mouth, but Zach caught her.

"Again," he ordered.

He gave another shove, and even though the unfinished hull tore at her fingertips, this time she held fast.

Then she was lying diagonally atop the pirogue, her body begging for rest. But Zach was still in the water, now needing her. She rolled on her side and extended a hand. Zach took it and just held on for a minute, treading water, resting, gathering strength. She could barely see him, it had grown so dark, but the warmth of his fingers revived her stamina.

"Come up, Zach," she whispered, not sure he could hear her above the noise of the water.

He let go of her hand and started crawling up the hull. His weight caused the craft to tilt. For a horrible instant, Liz thought they might both roll off. Spasms coursed through her body—she would vomit very soon—and her muscles screamed from fatigue, but she knew if he fell back into the water, she'd go after him by her own volition. They would survive together . . . or go down together.

She scooted back, providing a counterbalance to his weight. The canoe leveled out, and he threw his other arm over the keel. Then his legs were up and he collapsed beside her, clinging fast and breathing in gasps. Liz wanted to fall upon him and feel how alive he was. She wanted to cry out her exultation that they'd survived.

Instead, she gave in to her retching stomach and emptied its contents into the swirling bayou.

*   *   *

They drifted for eons around the edge of the waning vortex, silent in the dark, spread-eagled over the gently curved hull of the pirogue. The canoe rocked gently now, providing safety for the moment, and neither possessed the endurance to swim to freedom, nor even suggested the possibility. Though thunder sometimes interrupted the stillness, Liz took comfort in Zach's presence; hoped he also took comfort in hers.

When the moon began to rise, she turned her head to gaze at him. His eyes were open, and she wondered how long he'd been looking at her.

"Better?" he asked, his voice raspy with fatigue.

She smiled wanly. "Much. How about you?"

"I'll live. For a while there I wasn't sure."

"Yeah."

Silence again. Liz almost nodded off.

"What were you thinking out there?" he asked. "You know, when you thought you might drown."

"What a question."

"Yeah. Not one that comes up every day."

"I'm not sure. Everything was so jumbled, emotions, thoughts . . . regrets." She hesitated. Keeping her feelings inside had become second nature. But in one afternoon, she'd made love with this man, almost drowned him in her panic, and let him hold her while she'd heaved her insides up. She could at least give him what he needed to hear. "Lots of regrets. About Mama and Papa . . ." She looked at him, at those ever-changing eyes that were now blue-gray beneath the muted moon. "If only I'd—"

He put his finger over her lips. "No, *cher*, no. The big lesson I learned tonight was 'ifs' were driving me crazy. The future's all that counts, though I figure this isn't the time to talk about it."

She let out a grim laugh and they lapsed into another silence. This time it was Liz who broke it.

"There was one other thing, Zach."

"What?"

"It's hard to begin . . . with all the rest, fighting the water, thinking about my parents . . . Another thought kept running through my head, almost like"—a shiver of revulsion swept through her body—"This sounds insane—but almost like someone was talking to me."

"A voice? What did it say?"

Thunder rumbled overhead like a drum roll, sending shivers down Liz's spine.

Turn back, guardian. You cannot prevail.

"There! There!" she said. "I just heard it again."

"That was thunder."

"Not the thunder." She repeated the words that had run through her head. When Zach responded with an alarmed pause, she hurried to fill it. "A hallucination, that must be what it is. I was terrified, fighting for my life, and now I'm exhausted. I'm sure that's it. This kind of thing happens, doesn't it, Zach?"

"Yeah, *cher*," he replied in a flat tone. "It happens."

His confirmation lifted her spirits a little, and she tried to kid herself into thinking he understood. She wanted to tell him of the malevolence the message carried, how it had panicked her almost as much as the pull of the water. But there'd been something slightly off in the tone of his responses, and she wondered if he wanted more discussion about their future.

Only . . .

In truth, his voice contained more dread than disappointment. But why wouldn't it? They were floating on a canoe in the far reaches of the swamp. No food, no water, no way to get help. Zach was a man who needed answers, and right now there were none to be found.

She saw him pat his back pocket, unconsciously checking for his flask, and wondered if his heavy drinking was one of his regrets. Then she felt an urge so strong she couldn't resist.

"You," she whispered into the starless night.

"Who?"

"It's you. I regretted not spending my life with you."

He reached out to stroke her cheek. "Liz, oh Liz. It's not too late."

Then he kissed her. Not a hungry kiss, not a greedy kiss. Just a soft brushing of his lips against hers, a pledge to a love that had been all but lost.

When he gathered her against his heart, she could hear it beating, each thrum assuring her she was loved. And though it wasn't comfortable lying sideways on the rough curved surface of the craft, nothing could lure her from his arms.

Stiff and cold and aching from exhaustion, taking heat from each other's bodies, they fell asleep.

A *thud*—and the sudden certainty she was going to fall—shocked Liz awake. She grabbed for wood, then for Zach.

He was gone.

She shot up and saw him sprawled in front of her, bathed in subdued moonlight and grinning like a madman.

"Land!" they cried at the same time.

Liz jumped up.

By then Zach was also up, staring at the terrain in front of them. He crouched down, bending to scoop up a pile of soil. Liz went to his side, taking in his view. Gray. Everything so gray. Gray soil, sparse and gray vegetation, a gray sky, a gray moon. Liz gasped.

"This isn't Louisiana."

"Well, *cher*, it is and it isn't." He lifted his arm and let a handful of gray dirt trickle through his fingers. "Welcome to Quadray Island. Seems it does exist after all."

Chapter Fifteen

"No, Zach," Liz replied in horror. "We're exhausted. Our imaginations—"

"Stop talking that imagination crap! This is exactly what your ma described on the page next to the map. Don't try to convince me it isn't, even if I don't understand French all that well."

His shoulders sagged and his eyes dulled. He looked so weary that Liz wanted to say something encouraging, but as she scanned the island, she saw little to reassure them. Yards and yards of colorless soil, interspersed with only rusty chunks of lava rock and withered clumps of grass. Here and there she saw drooping cypress trees that were so covered with moss she wasn't sure they were still alive. And beneath the hazy sky through which the ghost moon dropped rays of baleful light, edges merged and blended to create a surrealistic landscape.

Zach was right. This was what her mother had described.

Turn back, Guardian. You cannot prevail.

She shivered. Exhaustion, mild hysteria, so many explanations, but none lifted the cloak of dread that fell upon her.

Turn back, Guardian.

"The pirogue," she said in a thin voice. "We have the pirogue."

"But no supplies. Worse, no water. If we find some, I doubt it would be fit to drink." He looked up grimly. "Even birds won't fly over Quadray Island. Your ma wrote that, too."

"Really, Zach, you're spouting superstition. I can't deny this island is different, but I'm sure—"

"Different?" He let out a choked laugh. "Take a gander, Liz. This is a wasteland in the middle of the wetlands. An anomaly of unexplainable proportions."

"There's a scientific explanation, I'm sure." She glanced back to the canoe. "Let's pull the pirogue ashore and see what's stored there. Papa used to keep tarps and canteens beneath the seat in the bow."

"They probably got washed away," Zach said dully. "The pole and paddles, too. Even if they aren't, we're too exhausted to row."

"A day without water won't kill us."

"Say that again when the sun comes up."

He needed her strength. He'd given all of his to

pull her out of the whirlpool. Now it was her turn. She closed the distance between them, and cupped his face in her hands.

"Kiss me," she demanded. "For luck."

Then she claimed his lips, almost brutally, wanting to affirm life and victory, and restore his sagging spirits. She ended the kiss as abruptly as she began it, then circled away and marched toward the pirogue.

"Are you going to help me?"

He looked a bit dazed, but he fell in behind her. Soon they had the craft far ashore and upright. "Well, one paddle survived," Zach said without enthusiasm.

Liz wasn't as interested in the paddle as she was in finding water and something to shelter them. They were soaked to the skin, and a biting breeze was in the air. "There's a tarp here!"

Yes, a tarp, wedged tightly beneath the seat. She fell to her knees and pulled, and when the cloth broke loose, something clattered to the floor of the canoe and rolled to strike her knee.

"Water!" A small bottle, the kind people were fond of carrying around these days. Maybe there was more. She unfurled the tarp and two more bottles fell out.

"Water, shelter," she said as cheerfully as she could manage. "What else could we hope for?"

"Food maybe," Zach said listlessly, taking the

tarp from her with one hand. With the other, he reached for his flask, deftly unscrewing the cap single-handedly before taking several gulps.

"It's no use, Liz," he said morosely. "We'll never escape."

She gathered up the water, then levered to her feet. What was going on? While Zach had been pessimistic about this trip from the beginning, and always more aware of the dangers than she, he'd never exhibited such a defeatist side. She bit her lip against warning him that alcohol would only dehydrate his body. He needed rest, not nagging. Rest and water.

"Let's find a tree to break the wind, so we can sleep. Tomorrow's another day."

"Scarlett O'Hara, I presume." His effort to shake off his funk encouraged her. He pointed at an unearthly cluster of moss-hung cypress, made more eerie by the gray light of the moon. Not her preferred choice, but she had to agree it was the best windbreak available.

"Okay," she said reluctantly, uncapping the first bottle of water she'd found. It was only half full, giving them two and a half bottles to last for who knew how long. They'd have to conserve.

She wanted to drink it down, but she took only a few sips, rolling it around her mouth first to wash away the bad taste, then offered it to Zach. He pocketed his flask, and took the bottle, glancing at the remaining two she carried.

"That's it?"

"Afraid so."

Like her, he took a few sparse sips, then gave the bottle back. In turn, he reached into his pant's pocket and pulled out a handful of the wrapped striped candies. "Least we'll have something to ward off hunger."

Half a dozen at the most, not terribly nourishing, and the way Zach offered them wasn't a particularly good sign. It showed how little faith he had that they'd escape the island. But she unwrapped the damp cellophane that had protected the mint from the water and popped it in her mouth.

A thought struck her. What if her father had crashed here, too? She unbuttoned the pocket where she'd kept his pills, relieved to find they were still there, and even more relieved when they jiggled around, apparently protected by the watertight container. The next thought that came to mind was the journal. A keepsake. Not important considering their situation, but . . .

She unbuttoned that pocket, too, pulled out the sealed plastic bag, and lifted it. The pale light revealed no sign of water, just the journal and the *gris-gris*. She let out a sigh.

"What're you doing?" Zach asked.

"Just, uh, just . . ." she said defensively, shoving

the bag into her pocket. "Nothing. I just wanted to be sure is all."

Considering his state of mind, she expected a sarcastic reminder of what she already knew, but he simply inclined his head and kept walking.

"When the sun comes up," she said, "we'll hunt for Papa. Maybe he made it here, too."

"If he did, he's gone," Zach replied impatiently. "Your pa's an expert swamper, and it didn't take him any two days to make this trip. Whatever his business, he's already finished it."

"But his heart . . ."

Zach breathed out a weary sigh. "Liz, don't we have enough problems without you inventing more?"

"I just want to be certain. Indulge me, okay?"

He sighed again. "Sure. Wouldn't dream of coming all this way, fighting off alligators and raccoons, surviving a near drowning, and not mount a wild-goose chase."

Satisfied with his grudging agreement, Liz ignored his tone. They were almost to the trees, and she saw the ground beneath them was sandy. No rocks to poke their backs, and that small serendipity lifted her spirits.

"Things will look better in the morning," she told Zach as they shook the residual water from the tarp, then laid it on the ground.

They collapsed together, their sighs of relief coming out in a single sound, and she felt his hand touch hers. She slipped her fingers inside his palm and held on.

"We better hang our wet clothes on a tree," he said, bringing a groan from Liz.

"We can't sleep in them," he insisted. "We'll be frozen by morning."

Every inch of her was scraped and bruised, her muscles cried out for sleep, but she saw his logic. She sat up to strip, then realized her Doc Martens probably contained water. Groaning again, she stood. "I'm not convinced this makes sense," she grumbled, spilling liquid out of her shoes. "We'll be just as cold sleeping naked."

"Not if we roll up and share body heat." He regarded her thoughtfully for the space of a breath, then grinned. "A delicious thought crossed my mind, but tonight you couldn't be safer if I were a monk."

He sat up and began pulling off his clothes while she stepped out of hers. The pale moonlight cast silken shadows on his defined muscles, and now he did look like a monk, celestial, otherworldly. The many aspects of this man fascinated her.

"You going to take all night?" he asked.

Quickly, she peeled off the remainder of her clothes and hung them on the tree.

Zach watched her strip, enthralled by the graceful lines of her body, the smooth upward tilt of her small breasts, the long concave curve between her ribs and her hips. The ethereal light gave her body a silvery shimmer that made her appear like an angel. An angel in the midst of hell.

"Hang these up, will you?" he said gruffly, handing over his shirt and jeans. The stirring between his legs unnerved him. His body was spent. How could he be having this urge? He'd heard that facing death aroused a primal need to perpetuate the species. Now he felt the truth of it.

When she turned back for his briefs and socks, her eyes grazed the length of his body, then hesitated.

"Get rid of those things, *cher*," he growled, "and come down here with me."

He reached out his arms. She threw the items on the limbs, then practically dove onto the tarp. He pulled one side of the canvas over himself, then reached across Liz for her side. This rolled them face-to-face. His erection pulsed between them, and he moved to taste her lips.

"You're no monk, Zach Fortier," she whispered just as their mouths touched.

And then primal hunger exploded. He slid inside her, filled her up, riding her as she bucked uncontrollably beneath him. This was hot and rough and dirty, filled with desperation, and neither tried to subdue their urgency. Eternity passed in so little time, and when fulfillment neared, Zach had only one thought, which he whispered in her ear.

"I love you, Liz."

She moaned his name, then shattered. He drank in her trembles, her shudders, and surrendered to his own. When the moment was over, he held on to her, filled with emotions, filled with love. Finally she shifted and he moved over, gathering the tarp more closely around them.

"Sleep, *cher*," he murmured, tucking her head on his shoulder. "Sleep."

She fell off almost instantly, and as he heard her even breathing, Zach looked up at the gloomy sky, finding that despite his exhaustion slumber wasn't easy to come by.

They faced death, and even now Liz hadn't said she loved him.

No birds twittered to greet Liz when she woke up. No bright round sun beamed down to celebrate their love. In fact the gray morning and its cold, dead silence could only be described as dreary. But as she snuggled next to Zach's warm body, her hand resting on his chest, her head touching his shoulder, she'd never felt so complete. Together they could face and overcome whatever was ahead. Together they could accomplish anything. Together they could escape this hellish island.

And then what? Go to Chicago with him? Introduce him to all the people who thought she came from a small Pennsylvania town? Expose the truth of who she'd been? She didn't understand why that terrified her so. What had she been hiding when she'd reinvented her beginnings? She should be proud of what she'd made of herself, so what forces had driven her to lie?

Zach rolled in agitation, turning his head from side to side. A frown creased the space between his eyebrows, and his chest rose and fell erratically. Goose bumps covered his skin, though the day was already growing warm.

A troubled sound passed from his lips.

She touched him and softly called his name. He didn't respond.

"Zach," she repeated.

"Unh!" He bolted upright. His eyes shot open and he looked around wildly, clearly unsure of where he was.

"It's okay," she said. "You had a bad dream."

He jerked his head toward her, his gaze unfocused. "Izzy?" He stroked her face with tender reverence. "You're safe. Thank God, you're safe."

"Yes, I'm safe," she said, smiling reassuringly. "It was a nightmare, that's all."

"A nightmare . . . Right." He slumped forward and wrapped his arms around his body, shivering. Spiders again, thousands, no, millions of them, and this time they'd been attacking Liz. "Christ, it seemed so real."

"Want to talk about it?"

"No, ma'am, I don't!" He could barely contain the shudders. The sooner he pushed it out of mind, the better. "It's bad enough dreaming it all the time."

"You've had this dream before?"

"More times than I want to count."

He could tell she wanted to pursue the topic, so he jumped to his feet. "We've gotta leave here right away," he said, taking his briefs off the tree.

"Look," Liz said unexpectedly, pointing inland. "This island is actually a mountain."

Zach looked in the direction of her finger. The futility and dread from his dream instantly reappeared in his waking life.

"A mountain in the middle of the swamp," he said leadenly. "Now that's one for the books." He scooped her clothing off the tree limbs and threw it down to her. "Get dressed right now. We're getting out of here."

She stared at him in dismay. "Papa . . ."

"Liz . . ." He went to his knees on the tarp, and put his hands on her shoulders, desperately needing to make her understand. "This place . . . it's not right. The longer we stay . . ."

"The better chance we have of finding Papa." She tilted her head, looking quite upset. But not as upset as she was going to be if they hung around too long. Why he was so certain of that, he couldn't quite say. Or maybe he could.

"You believe the legends!" Liz abruptly said, leaning away from him to shimmy into her overalls, then buttoning them as she talked. "That's why you're so scared. How could you swallow that crap? I'm stunned, completely stunned."

"Be stunned all you want," he said harshly, unwilling to waste a minute convincing her. "But take a look at the facts first. Don't you think it's weird that in the space of a day and a half, you were attacked by animals twice, and we nearly drowned in a sudden whirlpool? That's more disasters than I've come across in years, and I hunt crooks for a living."

"This is a swamp." She jerked on her shoes.

"Yeah, and it's where we grew up. The closest you ever came to being bit by an alligator is the time you stepped on one by mistake. And it just turned tail, if you remember."

"It was small and it wasn't mating—"

"Damn it all, Liz! Just finish dressing and let's get out of here!"

Zach leaped to his feet to yank on the rest of his clothing. Liz continued protesting, but since she was still getting dressed, he ignored her. He was sick of this hardheaded woman. He wanted the soft, pliant girl back, and though a whisper of Liz's accusations in the cypress swamp floated through his head, he shoved it away. This was her *life* he was thinking about. He'd lost her once and wouldn't let it happen again.

"I'm not going, Zach. Not until I'm sure Papa isn't here."

"Look around you! This place is a toxic dump! How would he survive even one day?" Christ, he had to stop shouting. It only made her more stubborn. "Look, *cher*, your pa knows what he's doing. He'll get home just fine, I guarantee it. But we're greenhorns. We can't make it in a place like this."

She regarded him for a long moment. The hazy light made her squint, causing her to look angrier than he suspected she was. So he waited, praying she'd abandon her fool's errand.

She got up and started folding the tarp, then turned, hugging it against her.

"All right. You've convinced me, but I still don't like it."

Her bitter acquiescence was good enough, and he'd sure as hell take it. He stepped into his jeans, buttoning them quickly, then reached for his jacket. God, he hoped that unopened pack of cigarettes hadn't gotten soaked. He didn't think he could endure the horrific trip back without them. Luck was with him, and he ripped off the cellophane, then reached into his shirt pocket for his lighter and lit up.

"We're in such a hurry, yet you take time to smoke," Liz said.

"You've never been a smoker, have you, *cher*?"

"No."

"Then don't comment on things you don't understand."

He got his pocket knife and began slicing a strong slender branch from the cypress, holding his cigarette between his teeth. From the corner of his eye, he saw that Liz had folded the tarp and was holding on to it while tapping her feet.

"I could have looked for him, all the time you're taking."

"Alone?"

He saw her glance around, and shrink right before his eyes. He held back a grim smile, and when the branch broke free, he scrapped off the twigs and leaves.

"Okay, we've got a pole now. Let's get hiking."

He started for the shore, and heard her trudging sullenly behind him. She'd get over it, soon as she saw her father safely back at his cabin. She'd get over it. Unfortunately, when and if they got back, he still had some snooping to do. Jed's death could not go unavenged, and the undeniable evidence of Frank's connection was still buttoned away in his windbreaker. He'd been begging for this break for years, and now he had it.

He sighed, took another puff from his cigarette,

and kept on walking. One thing he knew: If he took Liz's father in for questioning, she wouldn't get over that one quite so easily.

He was still lost in thought when Liz let out an alarmed squeak. His faraway thoughts slammed into the present, and as they did, he almost emitted a cry of his own.

The pirogue was gone.

Chapter Sixteen

"Guess I'm getting my way, after all." Liz felt no satisfaction in that fact.

"We pulled that thing so far up." Zach crouched in the vacant spot and picked up a handful of dirt, then tossed it down. "Water level didn't rise. There's no explanation."

As he stood, Liz saw an unspoken statement on his face. See? See what this place is like? In that instant, the old wives' tales she'd heard as a child flooded her mind. Ankouer, *le fantôme noir, la maladie maléfique, gris-gris* bags, candles of blessing, spells and chants, all of it, every one of them.

She squared her shoulders and lifted her chin. She refused to believe it, refused to even think of it. But that still left the vital question unanswered.

"What do we do now?"

Zach looked around. "I guess I could cut cypress

branches and use grass to tie them together so we could make a raft."

Liz nodded eagerly. "Okay."

He smiled with dark amusement. "Using my pen knife, it shouldn't take more than two or three days to cut enough branches. Weaving the grass shouldn't take much longer. Think we can last that long on two plus bottles of water and a handful of candy?"

"Do we have other options?"

"No. But after all that work, there's no guarantee it would float."

"We could light a big fire. Somebody might see it and send help."

She wasn't pleased that he responded by looking at her as if she were a child. "Nobody even thinks this place exists, Liz. Which means it's reasonable to conclude it can't be seen from the sky."

She nodded again, struck too dumb by the harsh realities to find more words. A large-mouth bass bumped belly-up against the sloping shore, and a bit farther out she saw the feathery remains of a little blue heron. There was nothing forgiving about this island. Death surrounded them. Waited for them.

Her despair felt like a weight, and she could see Zach was also taken in by it. Okay, she told herself, they were in a bad spot. But they couldn't just give in.

"Then let's get started."

"What?" Zach sounded as though she'd awakened him from a dream.

"Building a raft," she said.

"Why Miss Izzy, I do declare, you're the most optimistic critter I've run into in a long time."

But somehow her optimism seemed to catch on, and they returned to the cypress trees, where they put together a shaky plan. They traded turns with the knife, with Liz cutting grass when Zach rested after tearing off limbs. During one of Liz's rest periods, he suggested she read more of her mother's journal in hopes of discovering some survival techniques.

She opened the book, realizing that reading it made her feel closer to her mother and inspired her to go on, even though she was tired and hungry and wanted to drain the water bottles in one long gulp.

"Says here a certain blue buttercup will purify water," she informed Zach.

He lifted his head from his labor and arched his eyebrows. "What does the flower look like?"

"Who knows?" she said, then lamely added, "We might find some."

Wishing he'd lose that darkly cynical grin, she returned to the book, quickly encountering a dramatic heading.

Défaits le fantôme noir.

Defeating the black phantom. Nothing she needed to know, but she noticed it was poetry and decided to read it anyway. Zach was right. She had to stop railing against her parents' convictions, and it probably wouldn't hurt to know exactly what they were. Especially since Zach appeared to be catching their infection.

The guardian can never lose faith in good, purity, and beauty, though faith be not easy to come by in the face of the evil phantom, so I copy this prayer to help her. If she recites it each time her faith begins to wane, she can prevail.

Beneath this were some simple stanzas.

PRAYER OF PROTECTION

Power above, Power divine, I call to thee.
Shine your light upon my soul.
Wash over me a love so pure
My heart is cleansed of hate.
   Glow, glow, bright opal, free your fire.
   Illuminate the shadows. Pave my way.
   Pave my way, pave my way, so darkness does
   Not fall upon this earth.
By the fire within the stone I pledge
To hold love fast in this dark place.

The stanza repeated two more times without much change. In one, fear was substituted for hate. In the next one, sorrow was addressed. Liz read on eagerly, surprised at how much the poetry touched her heart, though she'd always been repelled by mysticism before. There was deep spiritual significance here, and she could almost hear her mother reciting it in her soft, gentle voice.

Zach's shadow fell across her and she looked up at him.

"This is so . . . oh, I don't know. Listen for a second."

When she finished reading, he remained silent for a moment, then told her it was a good thing she'd come across it. "You might need it later."

"Don't," she said.

He scanned their barren surroundings. "In a place like this, it's hard not to become a true believer."

"Believe what you want, Zach." She closed the book and climbed to her feet. "I plan to believe we'll get out of here."

"Good a thing as any, I guess." He handed over his knife and sat on the tarp to take his rest. Liz headed for the weeds, telling herself they would get out of here. They would.

Noon arrived. Zach finished cutting off another branch, added it to a pile of not much more than a dozen, then gave the knife back to Liz. Once more, she searched for clumps of suitable grass. Her task wasn't going smoothly either. Much of the time, the grass simply crumbled, and so far she'd cut barely enough to tie three branches together.

Gnats worried her neck and arms as she bent over another clump, this one looking a little greener than the rest.

"Izzy," someone called.

She looked at Zach, but he was lying on the tarp, an arm over his eyes.

"Izzy!"

She turned toward the mountain and saw a figure there.

"Zach," she yelled. "Maddie's here!"

A smile coming to his face, Zach bounced to his feet.

"Maddie!" he called.

The woman came rushing forward. "Izzy! Zacharie! Come quick. Your papa."

Liz's hand involuntarily clutched the pill bottle through the denim of her overalls. "His heart gave out." It wasn't a question. She'd known it, known it all along.

Maddie shook her head. "No, no," she gasped breathlessly. "He gone after Ankouer, and he sure to fall to *la maladie maléfique*. Help him, Izzy. You be the only one who can."

Maddie extended her hand, and Liz grabbed it,

forgetting in the moment how much she despised this woman.

"What's going on?" Zach yelled out as he crossed the distance between them.

"Papa," Liz explained. And then she was running with Maddie, running toward the center of the island, toward the mountain. Soon they reached a speckled rock wall, and Maddie veered around it, leading Liz into a sandy, sheltered alcove that was backed by a towering butte. Crates overflowing with supplies were stacked along the rocky wall, and an open bedroll lay on the ground. Otherwise the alcove was empty.

"Where's my father?" Liz demanded of Maddie.

The woman pointed to a spot high on the butte. "Up there. He go in the cave where Ankouer live."

Rugged outcroppings slanted across the face of the butte, and as Liz moved her eyes skyward, she encountered a large, dark hole in the speckled surface. Just then Zach entered the alcove. He asked about her father.

"Maddie says he's in that cave."

He stared wordlessly up at the entrance, then scanned the clearing, taking in the provisions, the bedroll, and Maddie's well-kept appearance. Liz had the definite impression that this was the investigator's eye at work. He put on a sudden lazy smile, but she saw a telltale narrowing of his eyes as he turned toward Maddie.

"How did you get here?"

Maddie assumed an expression that implied he'd asked a very stupid question. She shrugged. "Rowed out."

"You *rowed* out? In a pirogue?"

"You saying I'm lying?"

"I'm saying it's unlikely."

"You city Cajuns. Just cause the bayou hate you, don't mean it ain't friend to us who love it."

"Stop it, you two!" Liz ordered. "Papa's up there and we have to bring him out."

"Your father's a grown man, Liz," Zach countered. "Why are you always trying to save him?"

She wasn't sure of the answer herself. "His heart . . ."

"Right, and he forgot his pills. For all you know, he has another bottle. Hard as it is to take, he has managed without you all these years." She saw him glance longingly toward a crate where a loaf of French bread in a paper wrapper jutted out enticingly. She felt her stomach rumble.

"You must not talk of leaving him be, no," Maddie interjected. "Dangers are in there. *Le fantôme noir.*"

Liz saw a barely noticeable tightening in Zach's jaw at Maddie's crazy claim. He looked again at the cave, then back to the bread, then at the cave. "We haven't eaten in nearly twenty-four hours. How about waiting? If your pa went in, he'll come out."

"No! No!" Maddie cried. "He is in mortal danger!"

"Was he having chest pains?" Liz asked.

"Yes, bad pain," Maddie replied eagerly. "Very bad."

"How about his medicine? Does he have some?"

Maddie shook her head. "No, he forget it at the cabin."

Liz knew with absolute certainty that the woman had a hidden agenda, and didn't trust her answers. But in her pocket was her father's pills. If he didn't indeed have another supply, he was at risk while climbing through an airless cave.

"Go ahead and eat, Zach. I'll get him. Maddie, do you have a flashlight or something?"

"Frank took—"

Zach interrupted. "You can't go in there alone. I won't let you."

"—the flashlight," Maddie finished.

"You won't *let* me?" Liz asked.

"No."

"But there be candles," Maddie continued, as if Zach and Liz's conversation didn't exist.

"See," Zach said. "Candles. You especially can't go in with a candle. What if it went out?"

"She gotta go, Zach. Her daddy need her."

"If it goes out, I'll relight it," Liz asserted. "Now where are they?"

Assuming she'd find them in the crate, Liz

headed in that direction. Maddie and Zach flanked her, each yammering their concerns, and by the time she had matches and several stick candles in hand, Zach had found something else to delay her.

"He's got a lantern, Liz. At least take the lantern."

"It run outta fuel," Maddie informed them, "and we ain't refilled it yet."

"I don't want to wait," Liz objected. "The candles will do. It's not a very big mountain; the cave can't be that deep, since there's nothing but marsh underneath."

"No, Liz, you aren't going," he replied firmly, closing his hand around one of the candles in her hand. Although she held on stubbornly, it slid from her grasp. "I'll do it instead."

As it turned out, Liz so relentlessly insisted on coming along, that Zach agreed, winning only a single victory. She'd wait outside and wouldn't enter unless he called for help. Maddie weaseled out by crossing herself several times and claiming fear of *le fantôme*, and she had long since fallen from sight hidden by the natural barrier of rock to their left that blocked all view of the lower trail and the campsite.

He wished his pride permitted him to do the

same. He'd just committed to hiking through a black tunnel of unknown geography with only candlelight to guide him. Who knew what was in there? Lizards, maybe. Rats? Spiders?

Jesus, don't let there be spiders. He'd come awake itching from head to toe after his nightmare, and all through the day he'd plucked imaginary strands of web off his body. Please, no spiders.

He'd be better off without this train of thought, so he lit a cigarette. It didn't help his breathing on the steep trail any, but it sure helped his nerves. A sip of Smirnoff's couldn't hurt either, and he reached for his flask, pausing a fraction of a second to check Liz's reaction.

She didn't blink an eye, and he figured she was winded, too. The first part of the climb she'd talked nonstop, trying to convince him to let her go inside with him, but had fallen into silence about halfway up.

He uncapped the flask, taking a slow drink, his first for the day. Recognizing that alcohol caused dehydration, he'd eased up. But Frank had a good stock of water, and shoring up his courage was a better idea than going in the cave quivering like a coward. If there was anything he hated more than spiders, it was cowardice.

They rounded a large boulder on their right and met up with the mouth of the cave. That was exactly what it looked like, too. A mouth, round—gaping, and waiting to swallow him.

One more sip of vodka and he'd be off. He lingered with it, letting it sting his mouth pleasantly before swallowing, then recapped the bottle and put it away.

Liz put her hand on his arm, handing him her father's pill bottle. "Thanks for doing this."

"My pleasure."

She smiled, and said, "Liar," then kissed him briefly on the mouth.

"I take it you've forgiven me," he said.

"Oh, Zach, I'll always forgive you."

"Remember that, *cher*."

Then he took a couple of candles from her, shoved one in his pants pocket along with the vial, and lit the other. As he entered the cave, he had two simultaneous hopes. That he didn't run into any spiders. And that Frank Deveraux had an irrefutable explanation for the card case and fabric scrap found behind his house.

Water. It dripped from the low ceiling on his head and arms. Rusty, mineral-laden stuff that looked like blood drops in the flickering candlelight. The tunnel began veering off soon after he entered, and became as small and narrow as an enclosed viaduct, forcing him to stoop. The flame reflected off moist walls, only to be absorbed by dryer craggy areas thick with webs.

The fire quivered from the trembling of his hand, and he hesitated. Sunlight still filtered dimly through the opening; the way out was only a turn away. But Liz would just take the candle and go in his place.

Continue. He really had no other choice.

Pebbles crunched beneath his feet, the sound grating on his frayed nerve endings, and the flame in his hand provided only marginal relief because it revealed the heaps of bones cluttering the recesses in the walls. A stench emanated from one of the spots, a stomach-turning combination of rotting flesh and gasoline. When he got closer, he saw the scorched mask of a raccoon. He stumbled back, trying very hard to convince himself it was a coincidence. Ignoring the slime, he moved to the opposite wall of the cave and eased his way around the dead creature.

Ankouer wasn't very good to his servants, he thought. Used them, sucked their essence to sustain himself, then allowed them to crumble to dust. Was there no end to his need?

For a moment, these thoughts consumed him, and when he realized where they led, he halted them with a shock. That whispered legend meant to scare children into obedience had no credence even though everything around him, every event they'd endured, said it did.

Sunlight had vanished long ago, and Zach let the

flame be his guide. Outside its small circle the darkness was so complete it seemed he might encounter a vacuum by taking another step. The walls curved again, getting narrower and lower. Zach hunkered farther down, creeping slowly, wary of losing his footing on the patches of slimy moss that proved life could exist without light.

Water continued to fall, streaking down his face, and he wiped away a drop that caught on his eyebrow. As he rounded the curve, he heard flapping. A cluster of bats, disturbed by the flame, flew inside the ring of illumination guiding him, then swarmed around his head like gnats.

Zach recoiled, flailing his hands above his head to fight off the onslaught, testing his fragile purchase on the slick cave floor. In seconds, they were gone, repelled by the light, and he stopped for a minute to get a handle on his nerves. Vodka would help.

He was just slipping the flask back into his pocket when he felt it on his skin. Legs, crawling legs, straight out of his nightmares. He turned, his eyes wide with horror, and on the arm supporting the candle, he saw the spider. Big, nearly an inch in diameter, and, by God, he swore he heard it hiss.

"Ugh!" He jerked so violently the candle flew from his hand to land near a puddle on the floor. Reflexively, he divided his attention between cuffing the spider and recovering the candle. The spider flew from his arm at the precise instant the candle rolled into the puddle, sizzled, then went out.

Chapter Seventeen

Black, pure undiluted black, surrounded Zach, and it was heavy with the echoes of his rasping breath. He felt legs crawling all over his body, knew they were imaginary, but that didn't keep him from frantically brushing them away. He lost track of time. Eons, it seemed, passed before he got hold of himself enough to yank the backup candle from his pants pocket and reach for his cigarette lighter.

Tilting the candle, he flicked the lighter on, preparing to ignite it.

"Unh!"

There they were again, dozens of them. Big, spiny orb-weavers dangling from swinging strands of web. He instinctively recoiled and the lighter slipped from his fingers. With jumps and starts and gasps that disgusted him, he let go of the second candle. It landed with an explosive thud as he grabbed for the falling lighter.

He missed, and the lighter joined the candle with a reverberating thud of its own. Dropping to his knees and stifling his shudders of revulsion with little success, Zach searched the floor of the cave. Above him were the spiders, looking for dinner. Below him were piles of bones and rotting carcasses that he might join sooner than he thought. And he could see neither.

Not poisonous, he told himself. Orb-weavers were not poisonous. Just spiders. Just the stuff of nightmares, the stuff that had him waking in a sweat nearly every morning. Just spiders, just spiders.

The lighter had to be here somewhere. He'd heard it strike. Or had it hit the wall, to bounce off and land almost anywhere?

He hit an object about the right shape, closed his hand around it, then let go in repulsion. A fucking bone. He had the shakes bad. Real bad. And he struggled to overcome them.

But how the hell would he find these things in total darkness? He wouldn't, he couldn't. He might as well be hunting for a lost toddler at a Rolling Stones concert. At least there was help to be found at concerts. But none here.

His hand connected with something slimy, and he jerked it back.

No help. None at all.

Yes, there was.

"Frank!" he shouted. "Frank!"

Frank-ank-ank-ank-ank, echoed the walls.

"Frank!"

Another echo, but he kept on calling until he felt a tickle on his neck. Then another tickle. And another. He couldn't move, not an arm, not a hand, not a finger. And he wouldn't scream, wouldn't, wouldn't, wouldn't. . . .

Wouldn't.

The echoes of his wordless cry came back to him, again and again, and he joined it, renewed it, and he knew he was slipping into panic, and it would kill him more certainly, more surely, than the spiders crawling on his neck, across his shirt, creeping down his arms. He hated cowardice almost more than spiders, hated it, never gave into it, never, ever. . . .

This was Ankouer's power after all, to turn a man's mind into a mush of terror, to take away his courage and thus his soul.

Suddenly a refrain ran through Zach's mind. A stanza from the prayer Liz had read from the journal. Immediately, he felt his panic let go. Only slightly, way too slightly, but his thoughts weren't quite so jumbled. Not quite.

He forced his lips to move. " 'Power above,' " he mouthed. " 'Power divine, I call to thee. Shine your light upon my soul. . . .' " His mind went momentarily blank, something that never happened to him. He'd trained himself to remember the smallest detail, the smallest . . .

" 'W-Wash.' " Yes, that was it. " 'Wash over me a love so pure.' "

Pure-ure-ure, echoed the walls.

" 'A love so pure my heart is cleansed of fear.' "

At that instant, the snuffed candle reignited in a glorious blaze. More sounds left Zach's mouth, sounds of relief and joy. Volition returned to his body. He snatched the candle up, then prepared to swat away the spider menace.

They were gone, every one of them. Even the web strands had vanished. He didn't know how this could be, but damned if he'd question it. He'd just collect his lighter and the other candle, then turn back without Frank. The man knew a heap more about caves than he did.

He found the lighter, gleaming brightly red amid a pile of bleached bones. Pocketing it, he then plucked up the other candle, which lay in the middle of the path. After stuffing the items in his pockets, he took a step for the entrance.

He hesitated.

Liz. Liz was waiting out there, worried sick about her father.

Backward or forward?

Liz's face arose in his mind's eye.

Backward or forward?

Grateful, trusting, believing he'd succeed.

"Oh, hell," he muttered.

Hell-ell-ell-ell, echoed the walls. Damn straight, he thought, then marched to meet the sound.

Liz shifted her weight on the uneven rock she'd sat down on, and plucked her cotton top away from her skin. How could it be so hot with haze covering the sun? Just another puzzle surrounding Quadray Island, or whatever this place was. She glanced down at her watch for the hundredth time. It still said three-twenty-six, the hour it stopped after being flooded with too much water.

How long had it been? Half an hour? An hour? Two? Forever is what it seemed, and she could have sworn Zach had called for help.

Maybe.

Then maybe it had only been the echo of her own voice calling him. She got up and walked to the entrance. The sickly sunlight crept into the cavern, illuminating a pebble-covered floor, then getting lost in a dusky hole directly in front of her. A finger of alarm traced Liz's spine as she realized Zach had entered that narrow space.

An inviting place for those that craved the dark—bats, rats, spiders, snakes. . . . The finger suddenly grated on her nerves like a nail across a blackboard.

Unless he had found her father, he was all alone in there.

Returning to the rock, she climbed up to spy down on the clearing, but couldn't spot Maddie. Was she resting out of sight against the butte wall or simply not there? She'd suspected the woman's motives from the beginning, and had still let Zach go alone. What if her father wasn't even inside? Caves were often a maze of tunnels. What if Zach got lost?

Liz blew out a breath of air that made her curls bounce on her forehead. Brushing them back, she leaped off the boulder. Enough. Taking a candle and match from a pocket, she set it afire, then headed for the entrance to the cave. She was going in after him. He'd been gone too long. Way too long.

Zach moved slowly, cautiously, through the tunnel. The ceiling had risen, providing relief for his cramped, stooped shoulders, but he wanted to make certain he stepped on nothing slick . . . or rotting. One slip could cost him the candle again. It took awhile before he noticed that the darkness ahead wasn't so complete. Gray now, much like when he'd first entered. Moving forward into ever-paler shades of gray, he realized there was another source of light. Thus fortified, he picked up his step, curiosity overcoming caution and nearly wiping away his earlier horror.

He heard an echo. *Oor-oor—oor-oor.*

From a voice? Frank's voice?

He snuffed the candle, stashed it with the other, and broke into a lope. It *was* a voice. He was sure it was.

With the way now well lit, he traveled quickly, and soon entered a cave about the size of the one at the entrance. It opened to his right onto an enormous cavern.

Zach stopped a moment, listening.

"Give me the fire stone, phantom!" he heard Frank shout.

No one answered. Wanting to see what would happen next, he slid to the edge of the opening and waited quietly.

"No more!" Frank shouted further. "No more ones will die for you!" His voice softened almost to a plea—"Catherine. My own Ellie. And the other two."—then regained force. "You cannot have my Izzy, no!"

Zach had heard enough. And, damn, he wished it wasn't so. He stepped into the cavern, blinking from the bright light, and hazily saw Frank looking over a pool of water that filled most of the cavern.

"She will take the stone far away and trouble you with it no more." The echoes of Frank's shouts blocked out all other sound, and so far the man was clearly unaware of Zach's presence.

He took that opportunity to drink in the details around him.

Frank's line of sight was directed toward a high, shallow ledge that curved down and widened until it joined the level in front of the pool. Sunlight streamed through a round hole directly above, bathing the cavern with weak light, and clearly illuminating the opal that rested on the narrowest part of the ledge. At least Zach thought it was the opal. Almost fist-sized—large for such a gem—and from his vantage point it looked much like an uncut geode except for the spidery striations and color splotches that marked it as the fire stone.

So it was here, and Frank had come for it. Or brought it. But why? And who was responding to his words? The cavern's walls were smooth, not a nook or cranny anywhere. Except for the opal, the ledge was empty.

There was only one way to get his questions answered. And not for the first time, he wished he'd brought his weapon when he'd made that trip to the Deverauxs in Richard's rented boat.

"Who are you talking to?" he asked, walking forward. Frank swung away from the pool and met Zach's gaze with tortured eyes.

"Zacharie . . . Why are you here? Leave, leave this unholy place."

"I need answers, partner."

"How long you been standing there?"

"Long enough. Answer me. Who are you talking to and where is he?"

Frank darted his eyes wildly around the cavern. *"Le fantôme noir,"* he said, the name coming out as a whisper. "Not always can you see him. He some of the time have to be sensed. Now I sense him. Do you not?"

Zach shook his head, partly in answer to the question, and partly from his own dismay. Frank obviously believed he was speaking with Ankouer, but just as obviously, no one else was in the cave. Delusional. Homicidally so? Zach shook his head again. He'd never guessed that by coming to Port Chatre he'd learn that Liz's father had killed his brother. Not Frank Deveraux, not the same man who'd once strung his fishing line and pulled stickers out of his feet. Yet the damning evidence coming from the man's own mouth couldn't be ignored.

"You know something about what happened to my brother, don't you?"

Frank's broad shoulders slumped, the hands with strength enough to break a grown man's neck fell to his sides. He was a mess—a mirror image of himself, Zach supposed. His torn shirt hung from his shoulder. Spiderwebs and scraps of leaves clung to his hair and clothing. And his deeply shadowed, wild eyes added fuel to Zach's suspicions of insanity.

"*Oui*, I do. And the other *homme*, the one who run."

"The prisoner?"

Frank nodded uncertainly. "I send him to Quadray Island."

"What about Jed?"

"He came looking for the one that escape." Frank looked away, staring into the clear pool. "I tell him where to look, is all."

"And Ellie."

"*Le fantôme* come for her. Nothing I could do. Ankouer take their souls, all of them, and I can do nothing."

Sad, and the sadness of it weighed Zach down. A good man finally cracking, and taking the lives of other good people. It was the only rational explanation.

"Did you kill them, partner?"

Frank shook his head fiercely. "*Non! Non!* Ankouer, he suck away their life. *Le fantôme noir*, not me."

Zach stepped forward, one hand outstretched. "We're going out now." He kept his voice low and soothing, and put his hand on Frank's slack arm. "I'm sorry about this, sir, but I have to take you back for questioning about the murders of Jedediah Allen Fortier, Phillip John Surette, and possibly Eleanor Jean Deveraux. Even though I'm not a cop, it's only fair I tell you that anything you say can and will be used against you in a court of law."

Surprisingly, Frank didn't protest, in fact he didn't say a word, so Zach continued reading his rights. Nice, neat, legal, and he didn't know if his heart could withstand the pain.

When he turned to lead Frank out, he saw the reason for his prisoner's silence.

"Bastard!" Liz hissed with a malevolence he'd never heard from her. "You filthy, rotten bastard!"

Maddie waited for them at the bottom of the trail, and Liz's rage boiled anew when the woman rushed into her father's arms.

"Frank," she murmured fervidly. "Thank God, you is safe."

"*Oui, cher,* I am safe. Zacharie care good for me."

Liz exploded. "Good? He accused you of murder! He arrested you!"

"Murder?" Maddie repeated.

"He does what he got to, that's all," Frank said.

Liz's head jerked toward Zach. "You *had* to do this? Papa wouldn't murder Mama or Jed. He loved them." She looked back at her father. "Tell him, Papa, tell him you didn't do it."

"Liz," Zach said. "I didn't arrest Frank. I don't have that power. I'm just taking him back for formal questioning." He went for his windbreaker,

which he'd left by the supply crates before entering
the cave, and pulled two small clear envelopes from
a pocket. "I have evidence. I found Jed's card case,
a scrap of prison uniform . . . behind your parents'
cabin." He waved the envelopes near her face, but
she refused to look. Her father was still talking, too,
talking crazy.

"That not what count, Izzy—"

"Evidence, Liz. And I heard him talking to someone—"

"What count is you leaving the island before Ankouer—"

"Stop it! Stop these fairy tales, both of you! There
is no Ankouer. There is no curse. And you're not a
killer. Zach has just accused you of murder. Defend
yourself, for God's sake." She whirled toward Zach.
"And nothing you say, *nothing*, will convince me
my father is a killer!"

Zach's only response was to say her name again,
softly, sadly.

Her father said they'd talk later. "Alone, without
the lawman near. He read me my rights, so meantime I got nothing to say."

Zach became all business. "How did you get
here, Frank?"

"My fishing boat."

Clearly annoyed by the terse answer, Zach
barked, "Where'd you leave it?"

"It be anchored on the east shore."

"We'll pack up and go right away. It's early enough we can make the Port before dark."

"So you can put Papa in jail?" Liz asked caustically.

"No gas," Maddie said.

Zach ignored Liz's question. Giving Maddie a doubtful glance, he turned to Frank. "You didn't bring extra cans?"

"I did, *oui,* but raccoons throw it overboard while I unload."

"Raccoons?" Liz and Zach asked in tandem. He caught her gaze for just an instant, but she quickly averted her eyes. Damned if she'd share even this with him.

Frank nodded. "Most of them cans sink to the bottom, but I seen the neck of one sticking up near the shore. Them damn animals wouldn't let me get near it. Middle of the day, too."

"So that's what happened to our pirogue," Zach murmured, then asked, "Is one can enough to get us back?"

"*Non.*"

Zach sighed wearily. "Guess I'll have to dive for the rest. But I'm eating first."

Under other circumstances, Liz would have felt sorry for him. Under *any* other circumstances. But she did go to the crates and rummage for food, finding dried meat and canned fruit, and the loaf of bread she'd seen earlier.

As soon as the food was out, she went to the rock wall beside her father, leaning against it to gulp down her meal and ignoring Zach, who sat on a small boulder a distance away.

Distance . . . precisely what she wanted from him. But even as she ignored him, even as she ate, her eyes repeatedly glanced in his direction. When Zach finished eating, he stood up, taking a minute to close his flask.

"I'll dive for those cans now."

"Good plan." She wanted him away from camp for a while. "Take Maddie with you."

Maddie objected. "I will stay with Frank."

"Zach needs someone to watch for alligators and cotton mouths."

"You go then!"

"Absolutely not!" Liz snapped.

"Go with Zacharie, Maddie," her father said quietly.

Liz saw the woman's mouth open to protest again, but she hesitated, then apparently changed her mind. "Okay."

While Zach and Maddie emptied crates to carry the cans back in, Liz picked up a pan of water she'd set on the camp stove to boil, and left the alcove in search of a relatively private place to wash. She felt sticky and grimy from head to toe, and she stripped down to her underwear to tackle the dirt as best she could. She'd never get truly clean anyway, and what she'd really needed was a place to think.

More than anything, she wanted her father to say he hadn't murdered anyone. Of course, he hadn't, but she needed the denial from his own lips. How hateful to have even this small doubt, but she couldn't deny his actions suggested he was losing his grip on reality.

What if he had? No, that was absurd. The possibility wouldn't have entered her mind if not for Zach's reputation as a thorough investigator. Why had she read up on him anyway? His company wasn't even public. But she had, and the information she'd uncovered confirmed he wouldn't have accused her father without reason.

Sick at heart, she turned for her clothes, just in time to see Maddie picking up her overalls.

"What are you doing?" she asked sharply, wondering why she hadn't heard the woman approach.

"Looking for your mama's journal."

Liz stepped forward to snatch the shorts from Maddie's hand, relieved when she felt hard, square edges. "For what purpose?"

"Ankouer. I want to read on ways to hold him back."

"You decided to rummage through my clothes without my permission because you want to hold back a phantom that doesn't exist?" Liz bent for her T-shirt, tired of Maddie's nonsense, but too weary to get angry. As she slipped the shirt over her head, she added, "Even if this ridiculous fable were true, it doesn't matter. We're leaving soon. Shouldn't you be helping Zach?"

When the shirt settled around her neck, she found herself the object of Maddie's stare. "Maybe we leave, girl, maybe we don't. But I wouldn't count on that man you love so much if I was you."

With that, she swished her colorful skirt around her legs and flounced off, leaving Liz with no one to question about the meaning of those words. Seconds later, she dismissed the remark as a product of Maddie's twisted mind. She had no intentions of counting on Zach. What woman on earth would trust a man who'd charged her father with such unspeakable crimes?

Chapter Eighteen

When Liz returned, neither Zach nor Maddie were there, and her father was leaning against the cliff, asleep.

She replaced the pan on the camp stove burner to reheat. While she waited for the steam to rise, her thoughts returned unbidden to Maddie's remark. For some reason it still bothered her. Why? She tried to put a finger on the cause of her uneasy belief that Maddie meant something different, something yet to come. The woman's furtive manner? The secretive look on her face?

In disgust, she turned away and gathered up a cloth and towel. Maddie was always furtive and secretive. How could that mean anything?

The water was hot, so she dropped the cloth inside the pan and walked over to sit beside her father. She nudged him gently and he opened his eyes.

"How're you feeling?"

"*Très bien.*"

Very good. He didn't look all that good. Tired and defeated, actually, and his skin had an alarming gray pallor.

"Do you want a tablet?" As soon as she asked, she remembered Zach still had the vial.

"My heart is fine. I am tired, just tired."

Yes, she thought, that's probably all it was.

She leaned forward to work a twig out of his tangled hair. He smiled wanly. "I need a bath, yes?"

She pasted a return smile on her face. "This is a hard place to stay clean."

"*Oui.*"

She tested the water, then wrung out the cloth and began washing one of his hands. Dirt filled the lines of his knuckles and stained his calloused fingertips.

Dirty hands.

In more ways than one?

"Why does Zach think you killed Mama and Jed?" she blurted out. It wasn't the way she'd wanted to ask, but there it was.

"I cannot answer, but if I can, would you believe?" He took the cloth from her hands. "I think, no, you would not."

Leaning over, he dipped his hands in the water, splashing the liquid up his arms and scrubbing away the soil.

"You hear now, Izzy. Open your mind and hear. I have much to tell, and when I get done, maybe you will know why Zacharie think I am a killer of people I love."

Liz waited in dread.

"The fire stone come down a long line of women who are its guardian. It pass from mother to daughter like the torch, and it finally come to your *grandmère*. Each woman in her life does battle with Ankouer—"

"Ankouer doesn't exist," Liz said as gently as possible. "You're imagining him. Please try—"

"Let me finish, girl." He lifted his hand to stop her. Water trickled over his wrist and forearm, leaving streaks of clean skin that looked white against the gray dirt. "When I am done, you can say all you want about me imagining, but for now hear me out."

She'd get nothing else until she did, so Liz agreed.

"Ankouer seek the opal so he can be of flesh. But before he do, he must remove the last guardian from the book of man. You are the last one, Izzy, the one it is written can defeat him for all time. This is why he want to kill you."

Mild nausea churned in Liz's stomach as she listened to her father saying exactly what she'd hoped he wouldn't.

"And he got the opal. You got no hope to survive without it. So I come to Quadray Island and go in that sonuvabitching, stinking hole to get it for you." His dark eyes clouded with pain. "It is this way, you see. Every guardian got a defender. Your *grandmère*, she lost her man when she is young, and so Ankouer can get her easy. I was your *maman's* defender, me. But a defender's love, it gotta be pure." His voice thickened. "And, me, I got my mind clouded."

"Maddie," Liz said involuntarily, and with great bitterness.

"Ankouer, it were Ankouer. He make me not to see the right way, and so Ellie gotta fight him all alone. I seen them with my own eyes, but nothing I do will help her."

He scrubbed his hands and arms, hard, almost cruelly, and the water sloshed, forming a backdrop to his words. "Zacharie think I kill little Jed and that prisoner who got away. No, it were not me. Ankouer done that. But, God forgive me, I send them to him." He leaned forward and spoke with urgency. "You got to forgive him for making me under arrest. Let him do what a man, he must do. He is your defender. God bring you together to defeat Ankouer for all time. This place is for the final battle. If you and Zacharie lose, darkness will come over the world, and no one will be left to fight."

Oh, Papa. Losing her mother truly had taken his mind.

"Do not look at me with big sad eyes, girl. Looney, I am not. I been trying to make you believe what your heart knows all along. You been running from your duty. You can't run no more."

He pulled his hands abruptly from the pan, leaving the cloth in the pan, and Liz handed him the towel. He took a moment to blot the water away, finally giving her an opportunity to speak.

"I wish you would stop worrying about these things."

"Someone got to worry." He stroked her cheek, and she saw exhaustion in his face. The circles under his eyes were like dark stains, and he'd aged ten years in these few days. "When I done washing I think I will sleep, yes?"

"Good idea. You need your rest. We'll leave soon."

He shook his head. "I hafta see Ankouer again. He still got the fire stone."

"Papa, no! We have to leave!"

He looked at her for a long moment, then lifted the washcloth from the water and began washing his face.

"Papa?"

She wished she could see his dark eyes. They always revealed his true thoughts, and she suspected he knew it and had hidden his face to keep them from her.

Finally he lifted his head and let the cloth fall back into the water. Turning for the towel, he said, "Okay, Izzy. If that is what you want, we will do it. Now go get me my old tobacco box so's I can roll me a smoke before I rest."

"Your heart—"

"Izzy . . ." This was said in a warning tone, one she always obeyed.

He pointed at one of the crates stored with the many others by the base of the butte. Liz went to it, and easily found the box, which was tucked against the narrow end. As she picked it up she remembered the day she and Zach had worked out the design. Zach had executed the plan in wood shop, and later they had stained the wood, then waxed and polished it until it gleamed. It still gleamed, and she ran her fingers tenderly over the smooth surface, wondering how many other re-minders of the past she'd encounter before she got home.

After she handed her father the box, she took the washcloth out of the water, then picked up the towel and took them both to a tree to hang out to dry. Then she got the pan, and left the alcove to dump the dirty water. Murky inside that pan, so murky she couldn't see the bottom. Somewhat like the events of the last few days. Like Papa's warning about how Liz had run away. Maddie had said something similar, and so had someone else. Someone she respected. But who?

As she dumped the water, she again wondered why she wasn't able to cry. Tears were right there. In her chest, in her throat, behind her eyes, and yet they refused to flow. She wasn't sure how much longer she could bear the pain.

Perhaps it was for the best. If she gave into grief, she'd be unable to deal with the situation. Clearly, her father's mind had snapped, and he seemed almost unaware that Zach was preparing to take them back that afternoon. Had her father's insanity been there all along, just beneath the surface of his vital, laughing exterior? Had he really killed Jed and that prisoner?

Her mother and grandmother?

She turned away from the question, refusing to seek an answer. She only knew he thought his purpose was good, and that he needed medical treatment, not prosecution.

Without warning, her mind wandered to Zach. Was Maddie keeping careful watch for alligators and snakes? Was the water quiet or would another of those unexpected vortexes try to swallow him up?

Her father had told her to forgive Zach for accusing him, and she supposed she might owe him that. If she'd taken this journey without him, she undoubtedly would have died along the way. But he'd had the evidence he'd whipped from his pocket even before they'd boated from the cabin. He'd made love to her, sworn his love for her, when all along he'd planned to take her father back for questioning.

Even if she wanted to try, she doubted her forgiveness stretched that far.

"Izzy is a little bitch, no?"

Zach jerked his head from the oar he'd been poking in the water and regarded Maddie with annoyance.

Things weren't going well at all for his plans to leave Quadray Island that afternoon. Somehow the boat had lost anchor, and though Maddie greeted the news quite calmly, it scared the hell out of him. They'd found it about half a mile down, bobbing in the sullied water a good swim out, which Maddie graciously let him make alone.

He'd paddled the boat back in, and she'd climbed right inside, perching on the middle bench and continuing her nonstop complaints about her mistreatment at Liz's hand. This last one just about snapped his fraying patience.

"She's angry because I think her father might have committed murder." He jumped as something brushed his bare leg. Swamp grass, just swamp grass. "Keep an eye out for danger, would you?"

The oar hit an object. He reached in the water, and came up with a gas can. "Here," he said, handing it up. "Store this."

"You don't hafta ask so grumpy." She stood up and carried the can to the bow, her slight weight barely caused the boat to rock. "You gonna hang around and get them all?"

"Might as well. We're not going to make it out today anyway." He peeled a strip of grass from his hip and idly tossed it away. It floated very slowly downstream, tugged by unseen currents. Just like the mental one flowing between him and Maddie, he thought. "I'm surprised you aren't furious with me, too. I thought Frank meant a lot to you, and I did accuse him of horrible crimes."

She shrugged. "What you want me to say? He done it."

Zach felt a physical shock. Painful. He'd made the charges, sure, but only for questioning, and the woman's admission made him a bit sick.

"You willing to say that in a court of law?"

Maddie laughed. "No way."

"Then why tell me? They can force you to testify."

Her laughter faded, but a smile remained. "Not after Frank and me marry."

"I didn't know he asked you."

She looked down and flicked a leaf off her gauzy

gown. "He will. Frank will pop that old question soon, real soon."

Because she had leverage, Zach concluded, and he questioned her truthfulness. But she did seem confident, which meant she knew something Frank wouldn't want let out. So much weird stuff was going on, and it just didn't come together in a nice, neat bundle. Frank's one-sided conversation in the cavern hinted at hallucination and delusion. But the sudden influx of money? That implied illegal activity.

What if someone else really had been in the cavern? A contact, who'd been hidden and refused to answer. Drugs would be the most likely guess, but for all of his suspicions, Zach couldn't see Frank trading drugs. Money laundering, maybe. Whatever it was, it fit with his original theory that Jed had stumbled onto a crime ring.

Were Frank's crazy assertions about Ankouer just a coverup for what Zach had suspected all along? If so, that meant the man wasn't insane. But why would he kill his wife and mother-in-law? And some twenty years apart at that.

Links, links all over the place, and none of them connected. He wished now that his eagerness to resolve Jed's death hadn't caused him to act so hastily.

His oar struck another can, and he pulled it dripping from the water, then waded to the bow of the boat. "I'm giving it up," he said, putting the can in the crate with the others.

He'd stayed in too long anyway. Fighting his jitters at sloshing through stagnant water and hunting for rectangles filled with gas without the benefit of boots to protect his feet had kept his mind off the jigsaw puzzle. But not anymore. He had a question he should have asked long ago, one only Liz could answer. He was eager to ask it.

"Come on, Maddie," he said as he moved toward shore. "Let's drag the boat on land. I'm not taking a chance of it floating away again."

"A big man like you can't do it by himself?" she asked.

"Some help would be nice."

She kicked off her sandals, hiked up her skirt, and got in the water, pushing the stern as he heaved the bow onto dry land. After he dragged it safely to moor, he turned to put his clothes back on.

"Where's your pirogue, Maddie?" He pulled on his briefs and jeans, then slipped into his shirt. "I figure you want to tow it back."

"I leave it on the other side of the island. We can fetch it in the morning."

"Yeah," he replied, lighting a cigarette and preparing to leave. "That's where Liz and I left ours. Hope it hasn't met the same fate."

"It ain't," she said confidently.

As they headed back, each carrying a crate, it

occurred to him she sounded as if she knew theirs had disappeared. He asked her about it.

"What other could it be? If you had a boat, you'd'a gone before I found you, no?"

Zach accepted the answer as reasonable. Who would stay on this hellhole if they didn't have to?

As they rounded the alcove, Frank's voice came to his ears.

"Money. All the time we argue about it, me and your *maman*, with her saying if it come so easy, why not take it?"

"You did what was right," Liz said. "But I'm sorry you had to. Sorry about everything."

Maddie swatted her arm. "Shoo gnat!"

Liz turned abruptly, brushed Zach with a scathing look, then lapsed into silence. Her eye followed him as he and Maddie carried in the crates of gasoline cans and placed them with the other supplies.

Money, Zach thought. They'd been talking about money. Where had Frank gotten it? And was it connected to the murders?

Well, he'd soon find out.

Liz got up then and went to the butane stove, stirring something that smelled like canned beef stew. Zach waited until she returned, then told her they'd be staying until the morning. With a blank expression, she replied she'd made that assumption.

The smell of bubbling stew set his stomach growling. His hunger and weariness went bone deep, but before he fell asleep that night, he'd get his answer from Liz if he had to browbeat it from her.

"I need to talk to you," he told her later, dishing up his dinner as he spoke.

"About what?"

"To clear up something regarding your father."

Her eyes held more chill than an arctic winter and he was afraid he'd freeze before her answer came. "All right. I have some things to clear up myself."

He handed her the serving spoon and she dabbed a small amount of stew on her plate as he grabbed a chunk of bread. "After dinner, help me clean up," she said. "We can talk then."

"A smart way to get someone to wash dishes," he remarked, hoping to thaw the air. Instead it turned down a few degrees, and she picked up some bread, then walked away.

You sure do have a way with women, Fortier, he thought as he trudged to his unforgiving seat on the boulder to eat another lonely meal. He'd barely finished his stew when he saw Liz get up and go for the wash pan. Shoving one last chunk of bread in his mouth and forsaking his usual after-dinner smoke and drink, he went to join her.

He helped her dump the paper plates and left-over food into a plastic bag, then started scrubbing the cooking pan while she tied it up. They were outside of the alcove, near a hole Frank had dug for garbage, and out of earshot. Their shared task gave an illusion of easy companionship Zach was loath to disturb, but he couldn't put it off forever.

"Where does your father get his money?"

"That's the important information you need?" She shook the trash to the bottom of the bag, then twisted the top edge.

"It's more important than you think."

"He earns it by running his tour business. You should already know that." After securing the bag with a tie, she set it down and moved closer to him, crouching to stare into the soapsuds he swished in the pan.

"You answer one for me, Zach." Her face and voice were as even as they'd been that morning she'd encountered the destruction in her mother's kitchen. Somewhere between the time he'd left for the gasoline and returned, she'd regained that cool self-possession. "The authorities concluded that Jed accidentally drowned. Why are you so convinced he was murdered, and that my father did it? Couldn't the prisoner have hit him while trying to escape, causing them both to drown?"

Zach shook his head. "While they were handcuffed to each other? Besides, there's no irrefutable proof they drowned."

"But you said it was labeled a drowning."

Zach scrubbed a sticky portion inside the pan a bit harder than it needed. He was supposed to be asking the questions, but somehow the tables had turned. "The coroner based his conclusion partly on water and debris found in their lungs. But"—this was hard to talk about—"those corpses were all chewed up, holes in the lungs, holes all over, even in the heart. Water and other particles could easily have seeped in afterwards."

"And how does that lead to my father?"

He ceased his vigorous scrubbing and met her eyes. "That's what I'm trying to clear up, *cher*. Up there"—he gestured toward the mountain—"up there, I just as much heard your father confess he was responsible for people's deaths. He sounded . . . deranged. I thought my theory that Jed had been snuffed by a crime ring was wrong. That your father . . . that in his madness he was making sacrifices to this demon he talks about."

"Le fantôme noir," Liz said in a bitter tone.

Zach nodded. "But what doesn't add up is the money. He remodeled the cabin, installed plumbing, brought in electricity. That's a new boat and motor out there, and then there's my old house he owns and doesn't even live in. Port Chatre's no prime real estate spot, but it still takes some bucks to do all that."

She stared at him with an expression of outraged amazement. "And that's why you think he's a cold-blooded killer?"

"No, I don't think he did this with his own

hands, just that he hooked up with some real scum-bags. I mean, what was that little talk you two were having about money? The one you cut off so quick when Maddie and I came back."

"You want those answers, you'll have to ask my father." She abruptly turned away from him. A quick flash of anger ignited in Zach's belly, surprising him. He'd been feeling confused, sad, guilty, but only now did he realize how much Liz's refusal to listen enraged him. He darted out his hand and closed it over her shoulder.

"Let go of me, Zach," she demanded.

She resisted his attempt to turn her around but was no match for his strength. When she finally faced him, her eyes were narrowed with fury.

"Where did your pa get the money?" he repeated harshly.

"He didn't get it. I paid for the renovations, gave him the boat, even your old house."

"You? We're talking several hundred thousand here. Where'd you get that kind of money?"

"The stock market's done very well for me."

His immediate skepticism made Zach feel slightly sick. "Why didn't you just say so the first time I asked?"

She looked away a second, her temper obviously cooling.

"I feel treasonous even saying it now. You know how proud Papa is. He wouldn't want anyone knowing." Her voice took on a sad note. "He wouldn't even live in your house. And when I offered to buy him a new tour boat, he said it would ruin his image. Why are you making these awful accusations, Zach? Please tell me why?"

"If you'd . . . Those item . . ." He reached in his pocket and pulled out the evidence bag she'd refused to look at before. "I found these in your pa's yard, Liz! And the things he said inside the cave . . ." Now he looked away. His anger had faded, too, and he didn't even want to believe the words he was speaking. "He spoke of Jed, the prisoner too, and— Dammit all, Liz, he also talked about your mother and grandmother's death!"

"He believes Ankouer killed them, killed all of them."

"That's what worries me. I'm wanting to blame it on the money, on his getting mixed up with some bad types. I want to believe he's not directly responsible. But what if he's gone over the edge? Thinks he's protecting you from Ankouer. . . ."

A look of horror crossed Liz's face. *Dear God,* Zach realized, *she was asking herself the same questions!*

"I love you, *cher,*" he said softly, knowing exactly how she felt. "But I'm having a hard time believing you. If you know something, you'd better tell me now."

Horror faded from her face, replaced by rage. She

pointed her finger, then reached out and tapped him on the chest. "Well, you better believe this," she said. "Immodestly put, I'm filthy rich. If you're not careful, these wild accusations will lead you right into a court of law. I'll ruin you, Zach, take everything you ever worked for. You can count on it."

With that, she bent for the garbage bag, hurled it in the pit, then stormed away, leaving Zach with a pan full of dirty soapsuds and not an inch closer to his answers than he'd ever been. The hell of it was, his love for Liz remained as strong as ever. He even felt sorry for Frank, the poor, demented sonuvabitch. And his heart was coming apart at the seams. If only he could forget everything he'd learned over the past two days.

But he couldn't let personal feelings get in the way of duty. Jed deserved more from him. He deserved to be avenged. And nothing Zach felt for Liz and Frank would stop it.

Chapter Nineteen

Damn, *Zach. Damn him all to hell.* Liz repeated the words again and again as she marched back to camp, trying without much success to block out her other thought.

Zach's accusations had turned her stomach, but her own doubts turned it even more. His evidence was so compelling. Maybe not enough to convince a jury, or even a prosecutor, but it presented a clear danger. *Papa's in no condition to face such charges,* she thought. What if he babbled his theories about *le fantôme noir* to a lawyer, or even worse, to someone not bound by attorney-client privilege? Who'd believe he hadn't gone over the edge? She hardly believed it herself.

Now at the camp site, she stopped and lingered by the edge. Maddie and her father leaned against the rock wall, talking. Maddie laughed softly at something he said, and Liz's stomach did another somersault. What if that woman came to court, flaunting her relationship with Papa even as jurors were trying to decide if he killed his wife? Combined with Zach's evidence, the case against him would look even worse.

Liz knew her father, knew that even in a deranged condition he wouldn't kill anyone, but a jury wouldn't know that. With so much stacked against him, he might be convicted or end up in a state-run mental ward. She had to help him.

A seed of an idea slowly took form, one that didn't sit much better with her than the probabilities she'd been contemplating. But nothing better came to mind.

She coughed deliberately to let the pair know she was back, then approached them at a brisk pace.

"I want to leave as soon as the sun rises," she informed them, then turned toward Maddie. "Since we still have some light left, let's get your pirogue and tie it to the boat so we won't have to do it in the morning."

"We got plenty of time tomorrow," Maddie replied, a tinge of resentment in her voice.

"Liz is right, Maddie," her father said gently, rising to his feet. "We best be gone from this place soon as we can."

" 'Kay, okay," Maddie grumbled, also getting up.

Liz was about to ask her father to stay so Zach

wouldn't get alarmed if they were all gone, but at that moment Zach entered the clearing.

"Izzy want us to get my ol' pirogue," Maddie said to him. "A stupid idea you ask me."

"Not in my mind," Zach replied. "We can't pack out our supplies till morning because of the raccoons, and the less we have to do at that time the faster we'll get out of here."

"Right," Liz said curtly, wanting nothing to do with him even though he was defending her.

By the way he looked at her, she knew he noticed, and other than his quick defense he didn't regard her with much warmth either. He then suggested they gas up the boat at the same time. "Should have done it when I dredged up those cans," he said. "But I must've been tired, because I didn't think of it."

"Poor baby," Maddie said teasingly.

Zach's gaze drifted in her direction, but he didn't smile.

He walked over and picked up one of the crates holding the cans, then returned to the group, asking, "Where's the pirogue?"

"I show you," Maddie said sullenly.

They all fell in line behind her, traveling in strained silence. When they came to the little canoe, which was hidden behind some brush well away from the shore, Liz and Maddie helped her father carry it to his motor boat since Zach's hands were occupied with the crate of gas cans.

After the pirogue was tied to the back of the boat and the tank was filled, they headed back to camp. Maddie and her father walked ahead, chatting easily. Occasionally, Liz caught Zach looking at her. On other occasions, he caught her looking at him. But they spoke not a word.

Later, Liz lay on a bedroll, staring up at the haze-covered sky, and fought to stay awake until the others had fallen asleep. Oh, Zach, she thought, why did this have to happen just when we'd found each other again? She wanted to cry so badly her heart was about to burst with the agony of it. She loved him, oh she loved him. But she'd have to leave him behind, just as she had twenty years before. Only, unlike then, this time she knew the reason.

"Wake up." Liz shook her father, and when his eyes drifted open she put a finger over his mouth. "We're leaving."

She expected him to object, but instead he lumbered drowsily to his feet and followed her out of the alcove. As soon as they were far enough away, she clicked on the flashlight she'd taken from the storage crates. Although a round moon hung in the sky, the omnipresent haze dulled its power to that of a twenty-watt bulb, and a storm was brewing, as evidenced by infrequent flashes of lightning.

"Where're we going?" he asked.

"We're getting out of here."

Surprisingly, he chuckled. "So that is why you in so much hurry to get Maddie's pirogue outta hiding."

"I wanted to be sure she really came in it."

"You shoulda ask me."

"Well, I didn't, so there you are. Come on. We have to hurry."

He took the flashlight from her hand and moved in front of her. "I will lead. You do not know the land like me."

The trip to the shore was fairly easy, and soon they heard lapping water. The only other sounds came from the squishing silt beneath their heavy footsteps. No crickets, no frogs, no scurrying nocturnal creatures. But the absence of life no longer frightened her. They'd be gone soon.

Off Quadray Island, out of Port Chatre, out of Louisiana, and away from Zach. A replay of her threat came to mind. What unnecessary bravado. She had no intentions of taking Zach to court. Once she and her father reached Port Chatre—after a stop at his cabin to get the passport he'd acquired earlier for a family trip to England—she planned to drive to the nearest airport and buy two tickets to Chicago. From there, they'd head for France.

Another burst of lightning flashed, this time joined by the soft rumble of distant thunder. A chill ran down her spine.

What if Papa really had killed her mother and grandmother?

She hated that question, hated the way it came up so often. She'd just have to get him help. Europe abounded with wonderfully luxurious mental hospitals. Doctors there would help him understand his mind had been playing tricks.

"I gonna push the boat back in," her father said, when they arrived at the shore. They'd beached the boat when they'd tied on Maddie's canoe and filled the tank. Although Liz had paid for it, she'd never seen it before then and had been surprised at how large it was for a fishing boat. With two center benches, another in the stern, and one more in the bow, it could easily seat eight. Tonight it would carry only two.

He gave her the flashlight to hold and began dragging the boat toward the water.

"Don't forget to untie the pirogue."

"I was gonna get to that."

Of course he was, she thought, watching as he moved to the back of the boat. He'd no more deprive Maddie of a way off the island than she would Zach. But was the pirogue enough? She feared it wasn't, and this weighed heavy on her mind.

"You think Maddie can really get them back in this small canoe?" she asked, praying she'd get the answer she wanted.

He paused for a second, his face looking indistinct in the muted moonlight.

"Don't you worry. Maddie know the swamp like you know them stocks you mess around with."

Although she wondered how he could be so sure of how much she knew about stocks, she was nonetheless reassured by his confidence. If anyone knew Maddie's skills, he did. Just to be safe, though, she would notify the Louisiana authorities as soon as they reached Chicago, which if all went well would be the next night.

"Get in, Izzy," her father instructed tersely once the boat was in the water.

She stepped onto the center bench, causing the little craft to rock. Her father waited for her to sit, then as steadily as if he were on hard land, he took a seat in the stern and pulled the cord for the outboard motor. It sputtered and died. Liz's taut nerves pinged as she waited for him to pull it again, then relaxed when it coughed to life.

"You remember how to use the tiller and throttle?" he asked.

"Yes."

He inched forward, stepping over her seat, and moved to the bow. He clicked a switch, and the water ahead was immediately flooded with light.

"Keep a slow speed, hear?" He turned the tiller completely to the right, which Liz knew would send the boat straight out into the water. "And steer where the light fall. When you get out of Ankouer's evil fog, the moon will guide your way. Mind what I say and you get home safe."

A red light flashed in Liz's mind. "You make it sound like you're not going."

"He leaped into the shallow water, shoes and all, landing directly astern. "I am not. When I get the opal, then I come home."

"No! You can't!" Liz leaned forward, preparing to stand, but with two lightning-swift moves, her father rotated the throttle fully open and engaged the gearshift lever. The boat jumped forward, careening into deeper water.

The momentum flattened Liz against her seat, then sent her tumbling into the space between it and the next one. Her elbows hit cold metal, stinging like hell. Her rump slammed against the floor of the boat, sending shocks of pain up her spine. Stunned and confused, she scrambled to her feet, stumbling again as she headed for the tiller.

Finally she slid onto the seat and grabbed the throttle. She eased back on it, which slowed the speeding boat enough to turn back toward shore.

"Papa!" she shouted, searching for him in the light beaming from the front of the boat. "Papa!"

He didn't answer and she saw him nowhere.

"Papa!"

Lightning split the sky. Thunder boomed so loudly, she felt it rock the ground. And there, not far away, spun a funnel cloud, inky black against the pale gray sky and heading right toward Quadray Island.

Zach tossed and turned on his bedroll in the sultry night, journeying through the mist of his dreams. Thunder and lightning crashed above, just like the night he'd gotten them lost in the bayou. He, Izzy, and Jed had huddled beneath a narrow overhang carved from the shore during the big flood of a few years back. Below them, dead cypress reached black arms to the exploding sky as though offering up the mass of twigs and logs and six-pack rings each one held in its twisted limbs.

"Boogelly, boogelly, boogelly! I'll gitchoo!" Jed wiggled his fingers like little worms directly toward Izzy's face. "Half-Man. Half Man's gonna gitchoo!"

Izzy cringed against the wall of the muddy shelter, her scratched, bony knees drawn up to her chest, and stared at Jed in abject horror.

"Cut it out, twerp," Zach snapped. "Can't you see you're freaking her out?"

"What's the point in telling ghost stories if no one gets scared?" Jed asked indignantly.

"Shut up, Jed."

Zach scooted next to her, put his arm around her

shoulders, and pulled her close. "Jed was only kidding. There's no such thing as Half-Man."

She tightened her grip on her knees. Her lower lip trembled and her eyes stared blankly ahead, looking straight through Zach's little brother.

"Ankouer's a'coming."

"That's just another story *little boys*"—he looked pointedly at Jed—"use to scare girls."

She shook her head fervently. "It weren't Jed's story. I heard Ankouer inside my head. He talk to me. He say, 'Guardian, I'm gonna gitchoo.' Only that ain't quite how he say it. It were more cultured-like . . . and meaner."

"Ankouer isn't real, Izzy. Not any realer than Half-Man or the ghost of old Laffite."

"No, Zach." She shivered so violently he felt it in his own bones. "This is different for true. He's gonna come for me one day and nothing I can do about it."

Izzy's face blurred and vanished, and for eons Zach floated inside the mist. Then Liz's face appeared. "Really, Zach. You don't believe those old superstitions, do you?"

They were in a gray place, everything gray-upon-gray and half dead, and he wanted to say no, but something inside screamed, "Yes, yes, yes . . . and let's run, let's run like the devil was chasing us."

The mist enveloped him again. He floated, enjoying the peace, the absence of conflict, of fear, of

Ankouer. Suddenly he fell, plummeting, plummeting, plummeting into hundreds or thousands or millions of legs that wiggled like his kid brother's wormy fingers.

Tiny, they were very tiny, but he could see beady eyes staring evilly at him, and minuscule fangs dripping with venom. Sticky fibers oozed from their pendulous bodies, wrapping around him, entwining him. He twisted and jerked and fought with a fury, but his struggles caused the webs to tighten. When finally the creatures encased him like a mummy, they laughed. As one they laughed, and laughed and laughed.

Zach's own muffled screams awoke him, and he jerked upright to see the night ablaze with lightning. Thunder shook the sky. Every nook of the alcove was flooded with light, allowing him to see with no mistake that everyone but him was gone.

And in the distance a twister, black as death against the hazy sky, spiraled inexorably toward land.

The tornado roared like a tiger. Wind whipped the waters, pushing the boat back, and rain poured from the sky. Liz turned up the throttle and kept shouting, although she knew her father couldn't hear her above the storm. Even worse, she feared he wouldn't answer if he did hear. His moves had been calculated with cool sanity. He'd led her to believe he'd stay with her, when all along he'd planned to send her off alone.

For what purpose? Her conviction that he'd lost his mind suddenly rang false. Zach, she thought in alarm. If his accusations were on target, her father couldn't let him live. And if he had cold-bloodedly killed her mother and Jed, he wouldn't hesitate to do it again.

No! She refused to think such thoughts. It was the opal. Her father truly believed he had to get it back for her. She'd trust him, no matter what. She'd trust. . . .

Another wave hit the boat. Liz revved up the engine, but overestimated the tide's strength. The boat jumped ashore, and she had to grab the side to keep from flying over the stern. When she righted herself, she saw that the twister completely blocked the moon, hiding everything outside the path of the floodlight.

Then a shadow fell, splitting the beam in two, defying natural law. A head, huge, dark. Two large, powerful arms. Long legs that ate up the light as the form swirled toward her. A pair of red eyes blazed down at her as though she were a small insect, and a menacing drone accompanied its movements.

Liz closed her eyes, squeaks of terror hiccuping

from her throat, but when she opened them, the figure was still there.

Turn back, Guardian.

She screamed, the sound merging with an abrupt clap of thunder. Lightning streaked across the sky, allowing her to see her father running toward the boat.

"Izzy." She strained to hear him above the drone. "Leave. Leave now. You cannot win when you got no opal!"

The creature's noises rose to a high-pitched whine. It spun, directing red eyes toward shore. *Leave us, puny defender.*

But her father continued running, waving his hands, shouting, and the whine rose to a shriek. The creature abandoned its human form, spinning with dizzying speed directly toward her father.

Helpless little sounds spilled repeatedly from Liz's lips, her eardrums recoiled from the punishing noise, her eyes took in her father's moving mouth, saw his feet pounding the gray sand. Then the monster burst into hundreds of dancing flames, cooling the warm night with a blast of frigid air, and she saw it swallow her father's racing body, saw him fly into the air.

The last things she heard were scraps of words. "Power above . . . divine . . . I . . . to thee . . ."

Then nothing. The sky was vacant save for the

sickly moon. No sound, not even the splash of the once-turbulent water.

Liz opened her mouth and let out a scream so shrill it nearly ripped her throat apart.

Zach's feet barely touched the ground. His speed was much greater now that he wasn't trying to block out the earsplitting whine with his hands, but its sudden cessation alarmed him. When he heard Liz scream, his alarm escalated to full-scale panic and he pushed the last ounce of energy from his whirling legs.

Fat drops of rain splattered the dry earth, and thunder still rumbled far away, and through it shone a floodlight. The intensity blinded him for a moment, and when he recovered, he saw Liz climbing from the boat. She uttered pathetic mews and held herself so tightly he didn't know how her blood could flow.

"Liz!"

She jumped like a frightened mouse, then turned her wide, blank eyes on him. "My fath . . . Papa . . ."

Shock. He'd seen it before as a cop after reaching a scene of terrible violence. Terror and grief combining until the victim was little more than a shivering zombie.

He arrived at her side just as her legs gave out, and caught her easily while she sank, trembling, to the sand. His eyes automatically scoped out the barren land, the empty boat, as he crouched beside her.

"Where is he?" Zach wasn't certain Liz would even understand his question.

"T-The tornado . . . Ankouer—" She shook her head violently. "No, no, not Ank— The tornado picked him . . . picked him off the ground . . . li-li-like a s-s-stick."

She curled her arms around his forearm, clutching so hard her fingers bit his flesh, and her wide, tearless eyes stared as vacantly as they had in the dream he'd just awakened from. He could only guess what she'd seen. Her father caught in the storm, the twister spiraling down to pick him up, then lifting off to carry him away. Horrifying. Horrifying. No wonder she could barely speak.

"It's okay, Liz," he gently told her. "You don't have to talk about it."

"It b-b-burst into f-flames, Zach, ice-c-cold f-flames!"

Her description sent his mind traveling back in time, but he quickly slammed that door. "It was a tornado, Liz," he barked. "You're in shock, imagining things."

Zach's harsh words sliced through Liz's paralysis, and she looked up at him, her vision coming into focus. Rain was falling on them both, streaking down his worried face, and the floodlight showed stress lines between his brows and around the hard line of his mouth. A muscle twitched in his jaw and his blue eyes looked at her sternly, as if daring her to talk of these things again. She sensed a hard wall around him now, that despite her fog she knew hadn't been there a moment earlier.

She couldn't blame him.

The world she'd created for herself in Chicago excluded everything that she'd been taught during her first fifteen years of life—phantoms and ghosts, even God and higher powers—and it had just been shattered. As she met Zach's warning gaze, she felt her hold on sanity grow tenuous and slippery. She didn't know where Zach had gone or how he'd managed to erect his mental barrier, but she wanted to join him there.

Another explosion of lightning and thunder shook the sandy beach, and she gazed directly ahead, to the spot where her father had vanished, and told herself if she had any hope for survival, she'd better find the same protective place that Zach had entered. Madness would be so easy, too easy, and it was an indulgence she couldn't afford.

"We have to hunt for him." She tried to rise to her feet, but terror had cooked her legs to mush.

Zach leaned forward and slid his hands under her arms and lifted her. She quivered from head to toe, and he had to support her so she wouldn't fall again. Her breathing still came in tatters, interrupted now and then by the same small mews she'd been uttering when he'd found her. Raindrops trickled down her face. He gently brushed them away, but she hardly noticed.

Finally, her trembling subsided to infrequent shivers. "Did you hear me, Zach?" she asked. "We have to hunt for Papa."

"It's nearly pitch-black out here, Liz, and we're in danger from the lightning. We need to find shelter." He stepped away just slightly, testing the steadiness of her legs.

"Maybe the twister put him down somewhere."

"But we don't know where."

"I read about a cow once that was dropped gently on . . ." Her trailing voice hinted that she saw the futility of her suggestion.

"Yeah." If living things survived tornadoes often, newspapers wouldn't report them. But Liz had borne enough pain. He didn't have to agree with her that Frank had probably fallen with spine-fracturing force.

"In the morning. We'll search in the morning. When the storm's over and we have light. Okay?"

Her head bobbed up and down, and when he pulled her into his arm, bearing a great deal of her weight as they walked to camp, she said not another word.

Once in the alcove, Zach wrapped her in a blanket, then covered it with a tarp to protect her from the rain. She rocked back and forth under that insubstantial shelter, mewing again.

Using stones to secure the edges, he erected a flimsy lean-to against the rock wall, then dragged a sleeping bag beneath it. When he finished, he went to help Liz to her feet. Shock had stolen her strength again, and she could barely stand, so he carried her to the shelter, then stripped off her shoes and rewrapped her in the blanket. Then he returned to the shore to secure the boat. If it was lost, they'd both be doomed.

Afterward, he climbed under the lean-to. Liz was still awake, lying on her back, stiff and wide-eyed. He took her in his arms. "Sleep, *cher*," he whispered. "Tomorrow we'll search for your pa."

Her chin bumped his chest as she bobbed her head again, and a few minutes later he felt her relax. She still hadn't cried, he noticed. Raindrops on her cheeks, but not a tear, and he wondered if she ever did, and also wondered about the cost of holding back a lifetime of sorrow. Soon even that thought was forgotten. His own body relaxed as well, and he drifted asleep to the lullaby of his childhood sweetheart's breath.

Chapter Twenty

Liz pressed against the warmth of Zach's body. Rain drizzled on the roof of the lean-to. An occasional clap of thunder sounded overhead. The frequent lightning flashes turned everything as bright as day, and with each swath of light, snippets of her past played across the liver-toned canvas above. Mama singing her a lullaby in French. Papa hanging the truck tire to the giant cypress tree. Zach laughing as he put a worm on her fishing hook.

Then darker memories. *Grandmère* chanting over the body of a dying man. Mrs. Cormier looking left and right as she sneaked up the porch steps to get a potion to keep her man from cheating. And she knew with increasing dread that each recollected nugget was leading her to a night she'd wiped from her mind twenty years before.

Already the pieces were coming. Heat lightning

flashing through the sky. The air thick and sticky and hard to breathe. Liz rolled on her side, pushing away the images, pleading for sleep to take her back into its arms. Instead the images got crisper, more vivid, sweeping her irresistibly into the past . . . to the night she'd jerked from her sleep and shot upright in her narrow bed, calling her grandmother.

Lightning had swept like the path of a torch across the room Izzy shared with her grandmother, and her sweat-damp nightgown clung to her body. Though the shutters were open, no night breeze stirred the stuffy air inside the screened-in second floor, and she found it hard to breathe.

She saw *Grandmère* sitting on her bed, clutching a blanket to her chest, and wondered how she stood having it touch her skin on so hot a night.

"Grandmère," she whispered. *"Grandmère."*

The older woman didn't turn. Instead, she stared at an empty space, saying with uncharacteristic venom, "You cannot take the opal, no. I will die before you have it."

Then die you will, old one. The stone shall be mine.

The words in Izzy's mind sounded so like the warning she'd gotten the day she'd hidden from the storm with Zach and Jed that she trembled.

"Grandmère," she called again in a shaky voice. "Wake up. You're dreaming bad."

It was as though she hadn't spoken, wasn't there. Her grandmother's eyes remained transfixed on the vacant spot. Fear, thick and sticky as the hot air she breathed, permeated the room.

"Never! Never! Not if you summon demons from hell."

What could *Grandmère* be staring at, talking to, that unleashed such terror and caused such harsh words to come from her mouth? Again the voice sounded in Izzy's head.

I am hell. I am the unformed, the ravenous one that cannot be denied. I am hungry, old one. Give me the opal!

"Never! Again I speak never!" Her grandmother scrambled to her feet and stood on the bed, crying, "Power above, power divine, I call to thee in my hour of need!" Swaying on the sagging bedsprings, she lifted something above her head. Colors—gold and orange, blue and red and green—swirled through the room, bringing it alive with brilliant hues. The opal! Izzy realized. Why was it here in their bedroom instead of locked up in the sideboard downstairs?

A hiss sprang up, not of the mind, but real. Very real. Too real. Izzy shivered violently and grabbed for the muslin sheet at the foot of the bed, pulling it tight, frightened into paralysis.

Still not knowing what her grandmother battled, Izzy held her in a frozen stare. Her long, dark, gray-streaked hair fluttered behind her head as if stirred by wind, and her eyes looked toward heaven as she recited the prayer Izzy had heard so often she knew it by heart herself. With each word, the hissing got louder, longer, more frequent.

"Glow, glow bright opal, free your fire," *Grandmère* wailed.

You cannot win, ancient guardian. You have no defender. You're old and tired and weak. Release the stone. It is mine.

Grandmère trembled so badly the opal quivered in her hands and she stumbled over her words. "Cleanse . . . cleanse my . . . heart . . . of fear."

The sparkling globe in her hand flickered and dimmed with each stuttered syllable, with each quake of her body. Izzy couldn't stand it anymore. She adored *Grandmère*, had adored her all her life. She forced another call past her numb vocal chords. "*Grandmère!*"

"Izzy!" With eyes that were black dots of terror, *Grandmère* turned her head.

Ah, the seedling guardian. Come. Join the old one.

Her grandmother's expression abruptly changed to defiance. "Never, Ankouer! The child will defeat you in the end!"

Do not speak such drivel, foolish one.

Even in her terror, Izzy recognized that the mental voice contained an uncertainty that hadn't been there before, that somehow she could help. What she needed to do came to her in jerky, random thoughts. The prayer! She could help *Grandmère* say the prayer.

Still hugging the sheet tightly to her body, she began reciting in her high, sweet, young woman's voice. As her voice grew stronger, her grandmother's grew weaker.

"Izzy!" she called thinly.

And then the opal was hurling through the air. Such a small thing really, an irregular ball the size of a child's fist, weighing no more than a few ounces, but the light inside it sparkled like fragments of a fireworks show.

A silent scream rose from the unseen force, splitting her eardrums, making her hands want to fly up to cover them. But the stone was sailing toward her. She had to catch it, had to, had to. So fragile it was, and it would turn to powder if it struck the wooden floor.

And then the nothingness, the speaker in the mind, the hisser, the thing that terrified her *Grandmère* so, burst into flames. Izzy steeled herself against the heat. Instead, she felt the nip of cold. Creeping, seeping, biting at her sweat-damp skin, at her toes and fingers.

Her hands felt clumsy now as she cupped them to catch the opal. But she continued chanting the prayer— "Power above, power divine" —while waiting, waiting, waiting for the precious object to fall into a downward arc.

She heard *Grandmère*, knew she was speaking to her, but she couldn't look, couldn't, couldn't. If she did the stone would—

"Take care, you . . . for the fire stone."

Flames now engulfed the room with a fire that froze. They licked at her legs, her body, her small, child-woman's breasts, at the hands that waited for the soaring opal, making her movements jerky and hard to control. The fire stone. She must catch it before—

"You are . . . the last . . . the last guardian. It is up . . . up to you to defeat Ankouer."

I take the old one, came a voice from deep inside her mind. *For now. But you and I will meet again, seedling. I swear.*

"Power above, power divine," Izzy whispered.

The stone landed in her hands, soft and hard at the same time, and she closed her fingers around the glittering object and clutched it close.

With one last blinding flare, the flames vanished, allowing summer's heat to return to the room. She swooned, she must have swooned, because the next thing she knew morning had come. Her father sat beside her on the bed, uncurled the fingers she'd wrapped so tightly around the precious stone, and sadly told her that *Grandmère* had died in her sleep.

Even Mrs. Tricou's skillfully applied makeup couldn't hide the blue stain on her grandmother's lips as she lay against the soft white satin. And after they placed the coffin reverently in the vault, Izzy returned home, packed a few belongings in a paper bag, and went in search of Zach. But he scoffed at her fears and tried to talk her out of leaving. So, alone and scared and not yet 16, she paddled her pirogue out of Port Chatre, leaving the fire stone in her mother's care and doing her best to wipe out the memory of that terrifying night.

Abruptly, the canvas screen above came into sharp focus. The rain had stopped. The sun was rising. Liz idly stared at the fibers that bound the canvas together and finally saw the patchwork quilt of her entire life. The crazy events fell into place. The warnings in her mother's journal, her father's insane quest, even Maddie's curt chastisements. The obstacles Ankouer had placed in her and Zach's path.

And Harris. Suddenly she remembered everything he'd told her that night in his bar. She had run from duty, had fled the certain knowledge that Izzy held in her heart. Because of it, her mother had died as surely as if Liz had actually slaughtered her. With that crushing realization, she instantly knew where she'd find her father. Bolting to a sitting position, she leaned over.

"Zach," she said urgently, shaking him awake. "Zach."

His eyes fluttered open.

"I know why we're on Quadray Island," she told him. "We're here to destroy Ankouer."

Still half-asleep, Zach brought Liz's hands to his lips and stared into her ever-changing, amber eyes, trying to take in what she'd just said. Afraid of saying the wrong thing, he delayed his answer. She held his gaze and waited patiently.

"Liz," he said, breaking the silence. "You, well, you've lived through a terrible event. I can see why . . ."

She didn't argue and this uncharacteristic behavior troubled him more than her startling statement.

"I'll go hunt for your father's body," he said wearily. "Go back to sleep until I return."

"He's not dead, Zach. Ankouer took him. Don't you see? *Le fantôme noir* is luring me to his cavern by taking him there."

"In your own words, Liz, Ankouer doesn't exist."

"Yes, yes, he does." She covered the hand that held hers and brought it to her breasts. He felt a quickened heartbeat that belied her outer calm. "I remember, Zach. I remember why I left Port Chatre."

As she began her story, he found himself wanting to reach for the flask. Instead he pulled out a cigarette and listened to her tale with an increasingly sinking sensation in his stomach. The events she described stirred a memory.

He turned away from it. Yes, he believed the island was evil. He felt the very presence of that indefinable quality in the air he breathed. But to swallow the legend of *le fantôme noir*? In his philosophy, evil was a force, but it came from the dark impulses that resided in each man and woman's heart, not from some single supernatural entity one warred against like a marauding despot.

Sure, he found himself occasionally crossing himself, and once or twice he'd been tempted to throw salt over his shoulder. At times . . . at times the memory of his ill-fated journey for the orchid came flooding back. And the occurrences of this trip went well beyond rational explanation. But Liz was talking of fantastic things that science had long ago proven didn't exist.

She finished just about the time he stubbed out his smoke in the sand next to the lean-to. "Have you ever heard of confabulation, *cher*?"

"What?" She frowned as if the question was a non sequitur. "It sounds familiar, but I'm not sure what it means."

"When the mind encounters events that don't make sense, it makes up stuff to fill the holes. It's very common among Alzheimer's patients."

"I hardly have Alzheimer's, Zach."

"No, but you've had a shock, which is another cause of confabulation."

"I'm not making this up."

She responded calmly, as if nothing would shake

her conviction, and he realized he was wasting his breath. He turned to get his shoes and began slipping them on his feet.

"Are you still going?" she asked with surprise. "I told you already, Papa's in the cave."

"What about Maddie?"

"What about her?"

Zach reached for his jacket. It was caked with dirt, and so were his clothes. Particles of sand abraded every crevice of his body. He ached to get off this frigging island and have a shower. "She disappeared last night, too."

"Oh, it's worse than I thought," Liz exclaimed. "Maddie's probably dead, her soul feeding Ankouer's power."

It was all Zach could do not to roll his eyes. "Look, Liz, I'm going to check on the boat. While I'm out, I'll also search for bodies."

"You're wasting your time." She looked around the lean-to, finally coming upon her shoes, which she picked up. "I need to read more of Mama's journal, anyway. I missed so much of my training by running away."

"Reading that journal's the last thing you should do," he muttered.

But Liz was already unbuttoning the pocket on her dirt-splattered overalls.

Zach scooted from beneath the shelter and

climbed to his feet, doing his best to shake away the gritty sand that plagued him.

Just then Liz uttered a soft sound.

"Liz?"

"I'd forgotten about this," she said, displaying the chamois *gris-gris* bag. "Thank God, I didn't throw it away."

She loosened the drawstring and pulled out the macabre voodoo doll. The red dots glared out of its coal-black face. "It looks like Ankouer," she whispered apprehensively.

Oh, Liz, Zach thought sadly, turning away.

"I'll search the island," he said.

Too transfixed with the hideous effigy to acknowledge him, she slowly returned it to the bag, and he knew she'd read the journal despite his warnings.

The morning was getting warm, and the day was as bright as it ever got on Quadray Island, so he draped his jacket on a rock, then bent for his flask and tucked it in his rear pocket.

"Don't go anywhere," he instructed. "And if you're not going to sleep while I'm gone, you might pack up."

"Okay."

But she had already buried her nose in the journal, and Zach doubted she'd heard a word he'd said.

* * *

Liz was getting frustrated. What she'd read so far seemed so much of the same.

It starts. Ankouer has drank the souls of human sacrifices, and now he comes for me with his cold flame. Only the opal can defeat him, and then only if my heart is free of fear. But I tremble and shake at thinking of his approach.

It was all the more painful, reading this now, knowing she might have protected her mother from this evil if she hadn't run away. But it was too late now, and her own night of reckoning was drawing near. She had to prepare. How ironic that she alone of all the guardians had received no training, yet she was the last of the line, the final hope.

In the hands of a fearless guardian, the opal will snuff Ankouer's cold flame, and return him to the foul darkness of his own essence.

How did a guardian remain fearless? Liz flipped to the next page.

Ankouer comes from ceaseless need, and in his hands the fire stone feeds that need, unleashing his evil power on the——

Keep going. Keep going. It had to be here. She knew it did. Finally her eyes hit something she hadn't read before.

When the guardian holds the stone, it becomes like water on Ankouer's flame, and it begins to hiss the cry of death.

Liz's heart leaped with anticipation. Here, this was what she'd been searching for. Quickly she scanned the page.

To get to Ankouer's lair, she must first pass the gatekeepers who guard the narrow inward passage. The evil object, blacker than coal, with eyes aglow and a knife piercing his dark heart, defeats these foes.

Liz glanced at the *gris-gris* sack, secure once again inside the plastic bag. Odd that until now she'd forgotten that Harris had given it to her, along with his message that the doll alone was not enough. Look into your heart, he'd said, Izzy's heart.

The guardian shall walk into the darkest, blackest part of him. Blind and cold will she be, but onward she must go, offering the opal to heaven, and praying for protection with the fullness of love in her heart. Do not hate, guardian, do not hate. Ankouer loves hate like we love sugar and it feed his evil.

Was it possible to face evil with love? Liz wondered, reading on.

But alone the guardian cannot prevail. A defender whose love be pure, one who must battle his own demons on the way, shall stand by her side. If he fails, the guardian shall surely die. If he triumphs, the two shall fulfill the meaning of the verse.

Below this passage was the quatrain she'd come across early in the journey. She'd been skipping repetitive passages, but she was now too caught up in her swirling thoughts to move on. A defender whose love is pure. Without one, she would die.

Papa had been her mother's defender. He'd failed to defeat his demon in the form of sultry Maddie Catalon.

These new thoughts came with a certainty Liz didn't question as her mind moved on to Zach. His love was pure, she knew, untainted by the doubts she'd harbored. But his demons? What are they? His three former wives? His distant son? The flask in his back pocket? Or was it his sudden and complete rejection of ideas he'd once considered?

She couldn't blame him for believing she'd followed her father off the deep end. Were positions reversed, she didn't doubt she'd come to the same conclusion. Yet, even believing her mind had snapped, his love for her remained. It had survived the news that she had died. It had survived her fury at him for accusing her father.

A rueful smile crossed her face. How important it had seemed to preserve the image she'd built since leaving Louisiana. How important to defend her father, no matter the circumstances. With this new perspective, her former intensity seemed childlike and self-absorbed.

Through time, nearly thirty years, Zach had loved her, and contemplating the strength and endurance of his love made her feel safe, something she hadn't felt since putting foot in Port Chatre. Something she certainly had no reason to feel at this crucial moment. But to ask him to confront this horror as her defender. Lord, it was too much, just too much.

As she mulled over the challenge she'd just accepted, and the consequence to Zach that she hadn't considered until now, her eyes fell back to the quatrain.

Beasts lay panting on the trail.
The two keep the one at bay.
When the two join as one,
The soft overpower the strong.

Still as enigmatic as ever. In the name of heaven, what did this mean? Its title—The Key—implied it had great significance.

Where was the interpretation for this puzzle? Liz

leafed through the book, hunting for additional references. When she arrived at her mother's final entry without finding one, she repeated the action, this time from end to beginning.

Finally, she accepted the truth. There wasn't one. The interpretation was up to her. Out of the blue, Harris's words ran through her mind. *Look for what Izzy knew.* He'd said it was in the book.

In the book. What did Izzy, that clueless little girl, know that Liz did not? What? It was in the book. Once again Liz scoured the pages, hunting for something she knew as a girl.

Then it was there, clear as day, written again and again on every page in her mother's hand. *Love.* Izzy knew love. Izzy understood love. And only love could defeat *le fantôme noir.*

Zach went directly to the spot they'd left the boat, praying the storm hadn't blown it into the bayou. To his immense relief, it was still there. After pulling it a couple more yards from the water for good measure, he headed along the shore in search of Frank and Maddie.

The island wasn't much more than a mile around, and the lack of vegetation made the trip easy. Every now and then he turned his eyes inland, looking for a crumpled body. Each fruitless search led only to the small mountain rising from the island's center. When he finally got back to the beached boat, he was convinced Frank and his mistress were no longer there.

More pieces that didn't add up. Liz had hysterically declared that the tornado picked up her father, but Zach would've sworn the twister wasn't big enough to lift a grown man from the ground, much less carry him completely off the island.

With a smoothness born of habit, Zach reached for his back pocket. Not until he recapped the bottle did he realize what he'd done. On an empty stomach? Well, he needed something, that was for sure.

How had it come to this? How had Zach Fortier—son of Port Chatre's mayor and biggest employer, football star, homecoming king, everybody's fair-haired boy—how had he come to this? His life had promised great rewards. Nothing bad ever happened to Zach. Everyone said so.

But his father had died. Then his brother. His once-vibrant mother was a sad, empty shell. Three wives turned their backs on him. His children saw him as a walking checkbook. And the woman he'd loved all his life, the woman he'd once given up for dead, had either joined her father in his insanity or was covering up unspeakable crimes.

Had the whole tornado thing been a fortuitous smoke screen that came up just in time to allow Frank and Maddie to escape without pursuit?

That's when the pieces clicked. Drugs. He'd rejected the idea earlier, but it had to be drugs. Catherine and Ellie had probably gotten hooked, and eventually died from their indulgence. Jed and the prisoner had been tricked into or force-fed an overdose. And Frank, who was probably little more than a courier, had known what happened all along.

A lost fact wiggled in the back of Zach's mind, having something to do with blood test results, but it failed to surface and he spent no time digging it up. He'd given more than two years to the search for his brother's killer, and the mental tug of war caused by the conflicting evidence he'd uncovered over the last three days had exhausted him. It was time to face the truth. Either Frank Deveraux was an accessory to murder, or Ankouer really did live in that ominous mountain.

And those alternatives led to only one logical conclusion.

With heavy footsteps, he trudged back to the alcove to ask Liz some hard questions, scared to death that they would produce some equally hard answers.

She was sitting on a rock, reading, and lifted her head at his approach. At first she regarded him with a fuzzy gaze, then gave him a delighted smile.

A brilliant smile—warm, inviting, full of triumph—and begging for a response that was beyond him. Every muscle in his face felt the brutal pull of gravity.

"Zach," she cried, leaping up and rushing toward him. "We have to hurry. There's so much to do."

His heart ached so bad he couldn't answer.

"Did you hear me?" Her eyes filled up with urgency.

"I heard," he replied flatly. "And you can cut the act."

"Act? What are you talking about?"

"You can't kid me anymore, Liz. I know you helped your father escape."

Chapter Twenty-one

"**H**elped him . . ." Liz stared up at Zach with dismayed astonishment. "You can't believe that."

Clearly he did, because his voice turned harsher. "How did they get off the island, Liz, him and Maddie? And why didn't you leave with them? There must be a reason. He wouldn't leave you behind. So what are the three of you hiding?" At this he looked up at the mountain. "And what in God's name is in that cave?"

"Papa hasn't escaped," she told him. "He's still on the island. Ankouer took him just the way I told you."

"Stop lying to me, Liz," he countered, turning back to look at her. "You've been up north so long you think all Southerners are superstitious fools. But your ruse to make me think your pa's gone insane isn't working anymore. And then there's your sudden reversal. None of it rings true, Liz. Do you have any idea how nutty you're acting?"

She nodded. He'd squinted his eyes against the glare from the hazy sky, which made him look as hard and mean as he sounded. But this wasn't Zach. This was a hurt and tormented man, and not without reason. She dropped her gaze to the volume in her hand, then extended it toward him.

"Read this, Zach, please. It will ans—"

"Somehow your pa's responsible for your mother and grandmother's deaths," he interrupted. "Jed's death . . . that escaped con's. I'm going to prove it and bring him to justice." He took a frustrated half-step away from her, then turned back and fully met her eyes. "I love you, Liz, more than I can find words to say. But I swear, I truly swear, if you helped him, I'll take you down too."

"Please, Zach, listen to—"

"No! I've heard too many lies already. Maybe you can excuse your pa for killing two people you supposedly loved, but I can't give up on Jed." He chuckled bitterly. "Tell me, *cher*, how is it you can forgive him for murdering your ma and grandma, but you can't forgive me for finding it out?"

"He didn't do it, Zach. You've got to believe me. Our lives, his life, depends on it." She gestured toward the mountain. "Ankouer has Papa up there; he's using him to bait me . . . bait us." She stepped closer and tapped his chest with the journal. "Read this, please, please read this. Then you'll understand that if we don't stand together we're all doomed."

"Stop it!" he roared. "You're beginning to sound like your father!"

Liz felt the battle going on inside him. What unpalatable options he faced in trying to make sense of their situation. Either she was a criminal in league with her equally criminal father, or, also like him, she was going insane. And then there was the third one, which she was sure he'd also considered, the option she knew to be true: Ankouer did exist and was behind every inexplicable event they'd gone through.

"Just read what Mama had to say," she said in a whisper, pressing the book in his hand.

"Noooo!" He whirled and flung the book away, then stormed toward the place it fell.

Liz raced after him.

"Don't," she cried. She swooped down and rescued the volume just as he was preparing to stomp on it, and narrowly escaped getting her fingers crushed. She pulled it to her breasts and glared up at him. "Don't you *ever* do that again," she said with a hiss in her voice. "This was my mother's."

"It's making you crazy, Liz."

"No. No, it isn't." Liz shook her head sadly. It was no good arguing.

It amazed her that she understood his pain almost better than he did. He felt betrayed by her, possibly betrayed by life. The young Zach she'd loved had a clear and predictable future. He'd marry her, run his father's cannery, maybe someday become mayor of Port Chatre and after that, possibly state politics. They probably wouldn't have lived in luxury, but they would have had comfort, ease and respect. Lots of love. Good times.

Of course, none of that came to pass.

The silence between them stretched on for a long time, but finally Zach said, "We need to take our supplies to the boat so we can leave."

"We can't leave yet," she replied firmly.

"Yes, we can, Liz, and we are." At that, he slipped the ever-present flask rom his back pocket and took a long drink. After replacing the cap, he said. "And you're going to stick to me like glue, you hear? If you even try to get out of my sight, I'll tie you to me like a puppy on a leash."

She didn't doubt he meant it, and she supposed she could outwardly rebel. But why bother? Ankouer wouldn't let them leave the island, no matter what Zach thought or did.

He had waited a few seconds for a response, and when she didn't say anything, he shrugged, then turned, tucking away his flask at the same time.

The misty sky reflected darkly in the metal of the flask and caught Liz's attention. A second later the image disappeared into Zach's pocket. But in that instant, by some nebulous thought process, Liz saw what Zach's demon was. Unlike her father, who had only one, his were many. Dozens of losses, large and small, stacked one upon the other until they got so heavy he tried to numb them with liquor.

He'd probably managed to cage his anguish for most of his life, but Jed's death had finally forced the door open. Regardless of the reason, the demons swarmed around him now, and instead of dealing with them, he'd opted to keep them at bay with the contents of his flask.

He'd never defeat them unless he threw away his crutch, and that seemed so unlikely Liz dismissed the possibility as quickly as it arose.

She wanted to deny her part in his downfall, but wasn't able. One of the many abrupt changes in her makeup. Ever since her buried memories had resurfaced, she'd felt as if she'd somehow finally learned who she really was. An involuntary laugh escaped her throat. Of course she knew. She was the Guardian of the Opal . . . the *last* guardian.

"Something funny?" Zach asked.

While she'd been lost in thought, he'd been busying himself with returning loose supplies to the crates.

"Something crossed my mind, that's all."

"Well, instead of daydreaming, would you come

over here and give me a hand? Stuff's scattered all over the place."

Liz sighed sadly, shaking her head as she walked to join Zach. When she got there, he was rearranging items inside one of the crates, almost pointedly ignoring her. She watched him for a moment, then turned away and circled the camp, picking up stray items.

No, Zach wouldn't defeat his demons, at least not in time. He couldn't even face his biggest one, namely her. This meant she'd have to battle Ankouer alone, her only weapons a tiny, freakish voodoo doll and the gift from Izzy Deveraux's heart. No guardian had yet defeated Ankouer, and none without a defender survived her battle. But this time . . .

Liz could only pray.

They spent the morning lugging crates to the boat, returning to the clearing, then lugging more. They wouldn't be leaving Quadray Island today, of that Liz was certain. She wasn't going anywhere without her father, but even if she were so inclined, she knew events would conspire to stop them.

Already the mist was forming into ugly clouds. A wind had picked up, one strong enough to make their travels between the campsite and shore all the more difficult. She suggested that Zach leave the lean-to up in case it started to rain, and after examining the darkening sky he agreed.

When they were down to the cookstove, butane lantern and a crate that held some food, he said, "We'll eat lunch. After that, we go."

"Not without Papa and Maddie," she answered calmly, with a certainty that came from knowing her own mind.

"They've left the island. You know that as well as I do."

They hadn't left, but why argue, thought Liz. "Even if they have, I don't think the weather's on our side."

He looked up as if he were just now noticing the approaching storm, ran his fingers wearily through his windswept hair. Soft as a sigh, he said, "A man can always hope," and walked to the food crate.

Liz moved along with him. "Do you still have Papa's nitroglycerin tablets?" she asked, suddenly remembering he'd never given them back.

He frowned, patted his pockets, then finally pulled out the vial. "Here they are," he said, giving her a look that implied she was delusional.

Ignoring his expression, she thanked him, then bent to help take out the utensils. Zach handed her cheese, bread and a couple of apples, and she placed them on a plate, which she set on the ground. She wanted to get the journal before settling down to eat, and she'd left it in the shelter while she'd carried crates to the boat.

"Don't you think you've spent enough time with that book?" Zach asked curtly when she returned.

"I have to learn the prayer."

He snorted.

"Would you help me? I'm having a hard time memorizing it."

Considering his attitude, she was taking a wild leap by asking, but if she could just get him involved with the book maybe he'd read more. He gave her a wry look, but his pause indicated he might just agree to what he clearly thought was her insane impulse.

"Please, Zach. It won't take long."

"All right. But keep it short."

They moved to the cliff, leaning against the rock wall, and Zach put the plate of food between them. Liz tore off a hunk of bread, then sliced herself a thick piece of cheese before handing Zach the journal. Since the prayer was written in English, she'd be able to recite while he double-checked her.

"No," he said after only a few lines, "it's *shine* your light, not *beam* your light."

Liz nibbled on an apple, then on her lower lip. What was wrong with her? She could remember company stock exchange codes and prices after a single glance, but this relatively short poem seemed beyond her.

After several similar attempts, Zach gave her back the book. "Look," he said, running his fingers down the page. "Except for the last stanza, the lines are almost identical. This prayer is about hate, fear and pain. Just memorize it once, then repeat it by changing those words."

She saw he was right, and wondered why she hadn't noticed herself. It almost seemed as if something was clouding her mind. A grateful smile crossed her face. "You're pretty smart, know that?"

"It won't work, Liz."

"What won't work?" she asked distractedly, still absorbed in the lines of the prayer.

"Your charm. You're not getting me back in your clutches."

"My *clutches*? What bad movies have you been watching?" She slammed the book shut. "This isn't working. Just finish your meal. I'll do it myself."

"Fine with me."

Shaking off her irritation with no small effort, Liz worked hard at the memorization, now and then picking up a chunk of bread or slice of cheese. The apple was grainy and didn't have much flavor, but she hardly noticed, and had chewed it nearly to the core when the sprinkles appeared on the pages of the journal.

Zach let out a stream of curses, then grabbed the lantern and practically ordered her into the lean-to.

Again ignoring his bad attitude, she chose to pick up the food crate before she complied.

The wind picked up, flapping their canvas shelter. The day grew as dark as dusk, even though it was only noontime. Soon after that a downpour came, and Zach was visibly upset by the uncooperative weather.

Liz continued studying the poem under the light of the butane lantern. Thanks to Zach's astute observation she soon committed the first three stanzas to memory. That left only the final verse.

> *Power above, Power divine.*
> *Heed my call in my hour of need.*
> *Protect me from evil in this black place.*
>   *Power above, Power divine.*
>   *Heed my call. Heed my call.*

According to her mother's writing, this closing stanza was used only during the guardian's darkest hour.

Why couldn't it be like the others? When the time came, she'd probably have a hard enough time just remembering those three. How could she hope to dredge this one up during a moment of great terror?

Zach dozed while she read, or at least he seemed to, but once when she looked over she saw him staring at their makeshift ceiling. How sad and weary he looked. An irregular stubble on his face. New lines appearing around his eyes and mouth. And he was probably frightened. She loved him so and wished—

No, she couldn't let herself think about what might have been. Not now. Not here. Although she hadn't known it before, fate had directed her life all along. Had she remained in Port Chatre she would probably have died with her mother, and everything in the book she studied confirmed that her absence had served a purpose, keeping her safe for the fated battle ahead that was part of a bigger plan.

At just that moment, Zach caught her eyes. "Might as well go to sleep," he said. "We're not going anywhere until morning."

"I still have work to do."

"Why are you so obsessed with that poem?"

"You know. You just refuse to accept it." She felt the oddest urge to scoot closer to him and stroke the creases from his face, but she didn't succumb to it. Sometime soon she'd be compelled to march into hell. Alone. With no defender. She was so scared. If she could make him understand, then . . .

"You didn't ask for this, Zach," she went on, speaking softly. "And if I could change things, I would. But, as much as I wish it weren't so, I am the last guardian. What's more, whatever higher power is in charge of these events has sent you to

331

defend me. I'm preparing for that time and you should too."

"Oh, Liz," he said. He lifted his hand to stroke her cheek. "Either you've really gone bonkers, or you're the best damned conwoman I've ever come across."

With a slow shake of her head, she said, "Neither."

His expression softened, allowing yearning to enter his eyes. Slowly, he slid his hand down and closed it over her chin. His lips parted slightly.

Was he going to kiss her? Oh Lord, it seemed he was. And she wanted him to, wanted to feel his mouth on hers, his body inside her own.

This might be the last time. Words had not convinced him, and her night of reckoning was near. No guardian defeated Ankouer without a defender, and nothing he'd said or done indicated he'd be by her side during this terrible night. So why couldn't she have just this?

She could. She would.

Leaning into him, she parted her own lips.

A tremble rushed through Zach's body as he gazed at Liz's face. Her closed eyes, her quickening breath, her slightly parted mouth, all invited him to kiss her. If he had an ounce of sense, he'd roll over and slam the door on that invitation. But he hungered for her from the depths of his soul. He wanted her near him, wanted to feel her smooth luscious skin again.

Even more, he wanted to pretend none of this had happened . . . was happening. . . . If he kissed her, touched her, entered her, maybe he could wipe it all away. And yet . . .

He didn't believe she'd gone crazy, no longer even believed her father was crazy. There was some plan behind all these events, and they could only come from a scheming mind. Hers? He didn't want to believe so. But even if she wasn't a mastermind, in the end her father would go to jail, maybe get the chair if he turned out to be more than a henchman. How could he take her in his arms with this intent on his mind? Just as important, how could he consider loving her if there was even a possibility that her actions had brought about his brother's death?

A soft, eager sound left her lips, and in that instant he knew he was lost. He lowered his head and brushed her mouth with his, gentle as the touch of a kitten. A sigh passed between them. When he broke the kiss, he picked up her hand, put a kiss on her wrist, then took the other and did the same.

Then, tugging lightly, he led her to lay beside him. This was Liz, his childhood buddy, his teenage girlfriend, his friend, his lover, heart of his heart. He loved her, and somewhere he'd find it in himself to forgive her for whatever she'd done.

Liz sighed again, waiting for what Zach would do next. With a tenderness she'd never experienced before, he unbuttoned her overalls and slid them down. Next he slipped off her shirt, bending to kiss her nipples. Sensations coursed through her body, a bone-melting languidness that made her feel like she was floating.

He rose to kneel beside her, entwining his fingers through hers and pinning her hands above her head. His kisses traveled down, stopping in the valley beneath her breasts, at the slope of her ribs, then down her belly until they touched the apex of her thighs.

A sharp hiss escaped her lips, and she arched her back. Everything faded except the exquisite effects on her body.

"I love you, Zach," she whispered.

He stopped abruptly, then jerkily straightened up.

"Damn you!" The flickering lamplight emphasized his enraged expression as he glared down at her. "You tell me now? Now? How do you expect me to believe you?"

"I don't," she answered shakily. "But it's true. I do love you, Zach, I honestly do, and I wanted you to know."

Such beautiful and seductive sentiments, and ones he had forever yearned to hear. Only now they were too hard to accept. Light from the lantern filled their shelter, bouncing off the rough canvas above, off the layer of nylon bags below, only to be broken into geometric shapes by the shadows of their bodies. Zach found himself caught up in the play of light across Liz's body, caught up by her beauty. Those unruly dark curls, feathering out to brush her high cheekbones. Those almond-shaped eyes, glittering like amber. That soft, full mouth waiting for his kisses.

"Zach?" she said . . . soft, questioning.

So much to forgive this woman for. Desertions and lies. Possibly murder. Yet even as he urged himself to accept this, the deepest part of him cried out that Liz spoke the truth. *Le fantôme noir* waited in that mountain cave. Ankouer's net was out to drag them in. Nonsense.

Nonsense.

Nonsense. If he believed that, he'd have to believe in Liz's insanity, and in his own. He wouldn't. He'd protect them by sticking to reality. He'd protect them from danger, keep them safe by rejecting this otherworldly threat . . . keep them safe, keep *her* safe.

With a groan of utter frustration, he leaned forward and pressed her hard against the bedroll, then slid on top of her.

"God help me," he whispered hoarsely as he drove himself into her waiting, pliant body. "I love you too, Liz. I love you too. With all my heart."

Liz felt his agony, felt his need to bury himself inside her, so she opened completely to his love, to his fiercely hungry thrusting that was driving her wild.

She fed it, meeting his ferocity thrust for thrust, tightening her fingers around his until their hands seemed to meld as one. If never again they came together, they'd at least have this night together. This night.

This night . . .

For a long time afterward they stayed there, joined as one, holding each other, listening to the falling rain and the sounds of their own breathing. Zach stroked her hair; she kissed the smooth skin of his shoulder. Eventually, she slid from beneath him to snuggle under his arm, and wasn't even sure when she fell asleep. Sometime during her dreams, the voice came: *Tonight, Guardian.* But Zach was beside her, holding her, keeping her warm. She was safe, safe with him, as safe as she could possibly be.

She ignored the voice and moved closer to Zach. With him by her side, nothing could harm her.

Come forward, Guardian, this is your night of reckoning. Still half-asleep, Liz sat straight up and stared forward. The time was here; Ankouer had come for her.

Outside it was still light, but just barely. So heavy was the sky with clouds that only the faintest rays of sunlight made it through. Liz looked over at Zach. Thunder rumbled and the rain made a constant beat on the roof of the lean-to, but he slept peacefully. She ached to wake him up, to draw on the comfort she'd so strongly felt in the dreams. Maybe the dream was an omen, maybe he'd finally believe her.

No, she knew better. More likely he'd try to keep her from going. And she had to go. This wasn't about Zach, not even about her. So much more was at stake. *Other-the-wise*, Harris had said, *we all go back to the dark—man, woman, child, all fall into dark.*

She shivered nervously as she fumbled into her clothes, carefully avoiding bumping Zach. She'd just leaned for her shoes when a hand came from nowhere and clamped down on her mouth.

"Izzy," a familiar voice said.

She jerked around and met the dark, slanted eyes of Maddie Catalon.

Slapping the woman's hand away, Liz put her own finger over her mouth and glanced at Zach. Nodding, Maddie moved back and gave Liz room to get out.

"Where have you been?" Liz asked in a whisper.

Without answering, Maddie turned toward the trail to the cave. She appeared agitated, an uncommon occurrence that did little to ease Liz's own anxiety.

"Wait," Liz said. "We need the lantern."

Maddie shook her head. "Frank give me his flashlight. Come on now. We must hurry." Maddie pointed toward the cave. "He is bad off. Very bad. He need his medicine. You got it, don't you?"

"Yes." Liz instinctively checked for the vial, then moved on in search of the *gris-gris*. The bump reassured her somewhat, but her heart still pounded all the way to the cave.

"Hurry," Maddie said, ducking inside as soon as they got there.

This is it, Liz told herself with a shudder. This was the time to find every ounce of fortitude she possessed. Already she was drenched and cold, and the thought of what faced her chilled her even further.

The clouds scudded off the moon, temporarily bathing the clearing in paler than pale light. Taking advantage of it, Liz paused to take out the *gris-gris* and drop the contents into her hand. She had no idea how to use these items, nor did she even have much faith they'd work. But they were all she had.

She slipped the packet and stone back into her pocket, rather than into the bag. The voodoo doll she kept in her hand. Raindrops had already streaked its black-painted surface, giving it an eerie reflective quality. Were the moonlight bright enough, she fancied she'd probably see her own face inside the tiny torso.

Just then, something rustled. She jerked up her head, coming face-to-face with a powdery white mouth bearing a forked tongue and gleaming fangs.

Half paralyzed, she stared at the large cottonmouth snake, then shoved out a rubbery arm, and wiggled the doll. But now what was she supposed to do? What chant was she to utter?

"Depart!" The word had come from her mouth involuntarily.

The snake immediately uncoiled and fell to the ground. Astonished but wary, Liz crept closer, never taking her eyes off the creature. Alive. She could see the tongue twitching, see membranes close over the eyes. So still, still as death. The doll had done its magic.

A giddy laugh bubbled in her throat as she bolted for the cave, viewing it as a haven. The feeling of security died the instant her eyes saw the smaller, black opening. Her memory of what would greet her inside was still fresh in her mind. She licked her lips and walked closer, bending to see where Maddie had gone. A stream of light wobbled against glistening walls, and she saw the shadow of a slender figure.

"Maddie!" she called. "Wait!"

Her only answer came from the echoes of her own cry.

*   *   *

Heaven had exploded. The storm would take down their flimsy shelter at any second. Naked and shivering, Zach reached out for Liz.

His hand struck an empty space.

She's gone to the cave to meet Ankouer.

No, no, he thought, lurching upright and grabbing for his clothes. His drowsiness was ebbing now, taking his crazy conclusion with it. Liz probably had gone to the cave, all right, but not to meet Ankouer.

Zach dressed quickly, then rummaged for some matches in the food crate. After stuffing a back-up handful in his windbreaker pocket, he lit the lantern and left behind the flimsy protection of the lean-to.

The sky was awash with sounds. Crackling angry lightning. Booming thunder. And though the wind was heavy, rainfall had eased to a knifelike drizzle that fairly sliced his skin.

As much as he hated that stinking tunnel, he'd have to go through it again. Liz had gone to the cavern to rendezvous with Frank and Maddie, of that he had no doubt. This unpalatable truth weighed heavily on him, but he tried not to think of it as he bent his head against the wind and headed for the trail. The woman was a liar, a consummate actress. Even her animosity toward Maddie was feigned. He'd already realized it, had already told himself so, so how had he let her fool him into thinking she loved him?

A chill rushed up and down his spine, brought on by the rapidly dropping temperature. The boulder at the base of the trail provided some protection from the wind and rain, and Zach paused to open his flask and take a sip of liquid heat. Delaying tactics, he realized, but he took yet another moment to light a cigarette. Finally, holding the lantern high in the air for maximum light, he started climbing.

He was breathless when he reached the cave's dark mouth, and none too pleased to notice that the light made the opening pulsate in such a way that it appeared to be waiting for him to enter its digestive tract. After another nip from his flask—which was getting low—he steeled himself to enter the cave.

Just then, a gust of wind appeared. The flame inside the lantern sputtered and dimmed, and then was gone. Rain drizzling on his head, Zach stood stock-still in complete darkness, trying to find the guts to even reach for his supply of matches. Just as he made his move, the gas jets came to life again. But Zach's gratitude was short-lived. A mere fraction of a second later he stumbled backward, a cry of revulsion coming to his lips.

Sticky webs covered the yawning entrance, glistening evilly in the light. In the center waited a spider larger than his fist. Zach swallowed a second cry that lodged painfully in his throat as he backed into the boulder behind him. He jumped from the touch, convinced spiders were crawling all over him, already feeling their hairy legs on his skin.

"Well, partner," a male voice drawled from behind. "Seems you got yourself in quite a fix."

Chapter Twenty-two

Zach whirled to find Richard Cormier sitting arrogantly on top of the boulder, a wry smile of amusement on his lips. "You always were scared of spiders, Zach."

The final puzzle piece fell into place. Frank wasn't the only one in Port Chatre with a sudden upturn in financial fortune. Why hadn't he made the connection before? "So you're Frank's accomplice?"

"In a manner of speaking."

Zach frowned and stared up at Cormier, who balanced on top of a slick rock as though he were ensconced in an easy chair, and again wished he'd brought a weapon on this trip.

"Liz is inside. Maddie took her. Why don't you go after them, partner? It's what a man would do."

Zach looked over his shoulder. The spider had crawled down the web, closer to the ground.

"Then you never were much of a man. Scared of spiders, tsk, tsk, tsk."

Zach barely registered Richard's jibe, so caught up was he in eyeing the small space between him and the dark, spotted monster. His hand flew to his back pocket.

"That's it. A little more Smirnoff's and you can take on the world." Richard's syrupy drawl lingered in the air long after he'd stopped speaking. "Creepy things, spiders. Kind of make you want to piss your pants. But so small. You can wipe 'em out like this." Richard slapped the rock, causing Zach to recoil. "Go ahead, Zach. Take another drink. You'll find your guts in that bottle. You will. You know you will."

Zach's hand lingered over his pocket, poised to drop and pull. Such a tiny movement, and some of these jitters would ease. Richard was right. Richard was right.

"Hurry, Zach. Ankouer is waiting and he grows impatient."

Richard was wrong! Was everyone on this island crazy but him? Zach abruptly dropped his hand and whirled to face the web. The spider dropped to the ground and scuttled forward. With a hissed intake of breath, Zach brought up his foot and slammed it down. When he lifted it, only a small, spotted blob remained.

"I'm going in for Liz, Cormier," he said, still staring at his smashed opponent, thinking even as he spoke how truly easy it had been to kill it. "When we get back, I'll be coming for you."

Richard's laughter split the air, joined an instant later by a clap of thunder. Zach turned his head and saw in the flash of ensuing lightning that Richard had disappeared. He expected a shock of surprise, but it didn't come, and he supposed the many unexplained events had made him virtually immune.

Then he thought of Liz getting mixed up with this sleazeball just to protect her father. He'd put a stop to that right now. He'd go in there, drag her out by that short curly hair of hers and, if he had to, swim with her on his back all the way to Port Chatre.

He turned to face the web, fighting off waves of terror and revulsion. Dozens of small spiders had shown up in place of the larger one. Funny how Richard's taunts shored up his nerve, how notably absent it now was as he faced these tiny foes.

God, he hated spiders, hated them with a vengeance that stirred a fury he hadn't felt since the day he had identified Jed's tattered body. Filthy, crawling things! They didn't deserve to live!

With rage as his guide, he took a long deep breath that did more to boost his courage than a liter of vodka, and swung the lantern vehemently at the web.

*   *   *

Maddie still wasn't answering as Liz crept, stoop shouldered through the dripping, smelly cavern. The flashlight beam was not far ahead, and it reflected off the damp walls and shallow pools of water, creating a hazy glow that allowed her to see. She kept it in her sight, clutching the doll so tightly her palm was getting sweaty. She did her best not to allow her gaze to take in the clusters of bones and occasional decomposing animal, but sometimes she simply couldn't help herself. The final resting place for Ankouer's fallen servants, she thought, recalling the raccoons dragging away their dead companion.

At one point the tunnel curved and she lost the light. Small squeaks issued involuntarily from her throat, ricocheting off the walls until she jumped from her own sounds. Taking tiny steps, she rounded the curve an eternity later, and stepped straight into the path of a glaring mask.

Another raccoon. Its pointed snout curled over its small sharp teeth, and it approached with a snarl. Without thinking, Liz stuck out the doll. The creature continued bearing down on her.

What in the hell had she said before? Her mind refused to bring it up, and unintelligible sounds came from her mouth. What had she said? What?

"Go away, beast!" she shouted, although it didn't come out that way . . . more as a series of whispers.

Like the snake, the raccoon fell over. Lying supine and breathing heavily, it stared at her with small, dark eyes. Liz gaped at it, terrified to move, knowing she must.

Beasts lay panting on the trail.

The first line of the quatrain. Suddenly she realized the poem was a guidepost to let her know when she was taking the correct action. This realization allowed her to quickly hop over the raccoon, and with Maddie's flashlight as her beacon, she hurried down the tunnel with renewed courage.

Soon the beam vanished, but she wasn't in total darkness. Light flashed on and off, sometimes nearly as bright as day, and sounds of thunder again reached her ears. She walked on haltingly, moving only during the bursts of light, knowing she was nearing the cavern.

Then she heard Maddie screaming. "Leave it, Frank! Do not tempt Ankouer!"

Liz sprinted forward, holding the red-eyed doll in front of her and dashed through the opening.

"Frank, no!" Maddie cried, standing in front of the lake. Through the hole above, the storm-tossed sky spilled flashes of lightning, and raindrops struck the lake, causing ripples that were swallowed by dancing flames. As the fire sparked and ebbed, it sent out waves of icy air that told Liz she'd entered Ankouer's lair.

Liz followed Maddie's distraught gaze and saw her father creeping onto a narrow ledge. Just beyond him sat the lifeless fire opal. Above him, a swirling black shape sporadically formed itself into a parody of man.

"Papa!" she whimpered.

Her father jerked his head around. The apparition paused. A pair of blazing eyes appeared and fixed her with a stare.

"So, Guardian, prepare for your night of reckoning."

A surge of overwhelming malice swept over her, dulling the shocking realization that Ankouer's spoken threat must herald his transformation into human flesh.

Wisps of web and fried spiders still clung to the lantern, but Zach refused to look at them.

Would he make it through this stinking tunnel a second time, or would his resolve evaporate? Would he fail here as he'd failed with Carol, Rita, and Vera . . . with Zettie and Jeff . . . with Jed?

Would he turn back and take the easy way?

Liz would be okay. It wasn't as though she really was about to face the phantom. She'd come to meet her father, as Cormier's presence at the opening proved.

Where had the man gone? Where, in fact, had he come from? Storm or not, Zach had a sixth sense that usually alerted him to another's presence.

Well, obviously it hadn't come through this time.

His journey through the slimy, rotting tunnel had given him time to examine his thoughts, but he remained as confused as ever. Images of Liz talking quietly with Richard on his veranda came to mind. What had they been talking about? Of all those present at Ellie's wake, Cormier had seemed the least bewildered by Liz's sudden reappearance from the dead.

But no matter how he turned it over in his mind, Zach could not see Liz becoming involved with Richard. As a kid, the guy had tormented her unmercifully. Of course, there was the old saw about strange bedfellows, but the more likely guess was that Liz was only trying to protect Frank.

Could he blame her? Wouldn't he have done anything to save his father? Jed? Hell, wouldn't he have gone to his own grave before seeing his brother die?

At this moment he wasn't so sure.

He'd known how headstrong Jed was, yet he'd insisted on keeping his tryst before joining the manhunt. True, the lady had been delicious, but had he known what fate had in store, he would never have sacrificed his brother for her. And what about Liz? Maybe she was right, maybe he'd refused her plea to take her from Port Chatre the night of her grandmother's funeral. He'd only been a kid. Who could remember? The hell of it, though, was the ring of truth her accusation held. Didn't he feel like running now?

And what were these things that scared him so bad? Filthy, dripping water; rotting animal corpses and bleached bones; dead spiders and their sticky webs. Minor threats, none at all, in fact. So why did his gut keep screaming for him to turn back?

As he took step after tentative step toward the waiting cavern, quaking like a first-grader at the shadows in the tunnel, he thought of Liz traveling through it alone. What had she used for light? How had she withstood the darkness? Her courage suddenly put him to shame, and for the first time he wondered if he deserved her.

A sudden shiver reminded him he was wet and cold and he stopped for a moment. Despite the discomfort of standing in a hunched position, he pulled out his flask. He swallowed quickly, and the warmth eased his chill, absorbed some of the nagging doubts that plagued him. Or so he told himself as he cast a longing glance at the entrance to the tunnel.

He started to recap the flask, then hesitated. One more sip, he told himself. One more sip and he'd go on.

"Izzy! Run, girl! Run now!"

"What are you saying, Frank?" Maddie screamed, doubled over and clutching her knees. "Izzy is the one! Only she can save us!"

"Fool!" hissed Ankouer, his humanlike shape rippling with malice. "She is puny and untrained. You will die, all of you."

But Liz had eyes and ears only for her father. Even as he continued crawling along that narrow ledge, he repeatedly grabbed for his chest. His warnings came out as choked rasps. Should he manage to get the opal, she doubted he'd make it down.

With only one thought—he needed her—Liz raced across the cavern floor toward the slope leading to the ledge.

Suddenly, a man appeared to block her path.

"Richard!" Her whispered exclamation echoed back, and her mind spun. How had he gotten here?

"Go back, Izzy. Leave the stone to Ankouer. In return, he'll spare your pa's life and let you all go."

"The opal for my father?" she asked, looking up at the swirling shape above.

"That's the deal," Richard said.

Liz tilted her head, shivers of fear running through her body, but somehow she managed to calmly meet Richard's gaze. "Why should I believe you?"

A self-satisfied laugh—typically Richard—came from the man's lips. "What choice do you have?"

"This," she said. "Let me pass." Liz thrust out

the black doll and put her other hand on the needle protruding from its heart.

Ankouer gave out a choked cry, and Richard backed away, hands held up protectively. "There's more than me," he said. "That hunk of mud will keep you safe, but not for long."

Then his form faded, and in the blink of Liz's eyes, he disappeared. Ankouer wailed in rage; the dancing flames split into dozens more, bouncing over the water like sprites.

And still her father warned her away.

Her heart pounding like a congo drum, Liz resumed her ascent, leaping over small rocks that littered the path, ignoring Ankouer's angry sounds, Maddie's whimpers, her father's breathless warnings. His life was in danger, her life was in danger, and even the fate of the loathsome Maddie concerned her.

But greater danger awaited the world if the opal fell in Ankouer's hands, and she recognized that Richard's warning was not a threat but a statement of fact.

The figure above stared at her with dark, hot hate.

Gripping the voodoo doll ever tighter, she marched toward the ledge, toward the opal, feeling a responding hate sizzle within her breast.

Even as alarm bells rang in her head, she vowed

to let that hatred guide her until she sent Ankouer straight back to hell.

Zach swallowed another nip of Smirnoff's as he pressed himself to the walls of the cave, and stealthily made his way toward the cavern. He heard Maddie screaming, heard Frank's hoarse cries, and heard another voice as grating as a fingernail upon a blackboard. He started to rush through the opening, then his cop's training asserted itself and he halted, recapping and storing the flask and furtively moving toward the cavern.

He slipped soundlessly around the jagged edge of the entrance to assess the situation and saw something horrible and black hovering above a lake of fire. The sight staggered his mind, which pitched and reeled, shattering his precarious hold on reality. For a moment his vision went blank. He reached automatically for the flask.

But there was no time. He had to do something. But what? This wasn't life as he understood it. This was all his childhood fears rolled into one. This was his nightmares come to life.

His sight returned as quickly as it had left. He saw Maddie, bent over as if in pain, screeching toward someone clinging to a narrow ledge. Frank, he realized, grasping for the one solid fact to save his failing sanity.

Then he saw Liz. Dear God, Liz, leaping like a

mountain goat over rocks and small boulders to the tiny ledge that supported her father.

Suddenly, a man appeared in Liz's path. She stopped short and waved a dark object about. Allain! Doc Allain was here. Drawing on the rationale that had guided his choices until now, Zach tried to rearrange these events into something that made sense. Another accomplice. No, that didn't fit. A rescue party had arrived. No, not that either. His vision blurred once more, but he could still hear and, Lord, he wished he couldn't.

"Zacharie is below," the doctor said, chuckling darkly. "He is your defender, is it not so? Yet he trembles at the sight of me, the man who spanked his bottom when he first saw life."

The fog cleared from Zach's eyes and he saw Liz look down at him. Her eyes widened and she seemed encouraged by his presence.

"Take the offer, Izzy," the doctor went on in a softly seductive tone. "Your defender is a coward. He will not stand beside you."

"Yes, yes, he will," Frank moaned, rubbing his chest as though it sorely ached.

The doctor glanced up at Frank with scorn. "Ah, the fallen one. The failure. Tell Zacharie how it's done, Frank. Tell him of your impotence during your sweet Ellie's night of reckoning. Tell him how you failed her by loving another more than her."

"Non, non," Frank protested. "Do not listen, Zacharie. *Pas du tout."* Not at all. Then he launched into a volley of French that Zach understood only enough to know Liz needed him.

Nothing made sense, and he didn't know how to fight it. Men slinking in dark alleys, rough bars filled with violent criminals, courtrooms with slick defense attorneys, boardrooms with arrogant executives, those he could handle. But what was here? Illusions? Phantoms? Ghosts? What's more, he wanted to yank off his hand for creeping toward his back pocket against his will.

"See, Izzy, how the soothing liquid calls him. He loves it more than you. You cannot count on him." The doctor's voice turned harsh. "Take Ankouer's offer, so you and these puny men will live to see another sunrise. Refuse and you all die."

Liz's gaze lingered for an instant on the doctor's face, then slowly moved to scan the cavern. She stopped at Zach. He cringed beneath her scrutiny. Was the old doc right? Did he love his drink above all else? Had he really sunk so low?

"I'm here, Liz." But even as he swore it, he felt the draw of the flask. "What has Doc offered?"

"Our freedom," she said. "Our lives for the opal. But I've refused."

The opal for their lives? A small price. It was just a rock. Why did she hesitate?

"Give him the stone, Liz," he said, near to death from wanting another drink.

She dipped her head. A nod? Had she nodded? Was she agreeing? As she turned back to Allain, his breath stopped in anticipation.

Chapter Twenty-three

Liz gazed back at Zach, fearing he meant what he said, praying he didn't, and knowing deep in her heart that he still didn't understand the importance of the stone. She looked up at her father, at his ashen face and the way he clutched his chest and arm. She returned to Allain, taking in his sardonic expression, doubting he'd live up to the promise, but tempted, oh so tempted.

The stone for their safety.

A series of booms sounded inside the cavern, and her head spun in search of the source. Ankouer's evil eyes stared down from above, appearing to twinkle with mirth.

"No!" With that refusal, Liz extended the arm holding the doll out to its full length.

Why did Allain regard it so casually, as though it could not hurt him? The animals had simply curled up and let her pass. Then she remembered that Richard hadn't reacted until she'd reached for the needle.

"No! I will not hand it over!"

She gave the needle a vicious twist and instantly felt the sweetness of vengeance fulfilled. Allain gagged, reached for his chest, then tumbled over. Like the raccoon, he lay panting and staring up at her.

Ankouer howled and lost his human shape, reassuming the spiral of a cyclone. The fire on the lake flickered and dimmed. Above, beside her father, the opal sent out sparks of colored light. With her newly honed intuition, Liz realized Ankouer had been surprised, but that this opportunity would quickly pass. She circled around the doctor.

"Get the opal, Papa!" she cried, breaking into a sprint.

Already the flames had regrouped, intensified. Ankouer was twisting at a fierce speed. Time was running out.

She saw her father reach out, then lumber to his feet. Clinging to the rocky wall, he inched toward her, and Liz feared his heart would give out at any moment. She headed upward, ever upward, arms outstretched and urging him on.

Then Zach was calling to her, running toward her, running to help, and she whirled to greet him. When he was halfway up, a gale arose. It ripped at his hair and clothes, and he couldn't run fast enough or strong enough to overcome the force.

The wind plastered her overalls to her body. Maintaining her balance took every ounce of energy. She inched her feet forward, but for every step forward, the wind blew her back another. And above, his shaggy hair so wind tossed it nearly stood on end, her father clung to the wall for his life.

Then he turned, supported by a single hand, and teetered on the brink of the ledge with the opal in his hand.

"Izzy!" he bellowed. "The fire stone!"

The gale instantly stopped. Ankouer whirled in fury, then dipped and struck her father's arm. He staggered, weaving back and forth with precarious balance. Just as he tumbled, he let the opal fly from his hands.

"Zacharie! Get Frank!" Liz heard Maddie scream, but there wasn't time to think of anything but the stone soaring in her direction. She raced to the edge of the ramp until she stood on its very lip.

The voodoo doll had been her lifeline, and at first her hand refused to release it. Nearer the opal came, nearer and nearer, and still she couldn't force herself to let go. In desperation, she drove the needle completely through the doll's heart. Ankouer screeched. Her fingers uncurled, and the doll plunged toward the lake.

Stretching to her tiptoes, she opened her hands for the gem. It was falling short, too short. She dropped to her belly, stretching out, straining, waiting. . . .

A small sob escaped her throat as the stone struck her hands. She clenched them into tight fists and eased back, gasping, onto the ramp. She had it now. She had it.

The shriek that followed turned her blood to ice. She lifted her head, saw hundreds of black pieces shooting out from Ankouer's spinning form. Swarming bats instantly filled the cavern. They swooped toward the lake, where Zach supported her father while he struggled to reach the shore.

Then they were on her, too, dozens of them, flying at her hair, at her arms, at the hands grasping the opal. Their sharp little claws scraped at her fingers, which she clutched with fierce determination. But despite her will, her grip slowly weakened and the opal slipped away.

"Nooooo!"

The fragile gem plummeted over the lip of the ramp.

A split second later, Ankouer resumed human shape. He dove toward the falling stone, a whirling hand thrust out to catch it, new booms rising from his center.

But Zach had caught the voodoo doll. Even as the stone fell, even as Ankouer boomed his gallows laugh, he twisted the needle in the clay figure's heart. Again and again he twisted, expressing a violence Liz found both shocking and gratifying.

The fire ebbed and Ankouer's booms turned into another shriek. The bats soared back to their source, merging with Ankouer's slowing spiral. The monster rose toward the hole in the cavern's ceiling. Rising and rising, fading as he rose, fading . . . fading. . . .

A new flash of lightning crackled just as his spiral faded into nothing, clearly illuminating his absence.

Liz stared at the empty space with a mixture of triumph and terror. This wasn't over. Her father was still in the water with a heart that could go at any second. The opal had rolled to a stop not far from the water's edge, and she gave thanks that the fall hadn't shattered it. Its brilliance had ebbed, and now it looked unlike any other stone, although the striations were quite visible under the glow of a lantern that Zach must have brought.

Liz climbed to her feet and descended the ramp on shaky legs. Zach was still in the water holding her father's head above the surface. Maddie lay on the ground with her hands extended, sobbing. At the sight of Liz, she got up and rushed forward.

"Help your daddy, Izzy. Help him."

Without a moment's reflection, Liz kicked off her shoes and made a move to dive in after the men.

"Wait!" Maddie cried. "Do not chance your mama's book in the water."

"It's survived worse."

"But you are running out of luck, no?"

Liz divided her gaze between Maddie and the men, who were already closing in on the shore. They didn't seem to need her help. But in case they did, she might as well keep the journal dry. She reached in her pocket for the plastic bag containing the book, and as she started to hand it over she noticed a sly expression on Maddie's face.

"Just a second," she said. "Why don't you dive in and help them?"

Maddie shrugged and reached toward the journal. "Can't swim."

"Can't . . ." A swamp rat unable to swim? "What's going on here, Maddie?"

The woman laughed, and before Liz could react, Maddie had snatched away the journal. Liz reached out to yank it back, but Maddie whirled toward the water. In a few long strides, she swept down on the opal, then turned back and lifted it high in the air.

"I give you the guardian, master, just like I promise. Take her, take her now."

The opal flashed, and Maddie uttered a small shriek of pain, but held fast to the stone. Liz charged toward her, reaching up to tear the opal from the bitch's clutching hands.

An unseen force pushed at her arms, holding

them back. Maddie laughed in riotous triumph. A shrill whine filled the cavern. Instantly, Liz's entire body grew leaden. She involuntarily sank to the ground, crumpled in a heap at the crowing Maddie's feet, where she choked out, "Why?"

"Ankouer promise it all to me. Your daddy, your house, the magic that once were Ellie's. I only have to give him you. It were my pleasure. All these years I be second best. Now I get it all. I get what were yours and your mama's. Think of that when Ankouer is chewing on you."

Liz listened with much greater surprise than she probably should have. It shouldn't have been too hard to predict Maddie's actions. But despite her hatred, Liz had never once suspected the woman of treachery. Of tempting her father, yes, but not of being in league with Ankouer. Her love for Liz's father seemed too great to permit her to hurt anyone he cared about.

The whine increased, and Maddie looked up. Liz forced her heavy neck to lift so she could follow the gaze. *Le fantôme noir* was spiraling down from the overhead opening, slowly, leisurely, apparently in no hurry.

"I-I k-killed Ankouer," Liz stuttered thickly.

"Your uppity ways done get you in trouble," Maddie replied. "Ankouer not die so easy, no, not him."

Liz barely heard the words. She felt languid and

sleepy, and wasn't quite so cold anymore. Something splashed in the background, but she was certain it had nothing to do with her.

Then Maddie shrieked, and Liz snapped back from the lure of slumber. In her peripheral vision, she saw her father on the ground by the lake, heaving for breath. Above her, Zach fought Maddie for the opal. The woman kicked him, aiming for his groin, but Zach sidestepped, then spun around, taking Maddie's arm with him. He bent her forward, trying to wrench the stone from her hand.

"Come to my side, Ankouer," Maddie cried, even as her backward kick landed in the center of Zach's belly. "Quickly, master, come to my side!"

Zach let out a grunt and doubled over.

The phantom boomed a macabre laugh that sent further chill through the cavern. "You're doing well, servant. I give you the defender to do with as you wish."

Maddie picked up a rock and threw it at Zach, then another, and another. Her fury made her aim poor, but one glanced off his head. Blood surged from the wound, staining his hair. His eyes glazed. He staggered.

Life was returning to Liz's numb limbs, and she reached out for Maddie's ankle. As her hand closed around it, the woman fell and lost hold of the opal. She rolled, yanking her leg free, then gave a kick that struck a glancing blow off Liz's head.

But not before Liz had retrieved the stone.

"Give it to me," Maddie shrieked, leaping to her feet. "Give it to me." With dizzying speed she plucked a heavy rock from the ground. The next instant she stood above Liz, the rock held high, ready to crash down.

Just as the rock descended, Zach charged forward, his arm deflecting the blow.

"Fool!" Maddie spat out. "My master will destroy you!"

At those words, the whine in the cavern rose to a hideous shriek. The funnel coalesced, forming a man-shape. Flames burst anew on the surface of the lake.

A head appeared out of the formerly swirling mass, then a torso, two arms, two legs. A man again. A man without skin or hair. A man absent of all features but hot red eyes and a gaping hole of a mouth. A man so tall his skull nearly reached the cavern's ceiling.

His billowing body dropped to the cavern floor, and he walked toward them, but his red eyes looked only at Liz. As he bore down, his footsteps made the floor shake and echo. Liz sought escape, but time had run out.

She shrank back as monstrous hands prepared to close over her body.

"Kill her," Maddie shrieked. "Kill the guardian!"

Liz felt a yank and reflexively jerked away. It was

Zach, and he'd pulled her back to safety just as the fingers closed over the space she'd occupied. But her startled reaction had jarred her fingers open. Even as she screamed in protest, the opal fell from her hand.

Maddie scooped it up. Whirling, she faced Ankouer and offered up the stone. "Your prize, master. It is here."

"*Non*, Maddie! Give it not to *le fantôme!*"

Maddie hesitated, turning to see Frank lumbering toward them. Before she could react, he snatched the opal.

Ankouer let out a piercing screech. He lashed out and sent Frank flying toward the edge of the pool. He struck with a funereal thud, then slithered bonelessly into a heap.

"Papa!" Liz screamed.

Blood trickled from his mouth, and his fingers uncurled, allowing the opal to roll slowly over the stone floor, where it stopped inches from Maddie's feet.

Maddie gave it no attention. With a wail, she rushed to Frank and fell to her knees, then abruptly jumped back up and ran to meet the advancing monster that now blocked Zach and Liz's way to Frank.

"You promise!" she screeched. "You promise me you will not hurt Frank!" She pounded at the creature, her fists disappearing into the ebony swirl, then reappearing to pound again.

"Cease, foolish servant?"

"Did I not use your power as you commanded? Did I not send the gator and the coons to destroy this guardian? Did I not create the waters to swallow her up?" Maddie's voice rose to a crescendo. "T'weren't my fault they still live!"

Maddie paused, glancing at Frank's crumpled body. "You kill my man! You kill him . . . you kill my Frank." She sank helplessly to her knees, overcome by sobs, looking up with grief-wracked defiance. "Where . . . where is your power, puny master . . . that you d-don't keep your promise?"

Liz caught Zach's eyes and they inched toward her father, hoping to go unnoticed as Ankouer's displeasure grew.

"You have not the power you say, phantom," Maddie professed heatedly. With a dramatic whirl, she bent for the opal, clutching it to her breasts as she again faced Ankouer. "Power above, power divine," she cried. The opal let out a flash of light, and this time Maddie gave no sign of pain.

"Servant, you try my patience." Even as he bellowed, Ankouer's dark shape visibly diminished in size.

Liz and Zach were nearly at her father's side when a punishing shriek escaped the hole that served as Ankouer's mouth. "You love your man so much," he roared. "Go to him!"

An enormous arm swung back, then sped toward

Maddie with brutal force. When the blow struck, she let out a single surprised grunt before collapsing beside Frank's motionless form. The fire stone rolled gently from her grip and came to rest between their crumpled bodies.

Liz let out a gasp. No matter how horribly Maddie had schemed, Liz never wanted this. By this time, Zach had reached her father and was bending over, listening for breath, but Liz's outcry had caught the phantom's attention. An icy gaze crept down her back, chilling her soul.

Come, Guardian. Your night of reckoning is here.

Liz didn't turn to face him; instead she called softly to Zach, "Is Papa alive?"

"He's breathing," Zach said solemnly, then inclined his head toward Maddie. "But I don't think Maddie made it."

Liz nodded. The woman's neck was cocked at an obscene angle. Undoubtedly snapped by the force of the blow. The opal rested quietly—no flash of light, no warm, protective glow—in the small space separating the two bodies. Liz took a step to retrieve it.

A chill swept over her and almost sent her to her knees, warning her that if she even tried, Zach and her father would not survive. Slowly, she turned to face Ankouer. He stood above her, a swirling mass, his red eyes gleaming with anticipation, the black hole of his mouth forming into something resembling a grin.

Liz reached into her pocket for her father's pills and tossed them toward Zach.

"Take care of him," she said, then went forth to meet *le fantôme noir.*

"Liz!" Zach bellowed. "No! You can't!"

But Liz barely heard his protest over the words from the journal echoing in her mind. *The guardian shall walk into his blackest part.* Destiny had finally overtaken her. Already she was touching the cold, cold flesh of Ankouer. It parted for her easily. She stepped inside without the opal, knowing certain death was ahead, but also knowing she'd just guaranteed Zach and her father's safety. As the wall closed behind her, she felt the rumble of a cruel chuckle.

"Welcome, Guardian," said Ankouer. "The battle begins."

Chapter Twenty-four

It happened so fast Zach could hardly take it in. One second he'd been checking Frank for a pulse that appeared nonexistent, the next second Liz stepped into Ankouer's swirling body, and in the next, that manlike body changed into a vortex.

"Liz!" he roared, charging the funnel, prepared to follow her in. He hit a solid wall that sent him sprawling. He stared up, his mind spinning in tandem with the shape that had swallowed the woman he loved.

Laboring to his feet, he approached the twister again, this time more cautiously, but his touch rebounded so forcefully he felt it clean to his shoulder. Again he tried, and again. In a final burst of frustration, he pounded on the unresponsive spinning wall, only to end up staggering from the recoil.

He gazed around the cavern, insanely hoping that

Liz would magically be there. She wasn't. A few flames still danced on the surface of the pool, and nearby was Maddie, stomach-down, her head jutting out at a grotesque angle. Her dark and lifeless eyes stared at him, and the silent plea they held echoed his own. Next to her lay Frank, his left arm also twisted. Clearly broken. Zach had lied to Liz when he's said he felt a breath—or exaggerated, anyway, because the faint brush of air had probably come from the phantom.

His eyes drifted to the pill vial, which had fallen not far from Frank's feet. Feeling hopeless, he nevertheless stood up and went to get it.

With a sense of futility he opened the nitro bottle and took out a pill. After tipping Frank's head back, he slipped his fingers between the man's lips and deposited a tablet under his tongue. The instructions on the label said to wait fifteen minutes, and if there was no response, try again.

Fifteen minutes. It seemed like an eternity.

He bent listlessly to pick up his windbreaker, which he'd dropped on the ground when he'd gone in the water after Frank. Sitting down, he took out a cigarette, the put his arms on his knees and hunkered down to smoke it.

Run. He should run. They were dead, all dead. Nothing to do but save himself. But the funnel cloud appeared to have no interest in him, which meant he was safe for now. And leaving . . . ? He couldn't leave Liz, not without being sure.

By his account, she'd reappeared from the dead just a few days before, and since then he'd snatched her from death's greedy claws so many times he'd lost count. But this time it appeared he'd finally lost her to its grasp.

Yes, there was no sense in running. Without her, he had nothing to run to. His loss ran so deep he dared not feel it. A heavy sigh went out on an exhale of smoke, and he leaned forward to pull his flask from his back pocket.

It felt light in his hand, half empty at least, but he might as well drink his fill. Maybe it would numb him sufficiently to face hauling corpses through the dank tunnel. For that was all that was left to do. Bury the dead and say a prayer for Liz.

He lifted the flask to his lips.

"Zacharie."

Turning, he saw that Frank's eyes were open, and he jumped so bad he almost dropped his flask. But as soon as his heart stopped pounding, it lifted, allowing entrance to a scrap of hope. He recapped the flask and went to Frank's side.

"Hey, partner," he said, kneeling beside the fallen man. "I thought we'd lost you. Looks like you broke your arm. How bad does it hurt?"

"Izzy . . ."

"She's fine," Zach lied. "Just fine."

"*Pas du tout*," Frank replied, then launched into whispered French.

"I can't understand you, Frank. Speak English."

"*Oui, oui.* You must be bold, *mon ami.* Izzy is inside Ankouer, yes?"

Since his lie had failed, Zach nodded grimly.

"Does she got the opal?"

Zach shook his head, tilting it toward the spot between Frank and Maddie. When Frank saw Maddie, a low moan left his lips. He reached out slowly, and touched her now-pale face. "*Adieu, mon amour.*"

Good-bye, my love. Even with his poor grasp of French, Zach understood, and he looked away, unwilling to intrude on this grieving man's moment.

"Zacharie," Frank said urgently. "You must listen good. Izzy got no hope without the fire stone. But you . . . her defender . . . you can take it to her."

"It's no good," Zach said. "I've tried to go after her more than a dozen times. The funnel keeps throwing me back."

"But not when you got the stone. You pass through easy."

"How do you know, partner?" Zach asked. "How can you be sure?"

"I been there," Frank answered in a choked voice, glancing briefly at Maddie.

Unspoken words hung in the air: *But Ellie died anyway, just like Maddie.*

Zach looked toward the spiral. Now and then it

issued a hiss or a wail, but it still appeared completely indifferent to their presence. When he looked back at Frank, the man's eyes were drifting shut.

"Frank," he implored, panicked.

"The arm, it hurt bad." Frank put his hand over a protruding spot. Compound fracture, Zach thought. They'd have to immobilize it before they carried him out.

With a start, Zach realized he was again thinking in terms of survival. His optimism was returning. A good sign. Surely a good sign.

But even as this thought crossed his mind, Frank's eyes fluttered shut.

"When two join as one, the soft overpower the strong," Frank murmured.

"Beg your pardon."

He received no answer. Frank had slipped away. Zach leaned close, checking to make sure he was breathing. Reassured, he stood up and took a final drag from his cigarette before tossing it away. Several feet away the opal waited for him to fetch it. The time for pure gut courage had arrived.

Uncapping his flask, Zach lifted it to his lips and drank deeply.

So quiet, Liz thought. Too quiet. Surely Ankouer hadn't lured her here to simply just ignore her. Where was he?

" 'Wash over me a love so pure,' " she said, her voice barely above a whisper. " 'My heart . . . my heart is—' "

Her memory choked.

" 'My heart . . .' " Oh, God in heaven, she wasn't even through the first stanza and she'd already forgotten the words.

She stood in a world of solid black, frozen, too terrified to move. She'd stepped through that wall full of fierce protectiveness. Now only electrifying terror remained, and it was so complete she couldn't find it within herself to take another step. She had no opal. She had no effigy with which to torment Ankouer. She had no defender by her side. The prayer was all she had for protection. And she couldn't remember the next line.

A sob left her lips.

The two keep the one at bay.

Her mother's voice. Her mother's voice, talking to her inside her head, giving her the next line of the quatrain. And she'd heard the line recently, from somebody else's lips.

Then it came back. In Harris's bar. He'd used those very words when he'd handed her the *gris-gris*. Suddenly Liz's panic wasn't quite so complete. She reached into her pocket for the chalcedony and the packet of rose dust. Guided only by her sense of touch, she ripped the cellophane with her teeth.

With no clue how to use them, she relied on her instincts.

Even as the paper tore, she felt the dust drifting down. Particles struck her arms, and soon she felt them on her ankles. The sweet smell of summer roses came to her nose.

A mild shiver shook the dark landscape of Ankouer's soul.

Encouraged, Liz overturned the packet and sprinkled dust in front of her. " 'My heart . . .' " she said. Another shiver jarred the support beneath her feet.

Two, she reminded herself. It took two. Again without a clue to its use, she rubbed the green stone with her thumb and repeated the only words of the prayer she could recall. The shudder escalated to a quake.

" 'My heart, my heart, my heart,' " she repeated fervently. Immediately, the remainder of the forgotten line came to her. " 'My heart is cleansed of fear.' "

She took a tentative step forward. " 'Glow, glow, bright opal, free your fire. Illuminate the shadows. Pave my way.' "

Although she had no fire stone, the total darkness lifted, permitting her to cross a black divide into a world of gray upon gray. Soundless, formless. Bleak and empty. And infinite, it seemed.

" 'Pave my way, pave my way, so darkness does not fall upon this earth.' " Cold air nipped at her bare arms and legs, at her face and neck, but at least she could see.

She finished the stanza, finding that the stillness sapped her spirit. She'd primed herself for battle, for clashing and screaming, for out-and-out conflict. She felt aimless, weary, and so terribly, terribly sad. Her legs were growing weak, begging for rest.

" 'Power above, Power divine, I call to thee,' " she cried, desperate to shake off her lethargy. " 'Shine your light upon my soul.' " Her weariness declined, and she rushed to spill out the next words. " 'Wash over me a love so pure, my heart is cleansed of sorrow.' "

Suddenly the fog came alive with darting, shrieking bats. Liz's spirits lifted. The challenge had arrived.

" 'Power above, Power divine—' "

"Stop that babbling, child!" One of the bats landed at her feet. With a small squeal it took Maddie's shape and wagged a finger at her. "You cannot win."

"Get out of my way," Liz ordered. "You're not real. Not real at all."

"Oh, I real enough."

Her animosity at Maddie rising, Liz turned her mind back to the prayer. " 'I call to thee.' "

Maddie put her hands over her ears. "Stop that, I say. Stop, stop, stop!"

" 'Wash over me—' "

With an outraged cry, Maddie vanished.

You think you're beyond my reach, Guardian? Do not believe such lies. My power has no limits.

Liz felt a surge of hate so intense it was palpable. "I'm here to kill you, phantom," she shouted into the bleak gray land. "You'll die before I leave."

One of us will die. His mocking laughter reverberated from every direction. The bats screeched with delight.

A shiver ran through Liz's body—not from fear, but from cold, alerting her that the phantom's powers were growing again. What had the journal warned her of? Ankouer fed on hate. And yet she could hardly contain hers.

"See, Izzy?" came Maddie's voice. "You cannot win."

" 'Wash over me,' " Liz responded, warring against the malice consuming her. " 'Wash over me a love so . . .' "—the words were coming so slowly—" 'a love so pure, my heart is cleansed—' "

Cleansed? Look into your heart again, Guardian.

Another bat flew up.

"You're tired, Izzy. Give up."

"Mama?"

It *was* her. She stood in front of Liz, one hand extended as if to smooth her brow. And though Liz knew this was just another of Ankouer's messengers, she became so filled with love and joy she rushed forward to embrace her.

No! bellowed Ankouer. *No!*

Liz threw her arms around her mother's body, then gasped as they went straight through. An illusion, only an illusion. A wave of despair nearly brought Liz to her knees. It was no use, no use at all. Maddie was right. Ankouer was right. She couldn't win. Nor could she remember the next line.

What did it matter anyway? What did it matter? What on earth had ever made her think she could defeat boundless evil just by reciting a stupid prayer?

Zach stood in front of Ankouer's spiraling form, listening, listening hard for Liz's voice. She needed him. He knew she needed him. But what weapons did he have to fight a monster? A pocket knife, a cigarette lighter, a nearly empty flask and a cryptic couplet. Not enough. But, of course he had enough, he reminded himself. He had more than Liz did.

He had the opal, and it still waited for him to pick it up.

"So, Defender, the woman or your bottle?"

Zach spun around. "Richard!"

"At your service. Here to see your downfall, actually. You don't have it in you, Zach. You know you don't. Give it up."

"You bastard! You've sold your soul!"

"Ankouer is the future. Your future. No turning away from him." Richard moved closer. His lips curved up in smug satisfaction. "And he has plans for you, Zach. Big plans."

"I don't have time for this." As before, Richard's taunt strengthened Zach's determination and he gave a half-turn toward the opal.

"Don't you want to know the rest?" Richard scurried to Zach's side, then gazed up at the slowly spinning cloud. "Soon as the master has defeated your lady, he'll come and take your body. Imagine this, Zach. Being host to Ankouer, destined to rule the world. Unlimited power . . . No reason to ever run."

Richard was so close now, his nose nearly touching Zach's, his breath heavy with foul promises. Foul, oh yes, but so enticing. Never running away. Never again. Ever.

Not like that night so long ago, that night he'd tried so hard to block from memory. That night that was suddenly flooding back.

He'd crept up the outer steps to the screened-in second-story *galerie* of the Deveraux cabin, planning to sweet-talk Izzy into joining him in the warm night so he could whisper sweet words and feel her grow hot for him again. He loved her, how he loved her, and in his arrogant youth he never doubted she'd one day be his wife.

"You thought you had it all, didn't you, Fortier?"

Zach's absorption in the memories was so thorough he barely registered Richard's question or the scathing words that followed. "Golden boy. Good looks, athletic prowess, rich parents and a disgustingly bright future. You had it all. Until that night."

He'd sneaked toward the room where Izzy slept with her grandmother Catherine. Quietly he moved—trusting the thunder to muffle his steps—and he was already hardening with anticipation. Then he'd heard the hum. Not loud, at first, more like the buzz of a June bug. But it escalated until it bounced in his head and drowned out all other thoughts.

Izzy shot straight up in her bed, and as he was about to call her name, she clapped her hands to her ears and sobbed, *"Grandmère! Grandmère!"*

It all seemed to happen at once. Missus Catherine spoke to someone unseen, and Izzy clutched the worn sheet to her breasts. Screams filled the air, but not from the women. Higher pitched than the hum, and piercing, so piercing, they nearly split apart his eardrums. Fire exploded, sending out searing cold.

"You just ran like hell." Richard used the battering tone of a cross-examiner. "Took off for home with your tail between your legs like a cur. Didn't you, Zach? Didn't you?"

Zach buried his face in his hands. He'd just turned eighteen. Only eighteen. And still too vividly recalling the day he'd gone after the yellow orchid. Still too terrified to face such horror again. Still too young to face Ankouer.

"Now you're thirty-nine. And you still want to run."

It never occurred to Zach to wonder how Richard knew what he'd been thinking because the seductiveness of the next words had him lifting his head from his hands.

"You'll never be afraid again. Think about it. No wrenching of your gut. No pounding of your heart. You'd be free of fear forever."

No fear. Forever.

"No fear, Zach. No fear at all. Never again will your innards quake and make you run away." Zach stared in fascination, growing hypnotized by Richard's voice.

Then another voice, soft and hesitant, cut through his daze.

" 'Cleanse my heart . . .' " It was Liz.

Liz.

Her trembling refrain seeped through the walls of the phantom's twisting shape. " 'Cleanse . . . my heart of' . . . God help me, I can't remember the words!"

Zach stared at Ankouer, then back at Richard, who confidently awaited his answer. He hesitated and absently reached for his back pocket.

Richard chuckled. "Go ahead. Steady the nerves. It's just what you need."

Right, just the ticket to get him through. He slipped the flask from his pocket, unscrewed the cap, and lifted it to his lips. Just as he started to drink he saw his distorted image in the smooth silver. His hair was completely matted to his head, except for two tufts that stood up like horns. His skin looked thick and pasty, with irregular blond stubble on his chin and jaw. And his eyes . . .

They weren't blue anymore, but a fiery, angry red, and they stared back at him with such malevolence his stomach rolled in revulsion.

Him. That was him if he accepted Ankouer's unholy bargain. It was who he would become. The worst of him unleased upon the world. Without fear, without remorse. Never a moment of creepy-crawlies, never a moment of hesitation, never that limb-paralyzing electric shiver. Invincible, invulnerable.

" 'Cleanse my heart of . . .' " Liz's words came out on a desperate sob, " '. . . my heart—' "

Zach spun and hurled the flask toward the lake. Vodka spilled as it soared, drenching Richard. Then the flask fell into the water, gurgling and sending up bubbles as it sank.

"You fucking idiot!" Richard hissed, his image getting weak. "You've ruined everything!"

Chapter Twenty-five

Liz was on her knees, doubled over, so weighed down by her burden of despair she couldn't lift her head.

She'd failed again, just as she had on her grandmother's night of reckoning. She was inadequate. She'd succumbed to fear, despair, and hate, and couldn't even remember a simple prayer. " 'Power above, Power divine, I call to—' " Call to what? You? Thou? Who was she calling?

And why didn't they answer?

Dead, all dead. *Grandmère*. Mama. Jed. Maddie. Dead. Soon she would be, too. And Papa. Maybe Zach. Once she was gone, Ankouer wouldn't let him live. She didn't even want to think of the larger picture, of the conqueror who would rise into the world and lead it into bloody warfare. She couldn't think of it.

" 'I c-call . . . I call to . . .' "

The gray world was more desolate than a sunless desert, and it rolled like the waves of a cheerless arctic sea, broken only by the dark, flitting bats that circled above.

"Give up," she heard Maddie say.

"Terminal," said a new voice. She lifted her eyes and saw Doc Allain's floating head.

"Ankouer wins," they droned in unison.

" 'I call . . .' " She was tired, soul weary, without hope or faith to guide her through.

She dropped her head to the floor that wasn't a floor, yet somehow supported her anyway, and rolled into a shivering ball. Her teeth chattered like gunshots in the deathly stillness. Her body shuddered violently. Control of it was beyond her now. She doubted she could get up, even if she'd wanted to.

But she didn't want to. No, she didn't want to. She'd lost. She'd accept her fate. After all, it was destiny, wasn't it?

Ankouer laughed triumphantly.

Do not worry, servant. That was merely the defender's first test.

Although the words came to Zach internally, Richard Cormier laughed. His fading body solidified.

Ignoring *le fantôme's* message, and certain he was up to the task, Zach turned to get the opal, then stumbled back. Two bulging eyes glared down on him. Eight spindly legs stabbed the air above a thickly swollen sac the size of a hot-air balloon. A pair of open fangs the length of carving knives dripped with venom.

Zach's mind rocked so violently he was certain his sanity would shatter. In a moment, he'd collapse on the cavern's stony floor and begin babbling and snatching at flies. Another test? Oh yes. And this time he wouldn't pass.

Just as his knees began to buckle as he'd predicted, he felt a gentle touch. A familiar voice said, "You can beat this, bro."

He'd recognize that carefree tone anywhere. Waves of relief swept over him as he turned.

Trendily dressed as usual in a soft, neutral, collarless shirt and linen pants that wrinkled fashionably around his ankles, the man smiled at him with contagious confidence.

"J-Jed?" he stammered, dividing his gaze between the specter of his brother and the dangling, monstrous spider.

"Take this creature away, master!" Richard bellowed.

"Yeah, man. I'm here. Isn't that what brothers are for?"

What brothers were for? Yes, but . . .

"I let you down, Jed, and you died because of it."

His brother shook his head. "All events led to this night."

"Away!" Richard roared again. "Take it away! Look how it empowers this sniveling cur! Forget Zach, master. He doesn't deserve your grace. Take me as your host. Take me in his place."

The shout drew Zach's attention, and fearful that Cormier's plea would be answered, he moved forward, aching to embrace his brother once again. His arms contacted warmth, a sense of peace, but nothing solid, nothing he could hang on to.

His brother paled before his eyes as he spoke again. "You have a weapon in your pocket and another on the ground. Use them, bro. Use them to defeat *le fantôme noir* for all time." Then he vanished.

"No! No!" Richard shrieked. "It's always Zach. It's always been Zach. When will my time come?"

Zach lingered only an instant to inhale the freshness left in his brother's wake, then once again turned to face Richard, whose form was fading and twisting and rising to rejoin Ankouer, even as his raging voice faded into nothingness. The spider twitched, a rumble of satisfaction surging from its mouth.

Zach hesitated only a second before scooping up the fallen opal. Then he pivoted to face the waiting spider. He had the opal now, but what was the weapon in his pocket? He had only one. His pen knife.

He reached into his pocket for the knife, then flicked it open. What a goddamn flimsy defense. Still, if his brother said it would work, that was good enough for Zach. So, clutching the opal in one hand and wielding the tiny pen knife in the other, Zach moved to meet the spider.

He hoped like hell that Jed hadn't been another of Ankouer's illusions.

A violent shudder rocked Liz back and forth. Bats shrieked with pain, and a chilling wail filled her ears. Ankouer had been wounded. Feeling a surge of hope she struggled to her knees.

" 'Power above, Power divine,' " she began anew. " 'I call to . . . *thee!* Shine your light upon my soul. Wash over me a love so pure, my heart is cleansed . . . cleansed . . .' "

" 'My heart is cleansed . . .' "

Just then a strong bass voice joined hers, providing the forgotten words. " 'My heart is cleansed of hate. Glow, glow, bright opal, free your fire. Illuminate the shadows. Pave my way.' "

Zach chanted as loud as he could, seeking Liz in the gray mist, carrying his small and bloody pocket knife before him like a shield, and cradling the opal in his other hand. Who would think Ankouer could bleed? A creature made of nothing but formless protoplasm? But this sign of the phantom's mortality had given him hope. " 'Pave my way, pave my way, so darkness shall not fall upon this earth.' "

He broke off and called Liz's name. She didn't answer and he resumed his chant, moving uncertainly through an endless fog. Had the phantom killed her already? Would he find her lifeless body staring up at him with those telltale blue lips? His fears chilled his already cold blood. He shivered, clinging to the knife as though it was his only hope. " 'By the fire within the stone I pledge to hold courage fast in this dark place.' "

Submit, Defender. The guardian is lost. I promise you no fear. Take my gift, and see if I am true to my word.

"No!" he shouted defiantly. He resumed the prayer. " 'By the fire within the stone I pledge to hold courage fast in this dark place.' "

The stone in his hand remained inert. He'd expected it to spark and flare as it had done when Liz had approached the ledge. He needed light. Needed it bad. He could see so little in all the gloom.

"Liz," he called again. "Liz. Liz-iz-iz-izzzzzz!"

Liz moved skittishly toward Zach's voice. The thick mist kept her from seeing her own feet, and though she repeated the prayer along with him, for some reason he couldn't hear her.

" 'By the fire within the stone,' " she echoed after

him, " 'I pledge to hold courage fast in this dark place.' "

The circling forms above shrieked and scattered. She felt more than heard the shuddering sob wracking the mist below her feet. She stumbled through the cloudy haze, guided by the rich cadence of Zach's voice.

" 'Power above, Power divine,' " he said, then called her name again.

"Zach," she cried in return. The vapor seemed endless. Finding him was hopeless, a lost cause, not worthy of their efforts. But as they moved into the stanza regarding sorrow, her heart lifted, cleansed of sorrow as the words proclaimed.

Then there he was, emerging from the mist like a warrior hero from a Scottish tale, stance wide, holding his tiny knife in front of him as he might a sword. Liz broke into a run, arms held wide, finally trusting that she wouldn't fall.

Zach, oh, Zach, her love, her life. Zach.

And he was running, too, his arms as wide as hers, his face alight with an adoring smile, and as they met, she started to leap into his arms.

She stopped short. What if . . . ?

"I'm real, Liz," he said shakily. "Honest."

With the opal between them, he crushed her against his hard chest, holding her so tightly she could barely breathe, whispering, "I'm sorry, Liz. Oh, God, I'm so sorry."

Fiery color exploded. Rainbow hues shot from between their bodies in every direction. Heat seeped from the opal and eased their chill.

Above them the bats swirled, chittering angrily, letting out shrieks that bothered them not at all. She was safe now, safe in Zach's arms. And she had no idea why he was apologizing, but she just allowed herself to receive his loving kisses, deposited so frantically she couldn't begin to return them.

Another shudder ran beneath their feet. Liz stumbled, but Zach righted her. He hadn't realized how small she was, how fragile. He'd seen her as this pillar of strength since their reunion, often wishing to find the vulnerable girl he'd loved instead. He saw now that he'd wed each of his clinging wives in an attempt to replace the girl, dooming their marriage to fail.

Now it was clear that it had never been Liz's weaknesses he'd loved. No, he'd loved her strength. He wanted to shore it up with his support and no longer cared if she loved him back. To give love, that was important, and no one he'd ever known deserved it more.

She slipped her arms around his neck and gazed up at him. Her golden eyes carried all the glittering undertones he'd seen in the opal earlier and were filled with reflections of his own emotions.

Ankouer wailed in rage. A fierce wind arose as his body writhed in anger. Zach let Liz go and stood beside her, putting the hand with the opal protectively over her shoulder and holding the knife with the other. Like fighting an elephant with a needle, he thought, as bats darted down from the sky, pecking at them as birds might. He slashed at them, one by one, and like the spider, they bled. With each one he felled, his hatred soared. Beside him, Liz fended off other creatures, her face an echo of his emotions.

Suddenly she dropped her hands. " 'Power above, Power divine,' " she began, her voice high and sweet. " 'I call to thee.' " Then she turned to Zach. "Stop fighting," she told him. "Ankouer feeds on hate."

But hate had hold of him now. He let go of Liz, let the opal fall. His fury at all his fears, at all he'd lost at this monster's hand, raged and raged, and he expressed it with every slash of his tiny knife.

" 'Shine your light upon my soul,' " Liz cried, falling to her knees to claw at the mist in search of the stone. Zach was in a frenzy he couldn't control. It was up to her, and she said a smaller prayer that this time words would not fail her.

" 'Wash over me a love so pure, my heart is cleansed of hate.' "

His slashes lost momentum, getting weaker and less frantic, but Liz kept searching. Finally her hand brushed a hard object.

With an exultant cry, she held the opal aloft, crying.

" 'Glow, glow, bright opal, free your fire. Illuminate the shadows. Pave my way. . . . Pave my way, pave my way, so darkness does not fall upon this earth.' "

He glanced at her, his blue eyes dark with pain and despair, and still she chanted. Her body grew weak with the ecstasy of love, and she sank back on her heels saying the prayer that was their only salvation. " 'By the fire within the stone, I pledge to hold love fast in this dark place.' "

Zach let his knife arm fall to his side. Then, suddenly, though bats still worried them and Ankouer still screeched, he was on his knees, enclosing her in his arms as she held the opal aloft, joining her in the final stanza of the prayer, the one she'd been told to recite in her darkest hour.

Power above, power divine.
Heed my call in my hour of need.
Protect me from evil in this black place.
Power above, Power divine.
Heed my call. Heed my call.

Emitting frightened squeals the bats swooped upward and away. An earthquake rumbled beneath. The gray sky darkened to a murky black, the bats formed into storm clouds. Streaks of red crawled across the black like greedy fingers, creating fearsome cracks.

The quaking increased, and Zach steadied Liz as she stared wide-eyed into the terrifying night, holding the radiant opal high above her head. A mournful wail slithered through the unnatural storm. And with it, Liz felt a weight descend. At last she understood. The phantom's fear, his sorrow, his hate. They had twisted him into darkness personified. She knew then how he yearned for the soft, the kind, the loving. That he drank the souls of men in search of it.

Next, Maddie floated in her mind, and she comprehended the intensity of the woman's obsessive love, and the depths to which she had sunk in order to obtain it.

It was all so clear now, so frighteningly, so sadly, so hatefully clear, and the arms holding the opal began to sag. Her elbows bent. She could no longer support the burden of the stone.

Then Zach began the prayer anew, and as he spoke, tears sprang to Liz's eyes. She let her elbows fall to his shoulders, let him brace her with his strength, as the unspeakable sadness of all she perceived took over.

Her first sob came as a hiccup, but another followed, and soon she was wracked with them. Zach took her arms and wrapped them around his neck, cupping her hands so the opal still shone on the dark, red-torn sky.

As he murmured the prayer in her ear, all the pain of her lifetime spilled from her eyes in salty tears. She wept for her grandmother's sorrow, her mother's sorrow, for Maddie. So much sorrow, she couldn't contain it. Finally, almost beyond her understanding, she cried with pity for Ankouer.

The phantom's wails became like cries of an abandoned infant, and as those sobs shook the stormy terrain, Zach held the trembling Liz close to his chest. He felt her sadness, felt the world's sadness.

Inside a single flash of red that tore the inky sky, Maddie and Richard stood before them, faces twisted in rage and terrible curses streaming from their mouths. But Zach felt Richard's anger not at all. Bathed in his love for Liz, he felt only the man's worry over his own inadequacies, his fear he'd never be as good as Zach, his yearning and his need.

And Liz felt only Maddie's love for her father, her genuine admiration for her mother, and the aching loneliness she'd lived with so long. Her empty womb, her empty bed, her empty, empty life spent in pursuit of a man who belonged to another.

She wept for Maddie, feeling no shame over the tears of love and pity streaming down her face.

As Zach saw her tears, his own eyes burned. He blinked, again and again. Then, with a weepy smile, he lowered one hand and softly blotted her beautiful, shining face.

The opal exploded with light. Blue-white streaks rose into the dark panorama and entwined with the red-hot bolts. They licked at one another like dueling rapiers, blue against red, white against black.

Zach held Liz tight, protecting her from the maelstrom. At each clash of light, a head emerged in the sky. Richard, still swearing allegiance to the black lord. Ellie, telling them both that love would prevail. Then the doctor, declaring their doom, and after him, Harris, rejoicing that Izzy had been found. Maddie proclaimed it would all be hers. And finally Jed, reminding Zach again that all events had led to this night.

The battle went on endlessly. And Liz clung to Zach, knowing her only stability amid this chaos was her love for him. So sweet, so pure with no hesitancy or doubt. She may never again have a chance to tell him how deep it ran. So she loosened her terrified hold on his neck and leaned back to capture his lips. "I love you, Zach," she breathed into the kiss. "I love you."

The clashing ceased momentarily, as if eyes were seeking the source of this interruption, then resumed with increased ferocity.

"And I love you, Liz," he murmured, brushing his mouth across hers with gentle urgency that told her he finally believed her.

Instantly, without fanfare, the jagged red bolts vanished. The light waves streaking from the opal transformed to dancing prisms of color. The dark sky lightened. Faces appeared again— Ellie, Harris, and Jed, with the others notably absent.

" 'The two join as one, and the soft overpower the strong,' " Zach whispered in awe.

The faces nodded together, and Harris spoke. "*Le fantôme noir*, he die now. We be in your debt."

Then they were gone.

The gray mist shuddered, faded, reemerged to shudder again, each time tossing Liz and Zach about. With a final and gut-wrenching quake, the mist shattered into millions of gray pieces.

Liz held on to Zach and Zach held on to Liz, each wanting to protect the other from the fall to come. The next thing they knew they were kneeling beside the crystal pool, watching pale fragments of Ankouer drop like rainfall into the water.

"Ankouer is dead!" Zach cried in triumph, hugging Liz fiercely.

"Yes," she said softly, sinking into his embrace.

He leaned back and looked at her in question.

"Papa?" was her response.

"He's okay. Winded and with a broken arm, but he'll be fine."

"Where is he?"

Surprised, Zach jerked toward the spot where Frank last lay. It was empty, totally empty. Next he scanned the cavern—the narrow ledge, the ascending ramp, the smaller lighted cave beyond. Finally he answered Liz's question.

"He's gone. And so is Maddie's body."

Chapter Twenty-six

Liz climbed to her feet, and checked the cavern herself, but she knew Zach wasn't mistaken. New tears sprang to her eyes and she let them flow. But these weren't healing tears—they were tears born of a rage so intense she couldn't express it any other way.

"It's not fair, Zach. We lost so much. Why my father, too? Why did we lose it all?"

"Maybe he carried Maddie from the cave." She heard no conviction in his voice, but he cupped her chin and lifted her face to meet his. "You're cold, wet, and exhausted. I'm going to take you out, then I'll come back and search for them."

Liz shook her head. "It's no use. Ankouer took them. You know it's true."

"You gotta have faith, *cher*," he said. "It protected us from *le fantôme noir*."

"Shh." She put her finger over his lips. "Talking about him . . . it scares me. Let's make a pact to never speak his names again." She glanced at the lake. Ankouer's fragments still sank slowly in the water. To dissolve into the void, she wondered, or to someday return to dark form? They followed the path of the pieces for a long moment, then Zach brought Liz around to face him.

"I vow, Liz," he whispered hoarsely, "as long as my love for you endures, I'll never speak his names. Which means forever."

His gaze bathed her in love, and Liz realized they hadn't lost it all; they still had each other. "As will mine," she answered, then sank into his embrace and let him kiss her tears away.

Moonlight flooded the cavern, but by the time they stepped from each other's arm, the moon had passed and its light grew weak. The only other illumination came from the softly glowing opal. Liz used it to guide her as she searched for her shoes. When she bent to slip them on, she saw a long, red-striped cylinder.

"The flashlight." As she picked it up and turned it on in preparation for the journey through the tunnel, a thought flitted through her mind.

"Where's the lantern?"

"I set it down at the base of the ramp," Zach said, looking over his shoulder. "It's not there."

"Oh, Zach!" Liz said excitedly, shoving her feet

into the Doc Marten's and rushing toward the tunnel. "You were right. He took Maddie out. Papa's alive. He is, I know he is!"

Zach found it hard to believe. Surely, Frank's broken arm couldn't sustain the weight of even Maddie's slight body. But Liz had already ducked into the tunnel, racing along at a break-neck speed Zach found hard to match in such a cramped position. The flashlight bobbed in front of her, weaving over the slick, damp surface, and clearly showing the sudden absence of decomposing carcasses or caches of bones. The air was cleaner, too, easier to breathe. When Liz rounded the curve to leave him momentarily in total darkness, he felt no panic.

"Zach!" she cried as he made it around the curve. "Zach!"

Frank sat in the middle of the tunnel, rocking back and forth with Maddie cradled in his arms. His face was a mask of agony that Zach knew came only partly from his broken limb.

"You done prevailed against Ankouer," he said weakly.

"By the power of the opal," Liz answered.

Zach bent to relieve Frank of his burden. "I'll take her, partner."

"*Non*, I want to hold her a while longer so her soul can pass to heaven."

Heaven? Liz caught Zach's eye.

"Poor Maddie," Frank continued. "Ankouer lure

her with false promises. She weren't evil, just a woman who has her needs too long denied."

"Why did you try to carry her out alone?" Zach asked. "With your arm and that bad ticker, you could've died, too."

Frank swayed back and forth, supporting Maddie's broken neck as if she were a baby. "I could not help you and my Izzy. But if Maddie had been there when he die, Ankouer would'a took her soul into the void." His pained eyes looked up at Liz. "I cheat her . . . and your *maman*, who it be too late to help. But this I can do for Maddie. Take her broken body home for a proper funeral."

Liz understood, and realized it was a testimony to how much the battle had changed her. No longer did she want to rail against his affair. While his betrayal was wrong, her father's fidelity to those he cherished could not be questioned.

"We have to go, Papa," she said after a time. "Let Zach help you."

And when Zach had lifted her father's burden, Liz helped him up, supporting him as they made the final leg of the journey out of Ankouer's lair.

"You sure you don't mind?" Liz asked, closing her father's wooden tobacco box on both the opal and her mother's journal.

"It is fine, Izzy. I told you. You won't let me smoke anyhow, so what difference do it make?" He was a bit cranky, and not without reason. Although Zach had fashioned a sling out of dish towels, it wasn't doing much to relieve the pain.

"Are you sure you're up to this?"

"*Oui*. It is a right end to this curse."

"Good."

She and Zach helped her father to his feet, supporting him as they made the short walk to the cypress trees that had sheltered them their first night on Quadray Island. How fitting that they'd also spend their last day in front of this spot where they'd shared their love.

Everything else was done. They'd exited the tunnel into the rising sun, and as it traveled up, everyone saw that the perpetual haze on Quadray Island had vanished.

After tending to her father's arm, Liz and Zach let him rest, choosing to forego sleep themselves so they could finish packing the boat. Later, Zach wrapped Maddie in a tarp, and her father said a small prayer in French, then remarked again that at least she'd be interred on consecrated ground.

Zach had dug a hole beneath the cypress trees earlier, and Liz now knelt beside it with a small piece of canvas and the tobacco box. She reverently wrapped the box in the canvas, feeling a pang at letting go of items belonging to her mother. But she'd talked it over with Zach and her father, and they all agreed to leave everything connected to Ankouer behind, although they refrained from speaking his name. Zach later told Liz that if not for her father's intense desire to carry back Maddie's body and the laws against it, he would have also suggested burying the woman there.

The air was so fresh and clean now, and a soft breeze kept the naked sun from beating too strongly on their shoulders. Small green shoots that hadn't been there before poked out of the soil. Life appeared to be renewing itself. As Liz leaned forward to place the canvas-wrapped box into the hole, she wept openly. And when she joined her father in another French prayer—with Zach haltingly trying to follow along—she noticed both men's voices were thick. Closure. They would finally have closure, and her last reservations about burying the cherished items disappeared.

When she got up, Zach shoveled dirt back into the hole, then tamped it down. Tears still trickled down Liz's cheeks as she silently watched him work. When at last he leaned the shovel against the tree, he wiped the sweat from his forehead, then walked over and traced his finger down Liz's cheek.

"Every tear you shed adds a year to your life, *cher.*"

"*Oui,*" her father said.

Liz smiled, taking in the two men she adored, and who clearly adored her in return. "Guess I'll be living well past a hundred."

Their laughter was subdued, but light-hearted.

"Everything's done," Zach then said. "It's time to go. My mouth's watering for some of Harris's gumbo, so let's make a stop on our way home."

"Harris?" Her father sounded puzzled. "His place ain't there no more. Burned down not so long after he die."

"We saw him, Papa," Liz protested. "Harris is fine. Still playing with his zydeco band."

"Been dead six, seven years at least."

The accompanying shake of his head told Liz her father spoke the truth.

"We should have known," Zach said. At Frank's questioning glance, he added, "He was there, inside . . . during the battle. So were Ellie and Jed."

The three exchanged solemn looks, then Zach went to claim the shovel. As he bent for it, he paused and tilted back his head. "I'll be damned."

"What is it?" Liz asked.

"Let's see."

He reached under a thick blanket of moss, and brought forth a ray of sunshine.

Liz stared blankly, not quite believing her eyes. Zach held a swirling mass of yellow, its outer petals streaked in pale color while the inner lobe was almost gold.

He walked toward her with an awed expression. "It took more than twenty years, *cher*, but here's the yellow orchid I promised to deliver."

Liz couldn't even speak, her throat was so thick and as Zach braided the stem of the incredible flower into her hair, new tears streamed down her face. Zach kissed them away as he pulled her into his arms. "I love you, Liz."

"And I love you," she whispered.

"Does that mean you two are gonna give me grandbabies?" her father asked.

Liz let out a choked laugh and turned to see him regarding them with obvious approval.

"Whoa, partner," Zach said. "One thing at a time. First I have a question to ask."

He cupped Liz's cheek and brought her face back to meet his eyes. They looked misty, Liz thought, as his next halting words came out. "Will you marry me, Liz? For forever and a day?"

"Yes," she whispered. "What took you so long?" She laughed at his wry grimace.

And then, in front of her father, beneath God and the big, bright sun on Quadray Island, she kissed him long and hard.

Epilogue

Three years later

Liz placed candlesticks on the gleaming cherrywood table, then inserted tapers. She'd light them later, after she dimmed the chandelier in the formal dining room. She had already opened the shutters to the *galerie* to allow in the fragrance of magnolias that hung in the balmy May night. From the kitchen came the spicy odors of simmering jambalaya, and peeled shrimp was marinating in a refrigerated bowl until she was ready to dump them in boiling water.

Everything was waiting for Zach's return.

Actually waiting felt pretty good these days. Waiting, and having to time think. So much had happened, so fast, after their safe return to Port Chatre. Even as they unloaded Maddie's body, people remarked uneasily that "bad luck comes in

threes." First, Ellie. Then Doc Allain—who had de
clined rapidly—aging almost overnight and dying
in his sleep before they'd arrived. Now Maddie
After a cursory investigation, her death was ruled
accidental, and later that week Liz comforted her
father while the priest performed the funeral rites.

Then came happier times. Liz took that first brave
step and admitted her lies to Stephen and their as
sociates and friends. Many had flown down to
watch her make her joyful promise to Zach. Zach's
children had attended, too, as well as his first wife
Rita, whom Liz wasn't surprised to find she liked.

Fulfilling Liz's girlhood dream and delighting her
father, who was glad to be rid of it, but even glad-
der to have her nearby again, they chose to live in
Zach's old house. She now conducted most of her
business by modem or telephone, with an occasional trip to Chicago to meet with Stephen and
renew acquaintances. This absolute perfection made
Liz realize how empty and alienated her former life
had been.

Giving the tapers another push to make certain
they were secure, she whirled joyously away from
the table. Never had she envisioned herself so
happy, and now tonight . . . tonight she'd take perfection to another level.

Just as she'd stepped back to appreciate her prep-
arations, she heard a car coming up the gravel

driveway. She pressed her hand gently against her stomach, then raced to the door.

"Hi," he said, "I missed you." He trotted up the veranda stairs, taking them two at a time, thinking Liz had never seemed more beautiful. Her cheeks glowed with color, and her dark hair curled in soft waves to her shoulders.

"I missed you, too." She threw herself into his arms with considerably more enthusiasm than usual, which was not all that easy, and kissed him fervently.

He took his time savoring her lips, and when he finally wrapped an arm around her shoulders to lead her back into the delicious-smelling house, he asked, "What's up?"

"Oh, nothing," she said breezily, a cryptic expression on her face. "Just glad you're home. Hungry?"

"Starved."

She gestured toward a chair at the head of the table. "Take a seat, and I'll put the shrimp on to boil." Then she dimmed the lights, lit the candles, and headed for the kitchen.

When she came back, she carried two flutes of a sparkling beverage, placed one in front of him, and settled in the chair next to his.

"What is this?" he asked, drinking deeply of the carbonated apple juice. He hadn't swallowed a drop of hard stuff since he'd thrown his flask away, and though he sometimes yearned for a stiff one, it was getting easier every day. "A celebration?"

"Just of your return. You were gone a long time."

He smiled, but felt a small guilty pang. "Is that a complaint?"

She laughed, and leaned forward, curling her fingers gracefully around the stem of the flute. "Your absence was keenly felt, my darling, but your happiness means more to me, and it's obvious you're enjoying your work."

"That's the truth. Want to hear about it?"

She nodded, and he went on to tell her about his problems installing surveillance equipment and hiring undercover men. One man came dangerously close to getting his cover blown, but they'd finally discovered the spy. "Still, it shouldn't have taken three weeks," he said ruefully. "After all, industrial espionage isn't the same as cracking a drug ring."

"But it's a whole lot safer." She gave the tip of his nose a butterfly kiss. "You don't really miss the dangerous work, do you?"

He paused reflectively, and Liz hoped he wasn't concerned that the truth would upset her. It would, of course, but if his choice was to return to hard investigation, she'd accept it.

"No," he finally said. "Not since . . ."

The words hung between them. Quadray Island. Ankouer. Never spoken and seldom thought of, but part of their shared history nonetheless. They had broken their pact only once. On their honeymoon, Zach haltingly confessed his cowardice the night he'd seen the phantom kill her grandmother. Liz comforted him and gave him solace, she hoped, by reminding him his fear had let him live long enough for the final battle. They talked late into the night, sharing tales of the specters who'd come to taunt and the loved ones who'd come to aid. But after that, they never mentioned that night again.

She looked away a second. "I was in Tricou's Grocery Store this morning, and Mrs. Tricou told me Richard Cormier put his house on the market."

To an outsider, her comment would have sounded like a non sequitur, but Zach knew its importance. "He hasn't been the same since he lost the store and the marina."

Make a deal with the devil and . . . Liz kept the thought to herself.

"You thinking we might want to buy it?" Zach asked.

"What? No! Why would we want a replica of a Creole house when we have the real thing?"

"That's what I think. So what else is new?"

She laughed softly. "You know what Papa told me the other day?"

"No, but it's got to be good."

"It is. He thinks it's time he moved into the nineties and bought sonar fishing equipment devices for the tour boats. I swear he isn't the same man since he took over Richard's marina."

Zach's laugh warmed her heart. So carefree and rich, with none of the cynical edge it once had. A timer buzzed in the kitchen, and she got up. "Dinner is served, my love."

Afterward, as they lingered at the table, Zach took Liz's hand. "So are you finally going to tell me your secret?"

She returned his question with a sphinxlike look. "What secret?"

"The one you've been dying to tell since I got home."

"Dying to tell? Oh, yes. Yes I have." She tightened her fingers around his. "It's finally happened. We're going to have a baby, Zach."

His eyes widened. "A b-baby? A baby! Really, Liz? A baby?"

He leaped to his feet, dragging Liz with him, and whirled her around the room. "A baby, a baby!" he exclaimed repeatedly. Finally he stopped and just held her close. "Oh, Liz"—he sighed—"things couldn't get any more perfect."

"My thoughts exactly."

Then she felt him stiffen slightly. "Is it a boy or a girl?"

"It's too early to tell."

"Oh, yeah, of course. But if it's a girl . . ."

His blue eyes darkened as she gazed into them,

comprehending the enormity of his fear. Inheritor to the guardian's throne . . . Not a fate one willingly passed on.

"She'll be just fine," she said reassuringly, believing every word. "Boy or girl, our baby will be just fine."

Zach held Liz at arm's length for a long time, searching her eyes for any sign of doubt. When he saw none, he exhaled a relieved sigh and pulled her close again.

"You're right, *cher*. She'll be just fine," he whispered. "We saw to that . . . we saw to that."

"Yes we did, Zach. And there's our proof."

She directed his gaze toward her mother's sideboard. Encased under glass, in the spot once occupied by the fire opal, sat the yellow orchid.

Still in bloom.